The Lives of Skeletons

S. A. Nicola

ISBN-13: 978-0615667959 (Mystic Cow Media)
ISBN-10: 0615667953

While inspired by a real event, the characters, locations, and situations depicted in The Lives of Skeletons *are purely fictional.*

1

"I'm about to become your savior," Dogger said. The further Dogger and Marty walked from the Dead Zone, the cleaner the street appeared, and the less friendly the faces.

"If you're the one leading me to salvation, I don't think I want to go," Marty said with a small laugh.

"Ouch," Dogger said, grimacing in a way that deepened his wrinkles. When combined with his nickname, Dogger's face allowed Marty's mind to easily see a man-size shar-pei walking beside him. Dogger's arm shot up, pointing ahead. "There's our money."

"The County Inn? We're holding up a pancake house?" Marty said. He slowed down his pace, almost stopping. It was one of the busiest restaurants in Mason, Iowa. Even at 10:00 PM, the parking lot was nearly full of cars.

"We aren't holding up anything," Dogger said. "We're just going to go get some coffee."

"I don't think that shower we took at the truck shop qualifies us to eat in a restaurant," Marty said, feeling the stiffness of his unwashed clothes. "They'll never even seat us."

As they neared the County Inn, Marty could see into the glowing windows of the restaurant. One family appeared to be placing their order with the waitress, a redheaded young woman whose forehead shone with sweat.

"Don't worry, we'll be in and out quickly," Dogger said. "I can see our money sitting on the tables right now. It's just waiting for us."

"Wait," Marty said. Marty stopped walking and stood on the curb of the small parking lot. "You can't do this."

"I can't have coffee?" Dogger said with clearly false incredulity. He turned to Marty, looking impatient.

"You can't steal their tips," Marty said. He quickly glanced around to ensure no one heard what he just said. There were no people in sight, just empty cars.

"They earn a paycheck," Dogger said. "The tips are just a bonus. Most of them probably don't deserve a tip. People just leave them because they feel like they have to."

"It just doesn't feel right," Marty said. "I don't want to take money out of the pocket of some waitress."

"You're right," Dogger said. "It would be dishonest, wouldn't it? OK, I have a better idea. Why don't you just call Sonny and ask if we can borrow a few bucks?"

"Right," Marty said. He couldn't look at Dogger, so he busied himself with gently kicking a loose rock off the curb. Marty made a confession to Dogger years ago. He didn't tell Dogger what exactly happened with his ex-wife and his son, but it was enough for Dogger to know that stories about Sonny were lies. It was enough for Dogger to call Marty a hypocrite at any opportune moment.

"What is he doing nowadays?" Dogger said. He laughed. "He's a doctor, right? Or did I hear you telling Samantha that he's a lawyer? Hell, why not both?"

"OK, I get it," Marty said, stepping down off the curb. The confession wasn't as freeing as Marty anticipated, perhaps because he didn't tell Dogger the full truth. "I never said I was the most honest guy in the world. Maybe I'm not even a good guy. But stealing tips just seems to cross a line."

"What line? Listen, you're overthinking this," Dogger said. "Let's keep it simple. Do you need money?"

Marty licked his lips. He did need money. Money meant whiskey.

"I don't know," Marty finally said. "Maybe."

"OK, then. Here is the safest and easiest way to get it. It's a perfect plan," Dogger said, pointing to the restaurant behind him. He stared at Marty for several moments, as if he were expecting a response. Dogger sighed and shook his head. "How about I go in alone? You just stay here and come get me if the police stop in for a dinner break."

"What exactly are you going to do in there?" Marty asked, his eyes once again scanning the parking lot.

"I'll order a coffee. I have enough change to pay for a coffee," Dogger said, jingling change in his pocket. "Then I'll time my exit so there are a number of tables with paper money, and I'll just causally pick it up on the way out. No problem."

"Then what?" Marty said.

"Then we'll run like hell," Dogger said. He laughed hoarsely. "To the liquor store."

⚡⚡⚡

3

Dogger pushed open the door to the County Inn restaurant, and the sweet smell of bacon met his nose. It had been many years since he had walked into this restaurant, but it looked exactly as he remembered. Yellow faux-leather booths lined the perimeter of the large dining room. Square tables with small yellow-padded chairs filled the center of the restaurant. The kitchen, where harried waitresses picked up orders, could be seen opposite the entrance through a long rectangular window.

"Can I help you?" A thin waitress with a sharp jawline and small lips approached Dogger as he stood in the doorway. She probably asked most people who walked in if they wanted a booth or a table. She stopped about five feet away from Dogger. She looked nervous.

"I'd like a table," Dogger said. He quickly scanned the restaurant again to assess where the optimal place to sit would be.

The waitress hesitated, as if she wasn't sure if Dogger was serious or if she should call a manager.

"I just want a cup of coffee," Dogger said. He reached his hand into his pocket and pulled out a handful of quarters, dimes, and nickels. "I have enough for coffee."

The waitress half-smiled and looked over her shoulder toward the seating area of the restaurant.

"I won't stay long," Dogger said.

The waitress looked at Dogger again, her feet unmoving. Maybe she was waiting for a manager to come and rescue her.

"You guys sure are busy tonight," Dogger said. He wanted it to appear as if he frequented the restaurant. "Will there be a wait for a table?"

"No," the waitress finally responded. "Follow me."

She turned and grabbed a menu from behind a podium that sat in the entryway and walked toward the dining area. Dogger followed. It might have been his imagination, but it seemed that as soon as he stepped into view of the other patrons he could hear the buzz of the restaurant chatter drop off into silence momentarily before slowly picking up again. The waitress gestured to a small table just inside the restaurant. Suddenly feeling self-conscious, Dogger almost took the table. Before he sat down, he quickly realized this would never work, as the table was only a few feet away from the front doors of the restaurant. He had to walk by other tables on the way out of the restaurant if he was going to grab any tips.

"I don't mean to be any trouble," Dogger said. The waitress's nostrils flared, and she audibly sighed before Dogger could even finish his sentence. "But would you mind if I sit in the back near the bathrooms?"

The waitress frowned but turned and led Dogger to another small empty table toward the back of the restaurant.

"I just thought this would be more inconspicuous," Dogger whispered. "I know I don't look like your average customer, so I thought it might be more comfortable for everyone if I were sitting in the back."

The waitress gave the same insincere-looking half-smile she had given before. She pulled the menu from under her arm and handed it to Dogger.

"Just a cup of coffee," Dogger said, waving his hand at the menu.

"I'll be right back with that," the waitress said, her eyes not looking at Dogger but instead scanning the restaurant. Perhaps she was still hoping to spot a manager. She quickly tucked the menu under her arm and walked away.

Dogger glanced around. His eyes met the eyes of a young man sitting with a woman who was probably his wife, a toddler, and a baby in a high chair. The young man looked down at his plate as soon as their eyes met.

Suddenly, Dogger had an overwhelming feeling that this was a bad idea.

✽ ✽ ✽

Marty sat behind the restaurant near the dumpsters. The area was poorly lit and felt like an easy place to blend in. Marty counted the number of states represented by license plate in the parking lot.

"California, Illinois, Ohio ..." Marty said under his breath as he counted on his fingers. People from eight different states were enjoying pancakes in Mason, Iowa, as Marty sat by the dumpsters.

Marty wondered what state Sonny lived in and let his mind build a house, a wife, and kids for his son, who would now be about twenty-nine. Perhaps they loved to travel and take family road trips on I–80. Maybe they had a dog, a mutt they'd rescued from the pound, who traveled with them and liked to hang his head out the car window and bite at the wind.

The low hum of a car and the crunching of tires on pavement shook Marty from his thoughts. Marty quickly leaned back into the darkness of the space between the dumpster and the restaurant. Headlights swung around the corner, and a slow-moving car pulled into view.

It was a small SUV with a license plate from Indiana. The windows were tinted, and the bottom edges of the otherwise white car were caked with dirt and mud from the road. The car pulled into one of only three empty spaces behind the restaurant as Marty watched.

As soon as the driver's side door opened, the sound of two children arguing could be heard.

"I want to watch *Nemo* next," the voice of a small girl whined.

"*Little Mermaid,*" another voice, which could either have been either a small girl or a small boy, squealed.

"We just watched *Little Mermaid,*" the first girl whined again. "I'm sick of *The Little Mermaid.*"

A large man stepped out of the driver's side of the car. He was built like an ex–football player and wore khaki pants and a navy polo shirt. After he stepped out, he immediately leaned back into the car, and Marty could hear his low muffled voice saying something, probably to the children.

A woman exited the other side of the car. After she closed the door, she looked at her reflection in the glass and fluffed her blonde hair. She and her husband pulled open the two back doors simultaneously, and like synchronized swimmers, they both dove into the backseat, leaving only their backsides and legs visible outside of the vehicle.

The woman reemerged with a small blonde girl in her arms. She was wearing a white shirt with a pink heart in the middle and pink pants. She was probably only two or three. The father, from the other side of the car, pulled out a girl with long light brown hair who was probably about five years old. She was wearing jean shorts, a dark green shirt, and dark green shoes.

"Olive shoes," Marty whispered under his breath. A surprising memory overcame him of his Sonya whispering "olive shoe" in Marty's ear when he came home from work.

The first time Marty worked up the courage to tell Sonya that he loved her, he quickly mumbled it in her ear during a long post-date embrace. The romance of the movie they had just seen still hung heavy in the air between them, and it seemed like the perfect time to make the leap from causal dating to a serious relationship. Sonya stepped back from their embrace and said, "Did you just say 'olive shoe'?" Marty was momentarily embarrassed, but then started laughing so hard he nearly had to sit down to steady himself.

He looked her in the eye, took a deep breath, and said, "No, I said I love you." Still laughing, Sonya gave him a kiss and said, "Olive shoe, too." The joke carried on for their entire relationship. Sonya even wore dark olive shoes under her long white wedding dress.

Marty slouched back further into the darkness. The further back he sat, the less likely the family was to see him. But the further back he sat, the more vagrant-like he would appear if they did see him.

The car doors slammed shut, and the five-year-old girl skipped ahead of her parents. They were going to have to walk by Marty to get to the front of the restaurant, the only entrance.

The little girl suddenly stopped skipping, and Marty's stomach tightened. Did she see him?

"Come on!" the girl called over her shoulder. "I'm hungry!"

Marty breathed sigh of relief. The father laughed and pointed his keys at the SUV, which chirped as he set the alarm. He jogged to catch up with his daughter, and the mother walked more slowly behind, holding the toddler's hand.

The family was going to soon walk right in front of Marty. If they saw him, they might tell the restaurant manager to call the police. Or the beefy-looking dad might decide to remove Marty from the premises himself if he was worried Marty had plans to break into their car and steal their copy of *The Little Mermaid*.

Marty scooted back further into the crevasse between the dumpster and the restaurant, hoping the darkness would completely disguise his presence. As he moved back, his foot slipped, and he kicked a small rock into the parking lot. Marty froze.

The mother, the father, and both little girls looked at Marty. The mother immediately picked up the toddler and walked quickly to catch up to her husband. The father stared at Marty for several moments.

"Hi," the five-year-old said to Marty.

"Hi," Marty said.

The father furrowed his brow as he looked at Marty. He grabbed his daughter's hand and led his family quickly around the building, looking back at Marty several times along the way.

Marty sat alone in the darkness. He wondered if he should go in and tell Dogger that a family had seen him hanging out back there and the owners might call the cops. He considered it seriously and stood up, staring at the Indiana license plate.

Marty was usually very good at reading people, but this family was tough. He could see the father wanting to play the hero in front of his wife and little girls by alerting the police to a loiterer. But these wealthy families sometimes prided themselves on being charitable and open-minded. Perhaps the mother would take it as an opportunity to teach the girls that there were many people less fortunate than they were. *There are people who don't have homes and SUVs with DVD players in the backseat. There are people with problems much larger than whether to watch* The Little Mermaid *or* Nemo.

Marty slowly sat back down, pushing himself back into the dark space between the dumpster and the restaurant. Since they were from out of town, they probably wouldn't say anything. They would probably just eat their pancakes quickly and leave. They'd have a story to tell their friends about the sad homeless man they saw and felt very sorry for in the town of Mason, Iowa.

Marty sat on the curb and leaned against the dumpster. The dark parking lot grew even darker. Although Marty tried to fight it, all he could think about was what could have been if Sonya had never left him. He could have been a protective father driving an SUV and eating pancakes with his family late at night.

"Run," Dogger whispered, jolting Marty from his thoughts. "Run fast."

2

Mrs. Barnes and her four-year-old son were finally leaving Fashionable Finds. She hadn't purchased anything, but the destruction she had done to the previously tidy sales floor would keep Angela and Kelly busy for a while. When Mrs. Barnes reached the door, Angela called out, "Thanks for shopping at Fashionable Finds! Have a great day!"

Mrs. Barnes seemed to not hear as she walked out the door, pulling her son behind her. Kelly, who was on the floor picking up fallen panties, rolled her eyes at Angela.

"What?" Angela said.

"Nice use of a corporate-approved customer send-off," Kelly said with a laugh. "You got that from the employee manual, didn't you?"

"It doesn't hurt to be nice to our best customer," Angela said.

"You're such a corporate ho," Kelly said.

"Hey, we have to get sales up around here," Angela said. She pulled her shoulder-length brown hair back and twisted it into a bun, holding it tenuously in place with a Fashionable Finds pen. "They've closed three stores in the last month alone due to dragging sales."

"The sad thing is, no one who works in corporate even knows you're their ho," Kelly said, sighing dramatically. "You've been working here too long to just be a sales associate."

"You sound like my mother," Angela said. "Except she probably wouldn't say 'ho' quite as much."

"She would if she knew her daughter worked as a professional corporate ho," Kelly said.

"By the way, I'm not a sales associate," Angela said, tapping her name badge. "I'm a *senior* sales associate."

"You're still just a sales associate," Kelly said. "The 'senior' title only means you've been here too long."

"I'm going to count down Register Two," Angela announced, anxious to change the topic. "So if we have any more customers before we lock up, just use Register One."

"Got it," Kelly said.

As Angela counted the money, her mind quickly wandered to a familiar topic. What would happen if she just took this money? What if, instead of making the bank drop at the end of the night, she just left town? Or she could tell people that one of the homeless guys from the edge of town mugged her. Then she could travel the world. She could buy a Kate Spade bag. Maybe she could even get a nose job so she didn't look part human, part pig.

"Do you want to go out to Hysteria after work?" Kelly said. She had apparently finished rearranging the panty table, but it still looked like a mess. At least everything was off the floor.

"I don't know." Angela stopped counting. She wrote down $1,220 on the notepad next to her. "I don't really want to run into Jason."

"Oh," Kelly said. "Lovers' quarrel?"

"No," Angela said. She already hated this conversation. "We'd have to be lovers to have a lovers' quarrel. We aren't lovers. We aren't anything. Besides, he gives a weird vibe."

"Weird how?" Kelly asked as she tried on necklaces, looking up into the small mirrors attached to the jewelry spinners.

"Weird like something is wrong with him," Angela said. "But I just can't put my finger on it."

"Do you think he's gay?" Kelly asked.

"What?" Angela said. "That's stupid."

"I don't know," Kelly said. "It's just one possibility."

"I don't think he's gay," Angela said.

"What's so weird about him?" Kelly asked. She stopped looking at herself in the jewelry spinner mirror and looked at Angela.

"Nothing, I guess," Angela said with a shrug. In reality, there were plenty of things weird about him. A handsome man in a nightclub who showed patient, consistent, and sober interest in Angela was weird. Jason didn't really fit in at Hysteria, either. He seemed too mature, too together, to be a regular at a trashy club filled with drunken twenty-somethings.

Kelly turned to Angela and pointed to two small barrettes covered with pink sparkling plastic gems in her hair. "Do you like these?"

"They look cute," Angela said. "Do you want to buy them?"

"No," Kelly said. "But I'll bring them back tomorrow, I swear."

"You don't work tomorrow," Angela said.

"Then I'll bring them back the next day," Kelly said. "Just keep this in the junk drawer under the register."

Angela took the black piece of plastic that the barrettes used to be attached to from Kelly. The price on the back read $5.99. Angela sighed and stuck the black piece of plastic in the drawer. She saw several other empty jewelry and hair accessory holders stuffed in the drawer. A few were the result of shoplifters, but most were the result of Kelly "borrowing" things to go out.

"Well, let's go ahead and lock up for the night," Angela said, glancing at her watch. Kelly nearly ran to the front door to pull the latch. She walked back to the registers and rested her head down on the counter.

"What can I do?" Kelly asked without lifting her head.

"I can finish up here," Angela said, just as she knew Kelly expected. "Why don't you go ahead and take off?"

"Are you sure?" Kelly asked, although she had already lifted herself off the counter and started walking toward the back room, probably to get her purse.

"Yeah, it's no problem," Angela said.

"You are such a doll," Kelly said as she disappeared into the back room. She quickly reemerged with her white leather purse in her hands. She gave herself a quick look as she walked past the fitting-room mirrors.

"Have fun at Hysteria," Angela said. Angela followed Kelly to the front door and watched her hurriedly unlatch the lock and trot out toward her yellow VW Beetle, which was parked in the otherwise empty parking lot next to Angela's black Chrysler Sebring. Angela locked the double front doors, pulling them once to ensure they were once again latched before returning to the registers.

The register printed a report showing the total number of transactions, listed the items sold by their SKU codes, and indicated the total dollar amount that should be in the register. Comparing the report with the bank deposit form, Angela realized the register was short. It was short $100.23.

Angela could feel her stomach sink. If the register was off by more than two dollars, it was reported to corporate. Angela would also have to file an incident report for her manager, Natasha.

Angela ran to the front door. Maybe Kelly took the money for her night out. When she reached the door and looked through the glass she saw her black Chrysler sitting alone in the dark parking lot. Kelly was gone.

Angela spun on her heel and ran back to the register. She could feel her heart pounding in her chest, which only added to her panic. She grabbed the phone and called Kelly's cell. The phone rang only once before going to voice mail. Angela could hear Kelly's upbeat voice saying, "Leave me a message, OK?" as she quickly hung up the phone before the voice mail could begin recording.

Angela stared at the phone, trying to slow her thoughts and think about the situation rationally. Kelly might have a habit of borrowing barrettes and bracelets from the store, but she had never stolen money before. Angela herself had witnessed easy opportunities for Kelly to steal from the store or from customers, but she had never even acted as if she were tempted to do so. She seemed to think that borrowing accessories was a perk of the job, and not at all the same as stealing.

Angela typed the request code into the register once again to get the daily transaction report. She pulled the register tape out just moments before it finished printing, causing the ink to smear on the last lines of the report. Despite the smudge marks, the number at the bottom of the receipt was clearly still the same as before, and it was still $100.23 more than what was on the bank deposit slip.

Angela leaned back against the wall, crumpling the receipt in her hands. It seemed very unlikely that Kelly would take a hundred dollars out of the register, especially when Angela was working.

It didn't matter that Angela hadn't stolen the hundred dollars; what mattered was that she would inevitably be blamed for the missing money. Angela could not be fired. She could feel panic begin to push into her mind. The twenty-three cents in change could be disregarded as human error. But one hundred dollars didn't look like an error. Angela doubted Natasha or corporate would assume it was an error.

Angela thought for a minute about how much money was in her purse. Maybe she could replenish the register with enough money that it wouldn't look so suspicious. Her purse, however, contained only four dollars.

Angela picked up the phone by the register and dialed Kelly's cell number once again. This time it rang twice, and Kelly answered.

"Hello?" Kelly said. In the background indistinct music was playing, which immediately faded as if the radio were hastily turned down. Kelly was probably still in her car.

"It's Angela," Angela said. She realized her voice was shaking. "There is a problem at the store."

"What happened?" Kelly said. "Are you OK?"

"Register One is short a hundred dollars," Angela said. She tried to smooth out the report that she had crumpled up earlier. "It's short $100.23."

"Oh, my God," Kelly said. She sounded genuinely surprised and concerned, making Angela feel guilty for even thinking she might have taken the money.

"I know," Angela said with a shaky sigh.

"Natasha is going to kill us," Kelly said. "What are you going to do?"

"Natasha is going to kill me, not you," Angela said.

"Well, aren't you lucky to be the senior sales associate," Kelly said with a small laugh. "Are you going to file a report tonight?"

"Only if I have to," Angela said. She opened her purse again and began to search for money hidden in any of the many small compartments sewn into the interior.

"What do you mean?" Kelly said. "I think you have to."

"If I file a report, I'll get fired," Angela said. Kelly was silent. "I'd be willing to replace that hundred dollars with my own money, if I can."

"Do you have a hundred dollars?" Kelly asked.

"No," Angela said. "I have four dollars."

"You could run out to the ATM," Kelly said. "There is a drive-up ATM at the bank where we make the drops."

"I only have about twenty dollars in my account," Angela said. She could feel her cheeks growing hot with embarrassment at this confession. "We don't get paid until Friday, so I am operating off credit right now."

"That sucks," Kelly said.

"Do you have any extra cash?" Angela asked, her voice stammering with hesitation.

"I'm broke," Kelly said. "Why do you think I had to borrow those barrettes?"

"But you are going out tonight," Angela said. She could hear her voice rising into a maternal tone that she hated. "How can you afford that?"

"I don't plan on buying any drinks," Kelly said with a laugh.

Of course not. Kelly never had to buy any of her drinks.

"I don't know what to do," Angela said, her eyes moving rapidly between the bank slip and the transaction report.

"Call your sister," Kelly said. "She's rich, right?"

"Richer than me," Angela said.

"I'm sure she'd be willing to help if she knew you could lose your job," Kelly said.

"Thanks, Kelly," Angela said with a heavy sigh.

"Sorry I can't help," Kelly said. "I'll say hi to Jason for you if I see him."

Angela hung up the phone. She didn't want to call her sister. Calling her sister would mean letting her in on details of her life that Angela never wanted her sister to know. It was embarrassing enough to tell Kelly she only had twenty-four dollars to her name, but if she told her sister, her sister would tell her parents. Her parents wouldn't tell anyone because they would be so embarrassed by their youngest daughter's latest failure in life.

If Angela wanted to keep her job, she knew she didn't have a choice. She picked up the phone.

"Hello," a tired-sounding voice answered, and Angela suddenly realized it was already 11:15 PM.

"Christine?" Angela said.

"What's wrong, Angela?" Christine asked.

"I'm sorry to call you so late," Angela said. "Could I borrow one hundred dollars? I promise I'll pay you back."

"What happened?" Christine sounded more awake now. Angela could hear another voice in the background, probably her husband, Jack. "It's my sister ..." Christine said, her voice trailing away from the phone.

"I'm closing the store, and the register is short by over one hundred dollars," Angela said quickly. "I know I'll get fired for this. I can't lose my job."

"A hundred dollars?" Christine said.

"Yes, I've counted it several times," Angela said. She added quickly, "Please don't tell Mom and Dad."

"I'm sure this happens all the time," Christine said.

"No, it doesn't," Angela said, frustrated that her sister was trying to minimize the significance of the situation. "I've worked here for four years, and the most I've ever seen a register off is by $18.50. And that required a written incident report for corporate."

"What do you think happened?" Christine asked.

"I'm not sure. It could have just been an honest mistake," Angela said. "Listen, I only have four dollars on me. If I could drive over and borrow the rest from you tonight, I promise I'll pay it back."

"I don't have any cash with me. But it doesn't matter. As the store manager, Natasha will probably have to take the fall for this," Christine said, "not you."

"What should I do?" Angela said. She could feel her eyes stinging as she tried to hold back tears. Some sisters would feel more empathy if their little sister was crying, but Christine would probably only become irritated and say that Angela was being melodramatic. Or worse, Christine might strangely enjoy hearing the distress in her voice.

"You mentioned an incident report?" Christine said. "Just file that, and call it a night. Follow the standard procedures. Don't try to cover it up."

"OK," Angela said. "Sorry again for calling so late. Please don't tell Mom and Dad."

"I know. I won't," Christine said. "Let me know how it turns out."

Angela scrolled through the receipt of transactions on the register. Maybe she could void a hundred-dollar cash transaction. The only problem was that they would see that a transaction had been voided after hours.

Angela felt sick. It didn't matter that she hadn't stolen one hundred dollars out of the register. What mattered was that it *looked* like she had stolen one hundred dollars out of the register. Angela wondered what her mom and dad would say. It didn't seem possible that they could be more embarrassed or disappointed in their daughter, but this would just be further evidence that their unplanned child had an unplanned and unsuccessful life.

3

Any guilt Marty felt quickly dissipated as they walked into the Route 1 Liquor and Cigarette Depot. Worry over an anonymous waitress not being able to pay her electric bills or scaring the Indiana family in the parking lot seemed fictional and distant now. They had gotten away with it, and the reward more than justified the means.

"Hey, Mr. Evans," Dogger said to the old man standing behind the register with crooked posture.

"Hello, Dogger." Mr. Evans looked Dogger up and down, and then Marty. "You fellas buying today, or are you just here to lick the floor?"

Dogger pulled a small stack of ones and fives out of this pocket and held it in front of Mr. Evans. Mr. Evans nodded.

"I don't even want to know how you got that," Mr. Evans said. He folded his arms and leaned against the wall. "Why don't you make your selection quickly, and then get out of here? I close in five minutes."

Marty licked his lips and walked immediately to the third aisle of the small store. The whiskey aisle. Marty's eyes moved excitedly up and down the row of whiskey bottles.

"How much do we have?" Marty asked Dogger, who was in the neighboring aisle.

"Twenty-one dollars," Dogger said.

"Wow," Marty said, swallowing back the saliva that was quickly filling his mouth. Marty found the largest and cheapest bottle of whiskey: Black and White. It was only $8.95 and one-and-a-half times the size of a regular bottle. Marty walked back to the register and put the bottle on the counter. Mr. Evans frowned and didn't move. He was still leaning against the wall with his arms folded.

"Move it, Dogger," Mr. Evans said.

"Hold up," Dogger called back. Marty was beginning to feel anxious. He just wanted to get the booze and go. If the County Inn had called the police, there was a good chance the cops would come around there looking for them. Unfortunately, most members of the Mason police force knew Marty and Dogger too well.

"Dogger, just grab some beer, and let's go," Marty said. Dogger spun around in the aisle a few times before ducking down. He stood up with a twelve-pack of Huber beer in his hand, holding it up at Marty. Marty nodded. "Good, let's go."

"That will be $15.75," Mr. Evans said, ringing up the beer before Dogger even put it on the counter.

"That's all?" Dogger said, putting down the beer on the counter. "Hold on."

Dogger trotted to the first aisle. Marty looked out the windows behind Mr. Evans. He was expecting the police to arrive at any minute looking for them.

"Dogger," Marty said. "We don't have to spend all the money now. Come on!"

"You'll thank me for it," Dogger said, trotting back to the register with a bag of chips in one hand and a can of Slim Jims in the other. Mr. Evans began punching things into the register.

"$20.53," Mr. Evans said, opening a paper bag.

Marty and Dogger walked quickly out of the Route 1 Liquor and Cigarette Depot. The paper bag crinkled around the form of the whiskey bottle as Marty held it close to his body. If he dropped it, they wouldn't have enough money to get another.

"To Hillside Park?" Dogger said, smiling at Marty.

"Perfect." Marty laughed. The men walked quickly down Route 1. They walked out of the innermost circle of Mason, past the restaurants and hotels, past the gas stations and the strip malls. The landscape quickly changed from commerce to residential. Marty licked his lips. They were getting close.

"The park closed hours ago," Dogger said. "We should have the place all to ourselves."

Marty laughed again, but he wasn't sure why. As he held the bag tighter he realized almost all the joy in his life revolved around Black and White Whiskey. It wasn't a sad or disturbing revelation. He was just pleased that there was something in this world that could still make him smile.

Marty and Dogger started running as they entered the park. Marty scanned the moonlit landscape. It appeared empty. The swing set, the slide, the picnic pavilion all sat unused.

"Merry-go-round," Dogger said as he continued to run. Marty didn't argue. The merry-go-round, while not enclosed, actually offered the best protection. The merry-go-round sat just behind a crest in the hill and was the one part of the park that could not be seen from the road. Dogger and Marty had passed out on the merry-go-round countless times in the past, and nothing sounded better than doing the same tonight.

Marty collapsed on the merry-go-round, and it began to spin slowly under his weight. Without taking the bottle out of the bag, or even getting comfortable first, Marty unscrewed the top with shaking hands and took a long drink. The whiskey felt warm and tingled as it went down his throat. Marty immediately relaxed.

Dogger sat on the merry-go-round next to Marty and tore the twelve-pack's thin cardboard skin He opened his beer and drank the entire can in one motion. Throwing the can aside, he looked at Marty with a suddenly serious look on his face. "When are you going to tell me what happened with your son?"

"Not this," Marty said. He took another long pull of whiskey. "Why do you always try to start these discussions when I'm just trying to have a good time?"

"I know your son isn't a doctor," Dogger said. "Or a lawyer."

"OK," Marty said.

"Is he a drug dealer?" Dogger said. "A meth head?"

"No," Marty said, although he wondered if that was true. "He's no criminal."

"Did Sonny kill someone?" Dogger said.

"What did I just say? And guessing isn't going to get you anywhere," Marty said.

"Wait a minute. Did you kill Sonny?" Dogger said.

Marty sat up and looked at Dogger. Dogger's eyes were wide; there was no hint of whimsy or play.

"What do you think?" Marty said.

"I'm just asking," Dogger said.

"No," Marty said. "I didn't kill Sonny." Dogger seemed to relax, and he opened another beer. Marty, taking another drink of whiskey, wondered if Sonny was somewhere right now telling lies of his own.

4

The incident reports looked aged, outdated, and incriminating. Peeling back the first layer of the report revealed several carbon-copy forms, ensuring that news of the incident was shared with all the key players. The shredder whirred as Angela destroyed the report she had completed longhand moments before. She wanted to come in early the next morning and talk to Natasha. If she put some thought into this, she might be able to make it seem as if nothing of significance happened.

Feeling claustrophobic in the back room and overwhelmed with the weight of the situation, Angela knew she had to leave. She locked the filing cabinet and the safe and set the alarm. Angela moved quickly from the back room to the front door, all while building a story in the back of her mind about Mrs. Barnes demanding a refund on merchandise she had bought the week before. It wasn't exactly lying; it was reorganizing the facts. Maybe, if she edited the story just right, an incident report wouldn't even be necessary. Angela only had fifteen seconds to get out of the store after the alarm was set.

Brushing quickly past the racks of clothes, the alarm chirped off the seconds as she made her way to the front of the store. Angela pushed open the glass door and was met with the warm summer night air. She turned and tugged at the door to double-check the lock and could hear the alarm chirping in quick succession, and then one long sustained beep. The store was secured and the alarm set. Angela spun on her heel and began walking to her car. The breeze felt cool and soothing on her tears.

"Dammit!" Angela yelled with sudden realization, her voice echoing in the empty parking lot. She had forgotten the most important thing. The money for the bank drop was still in the store.

She heard a couple of people laughing and squinted into the darkness, looking outside the periphery of the parking lot lights. It was probably just some drunks. There was a bar called Tommy's Tavern on the other side of the strip mall that seemed to attract the sort of drunks one would expect to find at a frat party if this were a college town. They were young and loud and liked to advertise their drunkenness with occasional outbursts of "Wooo" or "Yeah."

Angela had to go back into the store. If she forgot to make the bank drop, any story she came up with would look suspect.

Angela could hear more laughing from the parking lot. She quickly inserted her key and pushed open the door to the store. She turned and latched the door behind her as the alarm sounded, a shrill blast of beeps in machine-gun succession. Angela ran to the back room, knocking several blouses off a round rack as she ran by. She typed in the code and pressed Enter. The alarm stopped.

Angela turned and saw the path of clothing she had knocked onto the floor. She could feel tears burning her eyes. All she wanted to do was go home and forget about today, but it was as if everything and everyone in the world was working against her. She walked over to the register, carefully stepping over fallen clothes as she moved. The large zippered pouch was sitting on the counter next to Register One. At least the bank drop hadn't disappeared. She let out a shaky sigh and began picking up fallen clothes and straightening skewed racks.

The silence in the store was eerie. The metal hooks of the hangers clinked and scraped on the metal racks as she hung blouses. Angela thought she could hear one of the corporate-approved CDs playing, tinny and almost indistinct, in the background. She froze and carefully listened, but there was only silence.

"I think I'm losing it," Angela whispered. She couldn't help but smile when she realized that talking to herself only confirmed this suspicion.

Suddenly, a loud knocking sound made Angela jump. Two flashlight beams shone through the front door and searched the store sales floor. She squinted toward the lights and could see two police officers standing outside the front doors. Angela's stomach tightened. Why were they there? Angela waved and accidentally dropped the blouse she was holding in her hand. One of the officers motioned her to come to the door. Angela stared at the ground as she quickly walked to the front door. How could the police know about the missing money already? Did Christine call the police? She tried to smile, but neither the male nor the female officer smiled back.

5

The stars swirled in the sky, leaving incandescent trails in their wake. Marty could no longer tell if it was the merry-go-round or the whiskey that made the sky move in such a manner. He pulled himself up to see Dogger slumped against the nearby tree, and he realized the merry-go-round was motionless.

"Dogger," Marty whispered. He wasn't sure if Dogger was awake or passed out. The ground around him was littered with Huber beer cans.

"Yeah?" Dogger said without lifting his head.

"Got any beer left?" Marty asked.

"No," Dogger snorted. "You asked me that five minutes ago, and ten minutes ago, and fifteen minutes ago, and ..."

"Really?" Marty said. He didn't remember asking before. Maybe Dogger was just being a jerk.

"Really," Dogger said. He straightened himself up against the tree. "And you," he said, pointing at Marty, "do not have any whiskey left."

Marty knew that. His empty whiskey bottle sat in the middle of the merry-go-round. It had been a good night, but Marty always wanted more.

"Do you want to stay here tonight?" Marty asked.

"Do you think you could wake up before the sun rises?" Dogger said.

"Unlikely," Marty said with a small laugh. "Good point."

"Let's just relax here a little longer," Dogger said. "I don't even care if someone takes our sleeping spot in the Dead Zone."

Marty was about to lie back down when a light caught his eye. He turned and looked at the slide, which was partially illuminated by a bright light. The metal slide reflected brightly, shooting a wide beam of light into a nearby tree. Marty closed his eyes and looked again; the light was gone.

"Shh," Dogger said, although Marty wasn't saying anything. "I think I heard something."

Marty strained to listen. At first he heard nothing other than a lone cricket chirping, but as he listened more carefully he thought he could hear the low hum of a car idling. Marty couldn't see the street from where he was sitting. It's why they chose this spot to begin with; people driving by couldn't see the merry-go-round from the road. But it didn't sound like this car was driving by. It was sitting and waiting.

Marty inched his way to the edge of the merry-go-round. The sound of his body sliding along small bits of dirt and sand was deafening.

"Shh," Dogger said.

The shifting weight on the merry-go-round caused it to begin to swing around slowly. A low, rusty creak filled the air and seemed to echo off the trees. Dogger got up to his knees and grabbed the merry-go-round, stopping the motion and the sound instantly.

"Are you crazy?" Dogger said. "Just be quiet."

The light reappeared; it hit the top of the tree well above Marty's head. Then it moved to the picnic alcove and the swings. Marty finally realized what he saw was a spotlight.

"It's the cops," Marty whispered. He stood up off the merry-go-round and onto shaky ground. He stumbled, catching himself with his palms on the ground, and decided to stay low anyway. He looked over at Dogger. Dogger's eyes looked wide and fearful.

"I am not getting picked up tonight," Dogger whispered. The spotlight continued to search. It seemed to be getting dangerously close to Dogger and Marty as it began to systematically sweep back and forth throughout the park.

"They know we're here," Dogger said. He began a slow run, his head still tucked down. Marty followed. "We gotta run."

Marty looked back quickly at the pile of cans, scanning them to ensure they were all clearly open and empty. He was always left wanting a little bit more. It didn't matter that they needed to run. So long as he was conscious, he wanted more.

"Come on," Dogger said. He grabbed Marty's arm and pulled him. As Marty began trotting away, he continued looking behind himself. He was imagining and regretting even the smallest drops of alcohol they were leaving behind. The spotlight suddenly fell on the merry-go-round. The whiskey bottle sparkled like a bright beacon.

"They're here!" Marty said. The flash of the spotlight injected sobriety into his veins. Both Dogger and Marty instantly became upright and began running. Marty wasn't sure where they would run to, but he knew that if they ran down the hill behind the park they would be in a residential neighborhood. There were enough streets and cul-de-sacs that they might be able to evade the cops.

Marty ran, half out of control, down the hill. He could hear voices behind him. He knew it was the cops. Marty and Dogger had left behind evidence of a crime. Drinking in a public park. Open bottles. Closed park. Public intox. There were a thousand reasons the cops could justify taking them in and handling them as roughly as they pleased.

"Wait!" he could hear Dogger far behind him. Marty couldn't stop as fear propelled him out of the park.

⚡ ⚡ ⚡

Angela turned the radio on to the oldies station. It was comforting, mindless music, and she wanted to forget everything that had just taken place. The cops had been really mean about everything. They had followed her to the bank for the drop. It was as if they were ensuring she was making the bank drop instead of running off with the sacks of Fashionable Finds money. It was humiliating.

After she made the bank drop and waved blindly in the darkness to the police car behind her, there was only one comforting thought: the bank might miscount the money and accidentally add one hundred dollars to Register One's total. Angela knew it was unreasonable, yet found some hope in that thought. She convinced herself that the scenario of the bank accidentally adding one hundred dollars to the deposit was quite possible and, in fact, quite probable. She might not need to concoct a realistic story about Mrs. Barnes demanding an undocumented hundred-dollar refund.

Angela's car turned down Jewel Street, and the familiarity of the houses and the neighborhood was reassuring. It hadn't felt like she was going to make it through the day, but she had. It was 12:45 AM, and the streets were empty. Most of the houses were dark, with the exception of a few squares of dimly glowing windows.

Angela reached in her purse, which was sitting on the passenger's seat, and felt around for her cell phone. She pulled it out and dialed Kelly's number.

"Hey," Kelly answered. Loud music was playing in the background. She was obviously at Hysteria, probably getting free drinks from anyone she wanted.

"Hey," Angela said. "The night just got worse. I forgot to take the bank drop with me and set off the alarm."

"What?" Kelly yelled.

"I set off the alarm, and the police came," Angela said loudly.

"Police?" Kelly said. "What happened?"

"I set off the alarm," Angela repeated loudly.

"What?" Kelly said. The heavy beat of a techno song was pounding in the background.

"Forget it!" Angela yelled. "I'll talk to you tomorrow."

Angela turned off her phone and threw it in her purse. Kelly was useless in times of crisis. She turned the radio up and tapped her fingers to "Big Girls Don't Cry" as she turned down Bethel Street. She pressed gently on the gas. She was so close to home and to ending one of the worst days of her life. She could see the green street sign ahead for Herbert Street. Angela was proud to have bought a one-bedroom townhouse on the newest and cleanest street in Mason.

Suddenly, a dark shadow jumped out of the woods by the sidewalk and landed directly in front of Angela's car. A large thud and simultaneous crack sounded. The car jolted, slowing down greatly but not stopping. Angela stared at the hood of her car, mesmerized. Shocked. It wasn't real. There was a man hanging onto the hood of her car.

✕ ✕ ✕

Marty Freeman was still drunk, but adrenaline and pain sobered him up enough to realize that he had just been hit by a car. Marty's body was partly collapsed over the black hood of a Chrysler Sebring, his ripped shirt and skin embedded in the silver grill. At least it wasn't a cop car. Marty could feel a strong, warm summer breeze wildly tousling his hair from behind.

"Dogger," Marty said. "Help." Marty could barely speak. Dogger was probably still catching up. He could never keep up with Marty, especially when they were running from the police. Now that he was forced to stop running, Dogger could catch up to him. So could the cops.

As Marty's heart pumped more fear and panic throughout his body, he became aware of a terrible pain in his chest, his right arm, his neck, and his stomach. He couldn't feel his legs and wondered if they were still there. Maybe they were run over.

Marty tried to look down and expected to see nothing of his body below his torso. To his surprise and relief, his legs were still there, although they were twisted and broken—mostly concealed under the car. He couldn't see anything past his knees, where they disappeared completely under the car.

Marty's eyes strained to focus on his legs, and then on the ground. The road was blurring and swirling in the familiar way that whiskey repainted the world. Marty closed his eyes, concentrating on the relaxing sensation of the wind tugging his hair.

He reopened his eyes and stared once again at the ground. This time, it was clear. The pavement was moving beneath him at a dangerous speed. The summer breeze tousling his hair wasn't a summer breeze at all. A terrible chill overcame Marty's entire body. The car was still moving.

Marty tightened his grip on the hood of the car. Through the windshield, he could see the driver, a young woman with brown hair and dark, wide eyes. She was staring forward. Was it possible she didn't know she hit him? Marty realized he hadn't screamed or yelled or made any kind of sound. Maybe she just didn't realize what happened.

"Hey," Marty's voice was weak. His chest hurt sharply as he took in a large breath of air, hoping to build a stronger voice. "Hey, lady!"

The woman did not move. Her facial expression remained stoic, her eyes wide and locked forward. It seemed the reality of the situation had not registered with this woman.

"Hey," Marty called again. "Are you drunk? High?" There was no visible response from the young woman; the car continued to travel swiftly along the dark street. Marty knew a guy that was high on meth and didn't even realize he had cut his arm down to the bone with a chainsaw.

"Dogger," Marty called. The pain in his chest was suffocating. "Help!" Quickly scanning the darkness beyond the streetlights, Marty couldn't see Dogger or the police. They must still be in the park, or maybe they were arresting Dogger right now for public intox.

Marty felt the slight pull of g-force and strained to hold onto the hood of the car as it turned a corner. He knew if he let go and fell off the hood, the car would run him over and kill him instantly. Marty gripped the side of the crumpled hood with his left hand and the grill with his right hand. Although somewhat stable, it still felt like his flesh was moving and tearing as the car turned.

The car was in a residential neighborhood. One side of the street was undeveloped, and the other side was lined with townhouses. Marty looked through the windshield and out the back window of the car. He saw a figure burst out of the darkness and shamble quickly down the road. It had to be Dogger. The g-force once again tore at his chest and stomach. The car was pulling into a driveway.

"OK, lady," Marty whispered. "Maybe you just wanted to get me off the street before you stopped. Maybe you have a first-aid kit. Maybe you're a nurse."

The car pulled further up the driveway, and Marty could hear a loud motorized sound behind him. A garage door. He had to stay in the driveway if there was any chance of Dogger seeing him.

"Stop the car," Marty whispered. He could feel the sharp pain in his lungs as he whispered, but he was compelled to keep talking. If he kept talking to her like a rational person, then she must be a rational person. "Maybe you get into your house through the garage door. But stop the car here. Go call for help. Get your first-aid kit. Stop the car here in the driveway."

The car didn't stop. The sound and lighting around him changed distinctly as the car pulled into the garage. Marty squinted at the woman behind the wheel. Her face was unchanged, and her eyes were unmoving.

"That's OK," Marty said. He realized his back was gently brushing the wall of the garage behind him. "Maybe it is just force of habit. You always park in the garage, right? Leave the door up so Dogger can see me when he runs by. Just turn off the car, and go call for help."

The car turned off. Marty relaxed a little. The garage was still and quiet.

"Call for help," Marty whispered, pushing his voice as far as he could. The woman stared forward for a few minutes longer, as if she were studying a speck on the windshield. Then her eyes shifted, and she was looking at Marty. She reached up and pressed something on her visor. The garage door began to rumble and close.

"No," Marty whispered. He stared at the woman in the car. "Are you high, woman? Crazy?" She looked at Marty with what seemed to be a bizarre indifference. Marty was just a bug on her windshield.

✗ ✗ ✗

Angela Johnson had hit a man, and she knew it. She had never hit anything organic with her car, never a deer, raccoon, dog, or squirrel. She'd hit a mailbox once when she was fifteen and her dad was teaching her how to drive. It was a mistake, but she was grounded for a month as a result.

She stared at the man clinging to the front of her car. He stared back at her. Her car didn't lose control. It just suddenly happened. There was a sound and a feel to it, but it wasn't what Angela thought it would feel like to hit something large and living.

Angela slowly reached into her purse and touched her cell phone. She winced. Who could she call? Her sister? Never. It would mean voluntarily disowning herself from the family. The police? It seemed logical only momentarily. She realized she had already committed a crime. A big crime. Hit and run. Only she had taken her victim with her.

It appeared as if the man was whispering, but Angela couldn't hear what he was saying. There was a small amount of blood on his chest, or it could be dirt or grease. As Angela took a closer look, the man looked rough and unclean. He looked like one of the homeless. He looked crazy.

Angela's head felt heavy with apprehension, and she realized this man was likely out of his mind. Why else would he have run in front of her car at one o'clock in the morning? She felt an unexpected hostility toward this man, this thing clinging to her car. He forced her to commit a crime. He materialized out of nowhere. She could explain to him that it was his fault, but an insane man wouldn't understand that. In fact, no one would believe this accident wasn't Angela's fault.

Angela examined the man through the windshield. He didn't look too injured, just disoriented. He looked like he could get up, walk over to Angela, and break her neck with one angry twist.

The man's mouth was sneering and still moving. It was as if he were whispering threats or a homeless-man voodoo curse on her. Angela knew that once she got out of the car, she had to run into the house and lock the door to the garage behind her. This man probably wanted to kill her.

Angela opened her car door. As she stepped out, she could immediately smell him. The smell surrounded her and entrapped her momentarily. It smelled as if she had struck a beer keg and not a human being. Not only was this man insane and homeless, but he was also drunk.

"Run," the man whispered, jolting Angela. She quickly closed the car door. She could hear a strange wheezing. Angela forced her mind to believe it was the sound of her car cooling down. The sound filled the small garage. She didn't want to appear afraid, but she could feel her face twitching with anxiety.

"Call," the man said, his voice trailing off.

Angela looked down at her feet and focused on walking around the back of the car. She inched quickly through the space between the black Sebring and the garage door. A loud chirp sounded, causing Angela to flinch in surprise, banging her elbow loudly on the garage door. The car alarm had automatically set itself.

"Get," the man continued hoarsely. Angela kept walking. She walked up the single step and opened the door to her townhouse.

"Help," the man said. Without looking back, Angela closed and locked the door behind her.

6

Dogger could hear voices behind him, but he didn't dare turn and look. He knew the police were catching up. How did Marty always run so fast? He was probably halfway to the Dead Zone by now. It would be nice if he would let Dogger catch up, even if it meant they would both get caught.

Dogger emerged from the park, stopping just inches short of running into a streetlamp that cast a long yellow glow all around him. He wrapped his hands around the cool metal pole and steadied himself. He was surrounded by a quiet and sterile-looking residential neighborhood that rested at the bottom of the hill behind the park.

"Marty," Dogger whispered hoarsely as he scanned the empty streets and sidewalks. He usually just followed Marty, but right now he couldn't see him anywhere. He listened carefully for Marty's response. The distant sound of a car engine humming and crickets were all he could hear.

"Psst," Dogger hissed. "Hey, Marty." The pavement, the trees, and the houses all seemed to sway and undulate in a bizarre and unnatural dance. Dogger was overcome with the rare feeling of wishing he was sober.

Dogger listened once again for Marty's response. He realized the humming sound was not coming from a distant car but from the flickering yellow streetlight above him. He craned his neck upward and squinted into the light. The light swirled in a nauseating spiral, and Dogger felt his back begin to arch as if his head were extremely heavy and was pulling him to the ground backward. He shot out his arms to steady himself, laughing under his breath at his own drunken stupidity. Then Dogger froze. He was suddenly aware of the sound of twigs snapping behind him, as if the cops were right there and about to pounce.

Dogger quickly spun to his right, running down the sidewalk and away from the flickering yellow light of the streetlamp. The sidewalk curled around, and Dogger realized he was on a cul-de-sac. It was a dead end. Most houses were dark, and mercifully there were no streetlights illuminating this area.

Dogger turned and looked behind him. He saw the bouncing beam of a flashlight emerge from the park, quickly followed by one police officer, and then a second. He recognized one of them, even

29

from a distance. His large build and waddle were unmistakable. It was Henry Gates.

Henry Gates was one of the meanest police officers Dogger had ever known. People in town loved him, and he even played Santa Claus every year for the kids at Johnson's Department Store. But Dogger knew what the man was really like. He had a cold heart and seemed to take special pleasure in humiliating those he considered "unworthy of Mason." He was racist, he was mean, and his heavily pitted skin made him one of the ugliest men Dogger had ever seen. Right now, he looked like an animal on the prowl.

Dogger slowly backed off the sidewalk and onto a well-trimmed lawn, hoping the darkness would shield him. Henry Gates seemed to be talking to the other officer, like they were planning the attack. Planning the kill. Dogger felt ill and hoped he wouldn't throw up on the nicely manicured lawn. He grabbed his stomach and breathed as slowly and evenly as he could.

The smaller officer started trotting down the sidewalk in the opposite direction. Henry Gates turned and looked in Dogger's direction and began quickly waddling his way up the sidewalk. Without thinking, Dogger backed up further on the lawn and into the space between two dark and quiet houses.

Henry turned and shot his flashlight beam into the woods that lined the sidewalk. He was looking for Dogger, and he didn't look like he was leaving until he found him.

Dogger noticed that small pine bushes lined the side of the house, and he quickly crouched behind one. He felt sick and claustrophobic between the prickly bush and a window to the house. If Henry caught him there, he'd accuse Dogger of attempting to break and enter.

The dark and waddling figure of Henry continued along the sidewalk of the cul-de-sac. As he reached the row of homes that formed a semicircle, he slowed his pace. Dogger held his breath as Henry began searching the front yard of the first home with his flashlight. He made wide sweeping motions with the light, sometimes pausing on a bush or tree. Then he would move forward a few more steps. He stayed on the sidewalk, as if crossing into the front yard would be breaking some rule that would require paperwork.

As Henry grew closer, Dogger could hear the heavy and rhythmic cadence of his breath. Suddenly, the rustling of something moving through the grass startled Dogger. He turned to see a large yellow dog peering around the house.

"Shh," Dogger whispered. The dog responded with a low growl, and then a small sneeze. It looked like a young Labrador, not fully grown but large enough to have a big bark and a big bite.

Dogger glanced quickly back at Henry. His view was partially obstructed by the bushes, but he could see the bottom half of his legs standing in front of the house and his flashlight searching the front yard.

Dogger turned back to the young Labrador and tried to smile at it. These were supposed to be smart dogs—maybe he would know a smile was a sign of friendliness. The dog let out a high-pitched whine, and the beam of the flashlight suddenly shot up, illuminating the side of the house and the bushes.

The dog began barking in rapid fire and bounded toward Henry. Dogger crouched down lower, nearly lying on the ground, and looked under the lowest bush branches at Henry Gates. Past the bright glow of the flashlight, Henry's face was barely readable, but Dogger thought he saw a look of fear.

Something hit Dogger hard on the side of his face, and he struggled to not let out a yell of surprise. Shaking, he reached up and touched something cool and metallic pressing against his face, torso, and legs. It was a chain. Dogger looked through the bushes again and saw the Labrador was jumping and barking at Henry, straining at the end of the leash. Henry scowled and kept walking.

7

"I just wish Doug understood," Samantha said. "Is it a bad sign that I'm thinking about divorce scenarios before we even get married?"

"What scenarios?" Wendy said. A loud snort filled the air, and she glanced toward the three sleeping men lying on cots in the Fellowship Hall. One of the men rolled from his back to his side. Wendy leaned toward Samantha, wincing as the folding chair squeaked under her shifting weight. She repeated in a whisper, "What scenarios?"

"Here is one scenario: He gets jealous when I come home late from the soup kitchen or the overnight shelter," Samantha said. "That could end in divorce."

"Why would that end in a divorce?" Wendy asked, cocking her head so quickly that her jowls jiggled.

"Coming home late is a classic sign of having an affair," Samantha said.

"Sam!" Wendy said, letting out a loud laugh. Her eyes widened, and she looked over at the three men sleeping. They didn't seem to notice, but she whispered "Sorry" to them anyway. She turned back to Samantha. "That's ridiculous. Is he really that paranoid?"

"Doug is the one who told me that coming home late is a classic sign of a cheater," Samantha said.

"So, yes," Wendy said. "He really is that paranoid."

"Here is another scenario: He turns me in to the police for doing something marginally illegal."

"Are you a marginal criminal?"

"I mean like giving free day-old doughnuts to people or letting Marty and Dogger sleep at the truck stop. In that scenario I get both fired and divorced."

"So basically, you think he'll divorce you for helping the less fortunate," Wendy said.

"He's got a weird jealous side," Samantha said. "He's a simple man in most respects, except when it comes to jealousy. When it comes to jealousy, he is ridiculously complicated, and I have yet to fully understand him."

"He needs to know you are allowed to have a life outside of him and outside of Super T's Truck Stop," Wendy whispered back, shaking her head.

"I think he understands that in theory," Samantha said. "In practice, though, he's just resentful that I'm not home being bored and useless with him on the couch and jealous that I care so much about someone that isn't him."

"He should be proud that you care about your fellow man so much," Wendy said. "You've won the Mason community service award almost every year since they opened that trophy shop and started making the plaques. I don't know if I could be with a man who didn't understand my commitment to these people."

Wendy nodded toward the three sleeping men. Samantha only recognized two of the men. The third man, with red and gray hair, must be a traveler.

"Did Marty and Dogger come by tonight?" Wendy said.

"No, but I saw them earlier today at the truck stop," Samantha said. "They seemed excited about some plans tonight."

"That's almost never good," Wendy said with a small laugh.

"I let them use the truck stop shower, gave them a hot dog, and sent them on their way," Samantha said. "They may show up later tonight, but knowing them they will just pass out somewhere instead."

"I'll leave the light on for them," Wendy said with a wink.

"I'd better get going," Samantha said, standing up.

"Sorry I was late," Wendy said. She shifted her large body awkwardly in the metal folding chair to look at the clock on the wall behind her. "It's already almost one."

"Well, the pastor's number is right by the phone in the office. He can be here immediately if you have any trouble," Samantha said. "He knows you're here alone tonight. And, of course, you can call me, too."

"I'll be fine," Wendy said. "I have a nice stack of magazines to keep me company. It's a pretty tame group, anyway."

"I'd better call Doug," Samantha said.

"Good luck," Wendy said. She reached down into her bag and pulled out a *People* magazine. "You'd better run. No sense in making Doug angrier than he probably already is."

"Bye," Samantha said as she gathered up her purse and cell phone. "I'll see you at the soup kitchen this weekend."

Samantha walked as quietly as she could out of the fellowship hall, although her hard-soled shoes clicked noisily on the laminate floor. She pushed opened the doors and left the church. The warm summer night air felt good.

Samantha turned on her cell phone. Moments later, as she walked to her car, she heard a high-pitched beep. The screen on her phone read "3 New Messages," and her stomach instantly tightened. Doug was probably upset that she didn't have her cell phone on.

Samantha sat in her car and stared at the dimly lit stained glass on the side of the church building. An eerie blue glow was cast from the windows onto the sidewalks, giving the appearance of a flowing blue asphalt stream encompassing the church. Samantha wanted to stay in her car and watch the soft glow of the church all night, but she knew every moment that passed meant her fiancé was getting more upset. Samantha held the cell phone to her ear and gripped the steering wheel tightly with her left hand, as if she were bracing herself for a collision.

The first message began: "Hi, honey. I wasn't sure if you were going to be home for dinner tonight or not. Did you decide to go help at the shelter tonight? I hope not. I really want to spend some time together. Well, give me a call."

It was Doug, and he didn't sound too angry. The second message began: "Honey, it is about nine o'clock, so I guess you are at the Methodist Church shelter? I tried calling the office number, but it just rang and rang. You must not be by the phone. Call me when you get this message. I don't know if I should eat dinner or wait for you."

He sounded miffed, but not angry. Then the third message began. This time, the anger in Doug's voice was apparent from the first word: "Why haven't you called? It's 12:02 in the morning. This is ridiculous. I have to work tomorrow morning, and I should be in bed. Instead I'm up, worried about you. Call me."

Samantha turned off her phone. She knew exactly what was about to happen. The same scene had played out several times before. She would go home, and Doug would be up. Even though she left him a note telling him that she was going to be at the shelter, and even though she had told him in conversation that she was going to be at the shelter, he would act like he didn't know where she was all night. He'd start yelling as soon as she walked through the door.

Her fiancé was a good man, but he had well-practiced senses of selective hearing and memory. Doug would only hear and remember what he chose to hear and remember. If he disagreed with Samantha, he simply did not hear it.

Samantha started the car. The clock on her dashboard glowed 1:06 AM. She even knew exactly how the fight would end. He would sleep on the couch, and Samantha would cry herself to sleep, wondering if she had made a mistake getting engaged to a man that didn't understand her. Samantha began the slow drive home, dreading what she knew was about to come.

8

Dogger kept watching until Henry and the other police officer met up again under the streetlight at the bottom of the hill outside the park. It didn't look like they had picked up Marty, so he must be on his way back to the Dead Zone.

The Labrador watched Dogger but didn't bark or whine so long as Dogger didn't move. After Henry Gates and the other police officer disappeared into the park, Dogger counted slowly to one hundred.

One … two … three … four …

Dogger could feel his entire body shaking. He laid his face down on his arms and closed his eyes, and it felt like the ground was spinning underneath him. The smell of dirt and grass made him nauseous.

Twenty-two … twenty-three … twenty-four … twenty-five …

The dog's chain pulled away from the side of Dogger's body, and he could hear the sound of the Labrador's paws moving slowly through the grass. If the dog started barking now, Henry would probably hear it and come running back.

Thirty-three … thirty-four … thirty-five … thirty-six …

Dogger lifted his head up, and the Labrador let out a small whine. Dogger froze, not even allowing his eyes to move toward the Labrador.

Forty … forty-one … forty-two … forty-three …

In his peripheral vision, Dogger could see the Labrador was approaching him. He could hear the sound of sniffing as the dog put his nose to Dogger's shirt.

Fifty-five … fifty-six … fifty-seven … fifty-eight …

The Labrador finally stopped sniffing and lay down next to Dogger. Dogger relaxed a bit and wondered if Marty was already waiting for him under Berler Bridge in the Dead Zone.

Seventy-seven … seventy-eight … seventy-nine … eighty …

Marty and Dogger had been using Berler Bridge as their meeting spot for years now. Although they rarely got separated, they always quickly found each other when they did, thanks to their permanent plan.

Eighty-five … eighty-six … eighty-seven … eighty-eight …

Dogger began to pull his feet in so he could stand up. The Labrador stood up and immediately began whining.

Ninety-five … ninety-six … ninety-seven … ninety-eight …

The whining immediately switched to a low, deep growl. Dogger had only known this Labrador for a few minutes, and he already knew this dog's pattern. This was the low growl that precipitated the loud barking.

Ninety-nine … one hundred.

Dogger stood up quickly, so quickly that he was momentarily unable to see anything at all. He began blindly sprinting through the backyard as his vision slowly returned. The young dog began barking wildly, and Dogger could hear the chiming of his tangled chain being pulled quickly through the grass. Dogger didn't look back. He had made this run before, though this neighborhood, and he knew he was only a few backyards away from Frontage Road. Once he got to Frontage, he'd have a clear shot to the Dead Zone. Hopefully Henry Gates didn't know this favorite route, too.

He grunted up the steep incline of the final backyard before Frontage Road. The Labrador's frantic barking slowed, and then finally halted. Dogger's throat burned, and he wheezed with exhaustion as he dizzily stumbled up the embankment and stepped onto the gravel road.

Dogger's shoes scraped rhythmically on the gravel as he trotted. He could hear the cars on 1–80 roaring past Mason with steady succession. It almost sounded like a waterfall in the distance, powerful but calming and reassuring.

A light suddenly appeared at Dogger's feet, and a tingle shot through his spine. Headlights. The sound of a car crunching heavily on the gravel road grew nearer, and the headlights traveled up higher and higher. Henry Gates must have found Dogger, after all.

9

The lower half of his body was twisted in an unnatural way, his legs disappearing underneath the front of the car. It looked bizarre. His torso was turned too far to the left for his chest and head to be facing forward. A contortionist of average skill could do this, but not Marty Freeman.

Marty could not feel his legs. He strained to move his right foot and listened carefully. If his foot was moving it was likely to hit something and make a sound. He heard nothing. Marty tried again. The effort was frustrating—like when he was a kid and would try to bend spoons with his mind. He was convinced that if he just tried hard enough, he could do it. No amount of effort ever made those spoons bend.

Marty's arms burned with the effort of clinging to the partially crumpled hood of the car. He let go of the car, stiffening his body in anticipation of falling onto the cement floor. His body didn't move. He felt the heavy pressure and pain in his chest and stomach increase. Looking down, he realized his torso was deeply pierced and embedded in the car. A combination of his shirt and flesh held his body close to the bent wings of the Chrysler logo. He was stuck.

Marty imagined he would probably hear sirens soon. Paramedics would rush into the garage and treat him with cold medical professionalism as they detached him from the car, and then later tonight he and Dogger would share a laugh at Marty's expense over a few beers. Maybe the cops would even let Marty and Dogger off the hook for stealing tips, given the circumstances. The small garage was quiet, and the world outside seemed quieter still.

"Help," Marty whispered. A disturbing wheeze followed. "Get help, lady. I hope you are calling someone. Someone good."

The woman who hit him seemed so cold, so unhappy. She was just like Sonya. She looked so bitter, visibly forcing a distance between them. It was identical to that cold look that Sonya used to give when Marty was drinking.

He knew the pain would increase with sobriety. The longer he had to wait for help to arrive, the more painful his position would become. If this woman was anything like his ex-wife, she might not be calling for help. Sonya would force Marty to suffer alone for a while, just to teach him a lesson.

"Come back," Marty whispered. "Help me."

Marty drew a deep and shaking breath. It caused painful pressure to build in his chest. Just as the pain became unbearable, Marty forced his voice out as he exhaled. "Hey!"

His word was barely above a whisper. No one outside of the garage would hear it, and Marty could not manage anything louder. Maybe if he rested for a bit, he would have more of a voice. But for now, he had to find another way to make noise.

Instinctively, Marty hit the hood of the car with his fist. A loud thump could be heard, and Marty's chest exploded with pain. It felt as if metal shards were splintering throughout his torso. Marty's mouth gaped open in a wheezing but otherwise silent scream. He felt hot tears squeeze out from under his tightly shut eyes and fall down his cheeks. He had to breathe. He had to focus on breathing, not on the pain.

With shaking, wheezing breaths Marty was able to calm himself down. In his mind, he tried to replay the sound of his fist hitting the car, evaluating if the sound was loud enough to justify the pain. It seemed unlikely that someone would be listening right outside the garage with a water glass pressed to the door, so it was unlikely anyone would hear the sound. It wouldn't be loud enough to justify the pain.

His chest and stomach were twisted into the metal of the hood and grill. Any vibration would tear his flesh. Marty imagined a significant strike to the hood could even be fatal if it pushed the car deeper into him.

"Salvation," Marty whispered as his eyes landed on the folding chair leaning against the wall to his left. If he could reach the folding chair it would give his left arm enough extra length to hit the left side of the car, above the wheel well. Since the crumpled metal of the hood and the wheel well barely touched, it shouldn't cause the same reverberation. It shouldn't hurt so much. Plus, the metal folding chair would make a very loud noise against the car.

The folding lawn chair was approximately six inches away from the edge of the car. Marty's back lightly touched the back wall, so it was merely a matter of extending his arm perpendicular to the left and carefully grabbing the chair. Marty knew if he wasn't steady, if his fingers grazed the chair before he grabbed it, it would fall to the ground and would be out of reach. He only had one shot at it.

Marty strained to keep his head turned, fixing his eyes on the chair. His vision was blurring. He wasn't sure if it was the pain or the alcohol.

The way his vision was beginning to swim, he might still be drunker than he realized.

He picked his left arm up off the hood of the car, slowly rotating it to extend from the left side of his body and toward the chair. He moved his arm slowly and deliberately. His fingers were shaking wildly with nerves and pain. Finally, his arm fully extended, Marty reached for the chair.

"Yes," Marty whispered. "Salvation."

The small light, part of the garage-door mechanism, clicked off. His salvation disappeared into the black. Surrounded by darkness, Marty felt very alone.

10

The tires of Samantha's car slid to a stop on the gravel road. A cloud of dust rose up around her car, glowing in the headlights and creating the illusion that the man on the road ahead of her was an ethereal presence. Without looking back, the man stuck his arm out and motioned for her to pass on by.

While she could see the streaking lights of cars traveling on I–80 just a half-mile away, Frontage Road was vacant. This unpaved stretch of road led from downtown Mason to a few small neighborhoods and eventually ended abruptly in the Dead Zone. At this moment, Samantha and this running man were the only people within eyesight. Or earshot. Samantha hit the automatic door lock button and heard the reassuring snap of all her car doors locking in unison.

The gravel crunched and popped loudly beneath the tires as she slowly pulled alongside the running man to pass him. His jeans were browned with dirt, and his white T-shirt was yellowed with age and sweat. He was probably either a transient or one of the local homeless. Samantha carefully tilted her head and peered up through the passenger side window, trying to get a glimpse of the man's face. The round cheeks and bulbous nose she saw were unmistakably Dogger's. Samantha stopped the car again.

"Hey, Dogger," Samantha called as she rolled down the passenger side window. He kept running, quickly passing by the window. Samantha moved the car up five more feet to catch up with him.

"Dogger!" Samantha called. This time, Dogger stopped running. He bent over and looked into the car. When he saw Samantha, he grinned a wide, toothless smile.

"Good evening, Samantha," he said, his words slurring. No sooner did he speak than Samantha could smell the alcohol emanating from his breath and body.

"So I guess I know what your plans with Marty were tonight," Samantha said. "Were you two drinking with Marty's son?"

"No," Dogger cackled loudly, and he shook his head. "But I do have to confess that we were drinking."

"Where is Marty?" Samantha said. She quickly glanced in her rearview mirror to make sure no one was coming. Beyond the soft glow of her taillights, she could see nothing but darkness.

"Hell if I know," Dogger said. "I lost track of him, but we always meet up under Berler Bridge when we get separated."

"If you guys want a place to stay, the church is open tonight," Samantha said. "Wendy is there. She was hoping you and Marty might come by to get a good night's sleep."

"On a beautiful night like tonight?" Dogger said. "Forget it. We're fine."

"It was nice seeing you guys today," Samantha said. "You should come by the truck stop more often."

"Thanks," Dogger said. "I'll tell Marty you said so."

Samantha didn't offer Dogger a ride, nor did he ask for one. Dogger probably knew Samantha wouldn't want to drive to the heart of the Dead Zone in the middle of the night. Besides, every minute that Samantha was not home was another minute for Doug to build up his anger. As Samantha slowly drove away she watched Dogger continue to run with his head down and legs staggering, illuminated by the red glow of her taillights, and then disappearing into darkness.

11

Angela looked out her bedroom window and to Herbert Street below. The street was empty. Leaning so that her forehead pressed the cool glass, she looked down the row of townhouses that followed the gentle curve of the street to her left. To the right, the road disappeared into darkness. It didn't appear that any neighbors had a light on. Probably, nobody saw what happened.

Her small townhouse was still. It seemed impossible that there was a dangerous-looking man who was likely insane, drunk, and very pissed off in her garage right now. Even though she couldn't see him or hear him, Angela was sure that she could smell him. The scent of hard liquor, body odor, and something she couldn't put her finger on seemed to burn her nostrils every time she inhaled. That insane man smelled toxic.

What would lead a man to drink so much that the smell of liquor emanated from his body, alerting anyone that came within twenty feet of him of his condition? Maybe he wanted everyone to know that he was sick and dangerous. Maybe he liked the smell and saw getting drunk to the point of total incoherence as an achievement, like the men at Tommy's Tavern.

But what would make him run in front of a car? Maybe he was trying to attack Angela's car and rob her. Maybe he was suicidal. Maybe this is exactly what he wanted.

Angela continued to stare out the window. She imagined what she would do if she saw a police car pull up to her house right now. The answer came to her quickly. She'd run. She'd probably have to run out the back door and jump from the balcony, but it would be worth it. In her own mind, it was easy to justify what had happened, but the police probably wouldn't bother to hear her side of the story.

"It's really his fault that I'm in this situation," Angela whispered, looking up at an imaginary officer. "I had no control over the fact that he ran in front of my car. And he was so drunk and insane-looking, I knew that for my own protection I had to stay as far away from him as possible."

Angela knew the police would never believe her. They would just see right through her façade and know instantly that she was an unaccomplished, unmarried, unhappy woman who couldn't even succeed at something as simple as driving home.

Angela picked up her purse, which she had dropped to the floor, and dug her cell phone out. She couldn't call the police now, because too much time had passed. With every passing moment, any chance of the police siding with her had dissipated to nothing. She couldn't call her sister because her sister would call her parents, and her parents would call the police. She tossed the cell phone on her bed, and it bounced to the floor with a light thud.

The stillness of the house pressed onto her ears, creating a light ringing sound. As if to ensure the silence did not calm her, his odor still hung in the air. The smell either clung to her from the moment she stepped out of the car or it traveled from the garage through the air-conditioning vents to haunt and torment her. Angela got down on her knees and pressed her ear to the carpeted floor. She heard nothing.

"Get up, open the garage door, and just leave," Angela whispered. "I've locked the house door, so you have to leave through the garage door. You do know how to open a garage door, right?"

Based on appearances it was possible he had never lived in a house before, much less operated a garage door.

"Don't worry about the car," Angela continued to whisper as she pressed her ear to the carpet. "I'll make a deal with you. If you get up and leave now, I won't make you help me pay for the damage to the car. I'll bring it in for repairs and just say I hit a deer on the road. It happens all the time."

Angela stood up and took off her shoes but left her work clothes on. She lay down in her bed. The pink and orange flowers on her bedsheets seemed ridiculously cheerful given the situation, like flowers at a funeral. Angela stared at the bright petals on her bedding until they blurred into nondescript splotches of color.

No sooner had Angela closed her eyes than they snapped back open to the sound of a crash. It was a metallic crash, and then a little clatter, as if something had fallen. Angela sat up. She was unsure if the sound was real or if she had just begun dreaming. A barely audible moan followed. Angela wasn't dreaming. It must be the man in the garage. Maybe he was getting up to leave. Finally.

Running from her bedroom to the living room, she turned on the TV. She couldn't stand to hear anything else from that garage. Plus, if her neighbors heard, they might come over and ask if she was all right.

Angela quickly fantasized about how the conversation with her neighbors might go, and how she could probably convince them that this man had assaulted her car and that she was just a victim in the situation. She couldn't fill in all the visual gaps of this fantasy because she didn't even know what her neighbors looked like.

In the three years that she had lived there, she'd never once had a conversation with, or even seen, her neighbor, who lived in the end unit next door. All she knew was that he (or she) watched old game shows all day. She always imagined Bob Barker lived next door, because his was the voice she most often heard coming through the walls. Bob Barker was unlikely to respond even if he did hear a strange sound coming from Angela's garage.

"Bob Barker won't hear a thing," Angela said. "So you gotta help yourself out of this one. Just open the garage door and leave. It's that simple."

Angela reclined on the couch and turned up the TV. The elevator-style music of the Weather Channel almost covered the sound of the second low moan.

12

The rhythm of his footsteps almost lulled Dogger into a trance as he ran along Frontage Road. His head felt as if it were floating somewhere above his shoulders and someone else was doing all the physical work of running, yet he felt exhausted. The night already seemed like a blur, and he barely remembered the circumstances under which he and Marty were separated. All Dogger knew was that he had to get back to the Dead Zone, find Marty, and get to sleep.

Dogger stared at the ground, feeling neither the energy nor the interest to look up. The gravel on the road became sparser, and Dogger knew the end of Frontage Road was near. The town of Mason didn't bother to maintain this portion of the road that only led to the Dead Zone.

Barely glancing up to check that his internal bearings were correct, Dogger veered to the left. The gravel road changed to pavement. The pavement was broken and riddled with potholes, which Dogger ran around with practiced precision.

"Hey, Dogger!" a man called, startling Dogger. Dogger looked up, expecting to see Marty, even though the voice didn't sound quite right. Instead of Marty, he saw Richie. Richie was sitting outside the former Whatta Dish Diner, smoking a cigarette. A small lamp was next to him and illuminated a book on his lap. Dogger slowed down.

"Hey, Richie," Dogger said. "How's it going?"

"Where's Marty?" Richie said. Dogger slowed his pace and walked over to Richie.

"I'm meeting him over by Berler Bridge," Dogger said.

"Are you holding?" Richie asked, scratching his beard.

"Holding what?" Dogger asked.

"Anything," Richie said.

"No," Dogger said. "You know I don't mess with any drugs."

"But I bet you have something to drink," Richie said. He looked up at Dogger and smiled widely. "Something to share?"

Dogger had to think for a moment and reached his hands into the pocket of his pants in case he had a flask. Empty. He and Marty must have drank everything.

"No," Dogger said. "Nothing left, sorry."

"You never have anything left." Richie frowned. "Next time, save something for me, all right?"

"You'd better talk to Marty about that," Dogger said. "I gotta run."

"Why the hurry?" Richie said, carefully extinguishing his cigarette between two wetted fingers.

"Marty's waiting for me," Dogger said. "Hey, watch out for Henry Gates tonight. He's out looking for trouble."

Dogger turned and continued down the sidewalk, first walking, and then picking up his pace once more. He heard Richie say something behind him, but he just couldn't be bothered. Conversations with Richie always lasted too long and always centered around confusing stories about either when he'd lived in Florida or times when he'd been high. Dogger didn't want to keep Marty waiting. Marty was probably getting worried.

Dogger put his hand in the air and waved, hoping that would be a sufficient enough good-bye to keep Richie from looking for him later.

Dogger scanned the sidewalks on either side of the street as he ran deeper into the Dead Zone and toward Berler Bridge. The Dead Zone was dark, quiet, and almost entirely empty. The sooner he found Marty, the sooner they could call it a night and find somewhere to sleep. Hopefully Henry Gates wouldn't patrol the Dead Zone before they'd tucked themselves away.

To most people, Rochester Street in the Dead Zone would look completely empty. Dogger knew exactly where to look to see people hidden away in the darkness. Most of the faces were as familiar as family, but there were sometimes a few travelers he didn't recognize.

Dogger continued trotting down the middle of the street. Cars were such a rare sight in this neighborhood. They were almost always people off of I–80 that got lost finding the on-ramp, driving around wide-eyed and white-knuckled. If it wasn't a lost tourist, a car in the Dead Zone was the police looking for someone to harass.

The grainy outline of Berler Bridge could be seen coming out of the darkness up ahead. Dogger squinted, trying to make out the figures beneath the bridge. As he got closer, it became clear that the figures were those of Joe and Tommy. They were standing and talking heatedly about something, exchanging loud whispers that couldn't be fully deciphered. They stopped talking as Dogger neared them, and his footsteps probably became audible.

"Hey, guys," Dogger said.

"Hey," Tommy said. Joe didn't say anything, but he was staring at Tommy. It was probably another argument about either money or drugs. As much as Dogger sometimes felt like he and Marty acted like an old married couple, Tommy and Joe did so even more.

Dogger looked up under the bridge and could see the form of a person lying down and probably sleeping. Dogger walked up the incline, balancing himself with his hands on the cool concrete.

"Marty," Dogger whispered. The person didn't move, but Dogger could hear the sound of loud breathing, almost snoring, echoing off the overpass. Dogger inched closer.

"Marty," Dogger said again. The sound of the loud breathing suddenly stopped, and the body shifted.

"Marty ain't here." The man who was sleeping rolled over and propped himself up on his elbow. It was Otto. His deeply lined face crinkled and squinted at Dogger.

"Sorry, Otto," Dogger said. "Have you seen him?"

"Not since this morning," Otto said. Then he turned around, his back once again facing Dogger, and laid his head back down on his backpack.

Dogger walked down the cement incline several steps and sat down. How could it be that Marty didn't beat Dogger back? He was running so far ahead of Dogger, and plus, Dogger had to lose some time hiding from Henry Gates. Dogger sighed and leaned back on his elbows, scanning Rochester Street to his left and searching the dead end under the bridge with his eyes.

Tommy and Joe were arguing again in loud whispers, with very few words audible to Dogger. For the first time since Dogger could remember, he felt very alone.

13

Marty was a man with a low tolerance for pain, both of the physical and emotional varieties. He knew this about himself and had accepted it as fact years ago. Marty had determined that it did not in any way diminish his masculinity, but the lawn chair somehow managed to challenge this belief.

Marty couldn't see the garage floor, but it didn't matter. He knew his left hand could not reach the ground to retrieve the fallen lawn chair. Even if it defied all probabilities and had somehow fallen toward him instead of away from him, the fact that it was on the ground meant it was out of reach. Marty had failed at his only chance to save himself and was less of a man as a result. He was a helpless bug, an entomologist's specimen, pinned to the wall.

Marty was mercifully distracted from the pain of complete failure with building pain in his head and chest. The more he noticed it, the more it seemed to build upon itself, intensifying exponentially. He became more aware of his labored breathing, his breath wheezing in and out of his chest. He was likely going to die.

The darkness that surrounded Marty in the garage made him feel especially claustrophobic. It was impossible to see the walls around him, so it was easy to imagine they were pressing tightly around his body.

As his eyes slowly adjusted, he could see a long, thin line glowing yellow. The line appeared to be four feet long. It disappeared for a few feet behind the car, and then reappeared for another four- or five-foot segment. It must have been the light from the street coming in under the garage door. It was as if the outside world were trying to reassure Marty that there was still light and still hope. It wasn't too comforting, but Marty tried to pretend that it was.

As his eyes continued to adjust, he could see another thin line of dim light that was about two or three feet long and glowing through the darkness to his left. It seemed to be floating in the air, a couple of feet higher than the light under the garage door. The color was more bluish gray rather than yellow like the longer line. Marty squinted toward the light, unsure whether he was merely hallucinating or whether it was real. It took a moment to realize that what he was seeing was the door into the house. It was the door Sonya had disappeared through, back when Marty had thought she was going to get help.

Of course, Marty knew the woman wasn't Sonya. She couldn't be Sonya because Sonya had left town years ago. Someone would have told Marty if she moved back. But she looked like Sonya and was cruel like Sonya.

As the years passed, Marty had developed a caricature of his wife in his mind. Her bad qualities were exaggerated to almost impossible proportions, and her good qualities were dwarfed. The complicated truth about Sonya was buried deep in Marty's mind. It was buried so deep that he barely even considered it as he recalled his ex-wife as a two-dimensional monster who was cold and cruel for no reason more complex than to hurt Marty.

Sometimes, at unexpected moments, the truth would rush to the forefront of his mind, and Marty had to consciously fight to move it out of the way. It was too intellectually straining to allow his memories of Sonya to be anything other than the simple, cold, and cruel figure in his mind.

Marty stared toward the thin band of light. He expected to see a shadow break into the light as Sonya, or someone else, came to the door. But the light was unwavering. He found himself holding his breath and straining to hear any signs of someone coming to open the door.

"Sonya," Marty wheezed. "Help." The garage and the house were silent in response, telling Marty that he had already been forgotten.

14

The top floor of the three-story apartment building was the only floor with a light on. Doug was obviously awake and waiting for Samantha to come home. Samantha sat in her car, staring up into the window of their apartment and debating her options. She should just walk in and act like everything was fine, or she should come in prepared with an elaborate lie. There was always the chance that Doug was asleep, and if she was able to close the door to the apartment softly enough, she wouldn't have to talk to him until the morning.

Samantha took a deep breath, as if she were about to dive into a sea with unknown depths, and got out of the car. The sound of her car door closing echoed off the dirty white siding of the building. She looked up and saw a shadow appear at the window, and then quickly pull away. Doug was waiting.

Samantha was surprised to find her fingers were shaking as she tried to unlock the outside door to the apartment building. In the small foyer, she turned to the row of mailboxes. There were nine small rectangular brass doors attached to the walls, each with a number etched in a brass plate in the center and a last name taped on with an old-fashioned label maker. On mailbox number nine, it said "Lightfoot/Burns," as if advertising to the world their unmarried status.

Samantha slowly sorted her keychain in her fingers until she found the small golden mailbox key. She knew Doug would have already gotten their mail, but she turned the key in the lock and pulled open the door anyway. It was empty. She closed the mailbox and stared at it for a moment before turning toward the stairs.

As she rounded the steps from the first floor to the second, she could smell the familiar scent of must and stale cigarette smoke. It was an odor that always lingered in the air on the second floor and either dissipated by the third floor or your senses adapted to it by the time you reached the top of the stairs. It was a smell that used to bother her when she first moved into these apartments, but she had long learned to associate it with being home.

The sound of a door creaking open and quickly closing froze Samantha in her path. She turned and looked behind her, but all three apartments on the second floor were silent. She hadn't yet hit the landing of the stairs between the second and third floor, but she knew she would see Doug standing outside the apartment door, waiting, as she came up the last flight of stairs.

"Where the hell have you been?" Doug said, his low voice ricocheting off the walls of the small foyer. He was standing right outside the door to their apartment with his arms folded, as if he were going to block her entrance.

"Shh," Samantha said. "You'll wake the neighbors."

"Oh, how sweet of you to be worried about the neighbors," Doug said, his voice lowered to a loud whisper. "Well, I should be in bed, too, but you don't seem too concerned about keeping me up at all hours of the night worrying about you."

"You know where I've been," Samantha said. She gently pushed Doug aside and opened the door to their apartment. "I left you a note."

Doug's face was red, so red that even his light blond hair seemed to have taken a pinkish hue. He followed Samantha into the apartment and slammed the door closed behind them.

"What am I supposed to think when you're out late like this?" Doug asked. He shook his head from side to side as he stepped into their small kitchen area to the left of the front door. He sat down at the kitchen table and continued before Samantha could respond. "This is Monday. You don't work Monday evenings. I expected us to get to share dinner together, like a normal couple."

"I never said I'd be home for dinner," Samantha said, dropping her purse on the living room floor. "When did I say I'd be home for dinner?"

"So I make dinner," Doug continued, his face evolving from red to purple. "And I wait, and then you never show up or even call."

"I didn't call because I left you a note saying I was at the church shelter tonight," Samantha said. She sat down on the couch in the living room, the point furthest away from the kitchen table without retreating to the one bedroom in the small apartment.

"What note?" Doug said, darting his eyes around the apartment dramatically, and then looking under the kitchen table.

"On the kitchen counter," Samantha said. "Exactly where I always leave you notes. I can see from here that it's gone now, but it was there when I left this morning."

"I suppose that's my fault? That I didn't read your disappearing note?" Doug's temples visibly pulsed as if he were grinding his teeth.

"No," Samantha said. She could feel her hands shaking, and she shoved them under her legs to keep them still. "But you do tend to throw away everything you find off the kitchen counter when you clean. And you conveniently choose to clean whenever there is something on the kitchen counter you want to ignore."

"Are you seriously accusing me of cleaning the kitchen? Wow, how do you put up with this abuse?" Doug said. "You left me eating a cold dinner, alone, while wondering if you were in trouble. For all I know, you could have been out on a date."

"Yeah," Samantha said. She couldn't help but laugh. "I was on a date. You caught me."

"This is serious, Sam," Doug said. "If we're going to get married, I need to know that you are committed to this relationship."

"Fine," Samantha said. She opened her purse and pulled out her cell phone. She threw it across the apartment at Doug. Though she was aiming for his head, it fell three yards short of even making it to his feet. It landed with a loud crack but appeared to be in one piece. "Call Wendy. I was covering the first shift at the shelter, and she is doing the overnight. She can vouch for me."

"That's great. Of course you were at the shelter," Doug said, rubbing his hand through his hair vigorously before slamming it back down on the kitchen table with a look of exasperation.

"Call her if you don't believe me," Samantha said, gesturing toward her phone on the floor.

"God, you just don't get it," Doug said, his eyes wide and wet with tears. "I believe you. I mean, I knew that was where you had to be."

"So what's the problem?" Samantha said. She had to fight the urge to stand up and hug Doug and comfort him. She hated to see him cry, but she knew these were more likely tears of frustration and anger than tears of sadness.

"You spend four nights a week working the evening shift at the truck stop and two nights a week helping at the church shelter," Doug said, his voice rising. "And on the weekends, you're …"

"At the soup kitchen," Samantha said quietly. She stood up and walked toward Doug. He stood up, too, but instead of walking toward Samantha for an anticipated embrace, he walked past her and collapsed on the couch. Samantha knelt down and picked up her phone, shaking it to ensure nothing sounded loose or broken, and then stuck it in the pocket of her jeans.

"If you don't have room in your life for me," Doug said, "please have the decency to just tell me."

"I'm sorry," Samantha said. Doug rolled on the couch so his back was facing Samantha. "You're right. I need to make you a priority."

"I'm sick of hearing about poor people," Doug said, his voice muffled against the back of the couch.

"Well, volunteering is part of my life," Samantha said. "You knew I was into community service when we started dating. I always have been."

"I didn't know you'd spend more time with hobos than you would with your fiancé," Doug said, twisting his body partway around on the couch to look at Samantha. His eyes looked red.

"What are you saying, I can't do both?" Samantha said.

"It doesn't seem like it," Doug said.

"What do you want me to do?" Samantha said, sighing loudly and folding her arms.

"Think about whether you really want to get married," Doug said.

"Of course I want to get married," Samantha said, although she no longer knew whether she believed that. It could just be relationship inertia driving them to marriage, and not true compatibility and love.

"Well, I'm looking for a wife, not the queen of the Good Samaritans," Doug said, facing the back of the couch once more. "You need to decide which you want to be."

"That's ridiculous and unfair," Samantha said. Doug turned around and sat up on the couch.

"Sam," Doug said, his voice shaking. "This relationship needs your attention and presence. I can promise you there is no damn hobo out there who needs you as much as I need you right now."

15

"Sonya, Sonya, Sonya …" Marty whispered her name over and over again, as if it would call her back into the garage to help him. He did this until his throat burned and the horrible pain in his chest would not allow him to say another word. Then Marty was alone in the darkness, without even the sound of his own voice to keep him company.

Although Marty tried to fight it, he couldn't help but let his thoughts turn to Sonya. He seemed destined to remember her tonight. It started with seeing the little girl wearing olive shoes, and it ended with getting run over by a Sonya look-alike. In a way, it seemed so fitting that the monster that had destroyed his life and taken away his only child decided to come back to town and finally put an end to his existence. Perhaps the pain was making him irrational. The lucid part of his mind still knew the woman driving the car could not possibly be Sonya.

As much as Marty didn't allow himself to believe it, the truth was that he had never loved a woman like he loved Sonya. She wasn't always the monster she later became. Far from it. In their courtship, she was sweet and funny and had an infectious laugh that Marty adored hearing. She was proud of Marty and what he did. The more Marty allowed himself to remember, the more he realized that she was nothing like the caricature that had grown into a nemesis in his own mind in the last two decades.

Marty sighed a long and wheezing sigh. The sound seemed to rattle off the walls of the garage, and Marty had to force himself to believe that the sound hadn't come out of him. Back when Sonya was still a loving partner he thought he would grow old with, she would have told Marty that the wheeze was a good sign that he was still breathing.

Unexpectedly, Marty could feel a small smile cross his face. It was a long-forgotten truth about Sonya that she was truly an optimist. In fact, she was often optimistic to the point of annoying those around her. More than once she had been accused of making molehills out of mountains.

As part of her optimism, she loved the idea of new beginnings and reinventing herself. Every four months, she would get a new hairstyle or color just to see what it was like. Her favorite season was spring. She called it "the season of resurrection," as trees and perennials rose from the dead with buds promising a new beginning. She was always the happiest in the spring.

Marty had asked her to marry him at Hillside Park on the first day of spring. There was still a little snow on the ground, but most of the winter weather was melting and trickling away into the damp earth. Marty and Sonya both wore their winter coats and sat in the newly constructed picnic table pavilion, listening to the birds chirp for nearly an hour before deciding to eat lunch. Marty had put together a picnic basket complete with egg salad sandwiches, chips, lemonade, and a small Tupperware container with two cupcakes for dessert. In between the two cupcakes was a small white velvet box with a half-carat marquise-cut engagement ring inside. Sonya had thought it was the most romantic thing she had ever seen, and she'd bragged about the well-planned proposal to her friends.

It wasn't long after they were married that Marty lost his job. For a while, Sonya was supportive and tried to help Marty find work. Her optimism had died when Marty gave up and would go for days just sitting on the floor of their under-furnished apartment, watching television. When she became pregnant, she was even more unsure of Marty's ability to find work and get his life together. That was the beginning of the end.

Sonya was never the same after she became pregnant. Marty was excited to be a father and hoped the baby would help to bring a renewed focus and energy to their lives. Sonya, on the other hand, had lost her optimism.

Sonya blamed a lot on alcohol, but she didn't understand that alcohol didn't cause any of their problems. Alcohol was merely her favorite scapegoat when she didn't want to admit that she was part of the problem. The sudden change in her personality and her outlook on the world was what had caused their problems. She became cruel and judgmental, and that was the Sonya that Marty remembered best. She became, in Marty's mind, just like the caricature he had created. She was cold, unreasonable, and borderline evil.

Marty didn't miss Sonya as much as he missed what could have been with his son. Marty knew Sonya gave birth to Sonny not too long after she left Mason, but that was all he knew. He didn't even know if his name was Sonny, but it was easier to imagine he knew his child's name than to ever admit that he didn't.

Marty could have been a great father if he had been given the chance—he was sure of that. If he were given the same chance now,

Marty doubted he would even be an adequate babysitter, much less a great father. That time in his life had passed, and he couldn't imagine being a good role model or caregiver for any child at this point. If he had been given a chance at fatherhood, Marty knew his entire life would be different. It would be better.

Marty wondered what Sonny would think if he knew the fate of his old man. His value in this world turned out to be no more than a bug's. Marty wished he were more surprised or disappointed with this fact.

"I'm sorry, Sonny," Marty whispered.

Suddenly, the air changed. Marty knew he was not alone in the garage. He could feel the hairs on his neck and arms standing erect. Someone was with him in the darkness.

"Hello?" Marty said. Part of him felt ridiculous and embarrassed, as he knew logically no one had come into the garage. He squinted into the darkness. He couldn't see anything, but he felt warmth on his left side as if someone were standing only a foot away.

"Who is here?" Marty said. He looked to his left, staring into the air and unable to focus on anything.

Then he saw something in the darkness move. Marty's body jumped slightly in surprise, causing pain to shoot through his chest and stomach. He focused carefully on his breathing, trying to ignore the inhuman gurgle that sounded with every exhale.

"Were you in the car?" Marty said. He quickly reasoned that the only way a person could be in the garage with him is if there was someone in the backseat of the car. A passenger. Maybe this person had fallen asleep on the ride home, and the drugged-up Sonya-look-alike didn't bother to wake him up when she pulled into the garage. It wouldn't be too surprising. Sonya didn't bother to help Marty, either.

"Hello?" Marty said. "I didn't realize there was someone else in the car."

Marty listened and heard nothing. But he knew he wasn't alone.

"I'm glad you're here, though," Marty said. "Maybe you can help me."

There was no response.

"Listen," Marty said. "I know this wasn't your fault. It was an accident."

The person in the shadows was silent.

"And you can still make it right," Marty said. "Please help me. I can't move."

57

There was only silence and darkness.

"Are you still here?" Marty said. He began to wonder if his imagination and the pain were getting the better of him when suddenly the air shifted once more, and he felt definite warmth on his left side.

"I guess you are still here," Marty said.

Marty was certain that someone was standing inches away from him, just out of sight in the grainy black air that surrounded him.

"Well," Marty sighed, trying to sound calm. The absurdity of sounding causal in this situation was undeniable, yet Marty tried to force a conversational tone. "Got any ideas?"

16

Dogger tried to sit patiently under Berler Bridge and wait for Marty. He tried distracting himself by counting the number of loud heavy semis he could hear roaring by on nearby I–80. Dogger even tried to pass the time by trying to focus on moving each of his toes inside his dirty black boots individually. Despite his efforts, it seemed as if time were passing slower than ever before.

He tried to replay in his mind the last moment he saw Marty, but the entire night was covered in a heavy fog of alcohol. Maybe once he was sober again, he would remember more. Eventually, the sound of Otto snoring behind him and Tommy and Joe arguing in loud whispers over how much money Joe should have in his pocket felt oppressively loud. The sounds were bouncing off the bridge, repeating in Dogger's ears, and Dogger didn't even have Marty around to break the tension.

Dogger stood up and walked down the embankment and trotted past Tommy and Joe. They stopped whispering momentarily as Dogger brushed by, but resumed arguing when he was only a few feet away. Dogger wasn't sure at first where he was going, but he just couldn't sit and listen to the whispering or Otto's snoring any longer.

Dogger walked down the middle of Rochester Street. The third building away from the dead end underneath Berler Bridge used to be a thrift shop with an apartment on the second floor. Dogger quickly looked around to ensure no one was watching before he veered off the street, stepped up onto the sidewalk, and then walked down the dark and narrow space between the old thrift shop and the adjacent building. It was technically an alley, but wasn't wide enough to be functional for anything other than getting to the back of the building or hiding in the darkness.

"Coming through," Dogger muttered. He stuck his hand out in front of him and waved it as he walked. People rarely hung out back there or slept in the tight alley in the summer. The air was always too hot, and the wind rarely made its way in the right direction to help cool it off.

Dogger emerged on the other side, and the air instantly felt cooler. Up the backside of the thrift store was a metal staircase that led to the second floor. It was the old fire escape.

The main entrance to the apartment was through the front door on the other side of the building. There was a small foyer with two doors at the front of the shop, one to the thrift store and one up to the apartment. Henry Gates checked the lock on the front door almost nightly, but he very rarely made the effort to walk back to the fire escape and check the back door.

Dogger quickly scanned the small area behind the row of abandoned businesses. Although it was difficult to know for sure, it looked as if he were alone.

"Marty!" Dogger called up toward the apartment. "Marty!" Dogger listened but heard nothing in response. If Marty wasn't at Berler Bridge, this was the only other place he could think of that Marty might be. If he wasn't there, he might have gotten picked up by Henry Gates or possibly passed out somewhere.

Dogger's feet made a loud clanking sound as he ascended the metal staircase. With each step, he could feel the handrails shake, and the entire structure seemed to sway. Dogger never got used to these stairs. He was sure they would collapse someday, and Henry Gates would order the building torn down, and everyone in the Dead Zone would curse Dogger for destroying the best winter shelter they had. As Dogger reached the top of the stairs, he saw the door to the apartment was wide open.

"Marty?" Dogger whispered into the dark apartment. He cleared his throat and, more loudly, said, "Marty, it's me."

There was only silence. Dogger's stomach began to ache with a sick anticipation. Either someone had left the door open, or there was someone inside. Dogger held his breath and stepped inside.

The glow of the streetlight flickered through the window that faced the street and allowed for some eerie visibility inside the apartment at night. While Dogger was able to tread noiselessly on the worn carpet, he had already announced his arrival on the loud staircase and by calling for Marty. If there was someone in the apartment, they already knew he was there.

A sudden swooshing sound caused Dogger to jump and turn around in one less-than-graceful motion. There was no one at the door, and no one behind him. Dogger could feel his heart pounding inside his chest and was sure that anyone nearby could hear the loud and urgent thumping sound it made. Dogger felt dizzy with anxiety and took in a deep breath and tried to steady himself.

"Marty?" Dogger whispered. "Is that you?"

The swoosh sounded again, and this time Dogger could see the source. The large piece of cardboard that was usually propped up against the wall between the door and the window was sliding down. Dogger must have brushed by it on the way in.

Dogger picked up the cardboard, as he had many times before, and set it back up against the wall. Marty and Dogger were the only ones who seemed to take care of this place. If the cardboard were left on the floor, it would be trampled over and become useless. They needed it for the winter, so they could block the broken window.

Dogger turned and glanced up at the vent in the wall. It was where Marty and Dogger kept everything valuable. Extra clothes, food, Marty's Bible. It took two of them to open the vent; it was just barely out of fingertip's reach otherwise. Usually, Marty would get on Dogger's shoulders to take down whatever they needed from their stash. It was great in the summer, but in the winter it was harder to use because there were usually people hanging around in the apartment, trying to stay warm. So late in the fall, they had to take out everything they thought they would need for the winter just to ensure their stash was kept safe.

"Marty?" Dogger said one more time as he scanned the apartment. The small studio was empty. Dogger walked over to the window and looked down to the empty street below, hoping Marty would miraculously walk into view at that very moment.

Just as Dogger turned to walk away, he heard the sound of a car approaching, the engine humming and wheels kicking and crushing broken concrete. It could only be Henry Gates. Maybe he'd picked up Marty and was bringing him back to the Dead Zone.

Without thinking, Dogger sprinted toward the door and ran down the shaking metal staircase. He quickly inched his way through the narrow alley, this time without giving the courtesy of announcing his presence. When he emerged back on Rochester Street, he could see that the police car had pulled up near Berler Bridge. Tommy and Joe were gone, but he could just see the shadow of Otto still sleeping at the top of the embankment, right under the bridge.

The police car slowly backed up and turned around. Without allowing himself to be fearful or overthink things, Dogger ran toward the car. Even as he ran, part of him couldn't believe he was running toward Henry Gates rather than away from him.

The police car had finished making a U-turn and started driving toward Dogger. Dogger stopped running. His stomach suddenly tightened as he realized the insanity of what he was doing. Despite his apprehension, his feet refused to turn away. Dogger was left standing on the edge of the sidewalk, staring at the headlights of the police car driven by Henry Gates.

"Dogger." A loud voice startled Dogger, and he took a step back. The police car pulled alongside Dogger. The window was down, and Henry Gates was looking up at Dogger with a strange look on his thick, pockmarked face. Dogger could feel the cool breeze from the air-conditioning rush over his body.

"What are you up to tonight?" Henry Gates said without a hint of friendliness.

"Not much," Dogger said. "Just taking a walk."

"I see," Henry said. He coughed hoarsely. He was probably still worn out from chasing after Marty and Dogger. There was someone sitting in the front seat of the car next to Henry. It must have been that other officer Dogger saw come out of the park when he was hiding. Dogger leaned down, trying to see the face of the other officer.

"Have you been drinking?" Henry said, sniffing the air. Dogger straightened up immediately.

"No, sir," Dogger said. Dogger knew if he were asked to take a Breathalyzer, he'd fail. Then he could be picked up for public intox. "Not lately."

"Well," Henry said. He seemed to be reaching for something in the console next to him.

"Have you seen Marty?" Dogger quickly blurted out. Henry turned back and squinted at Dogger. "I mean tonight. Have you seen Marty tonight?"

"Why?" Henry said with a small laugh. "Did you lose track of your drinking buddy?"

Dogger stepped back from the car. He felt as if Henry were only seconds away from pulling out his Breathalyzer and forcing Dogger to prove his sobriety.

"Thanks anyway," Dogger said, backing up further. "Have a good night."

Dogger turned and walked quickly down the sidewalk, being mindful not to run. Running from the police when they could easily catch him was always a bad idea. Then they could say he was evading police officers. Dogger kept walking.

The sound of the police car slowly rolling over broken concrete felt as if it were right behind him. Dogger cautiously turned and looked over his shoulder. Henry Gates was driving away, down Rochester Street and out of the Dead Zone.

Dogger walked back up the embankment of Berler Bridge and sat down. He listened to the sound of Otto snoring and leaned back on his elbows. He was tired, too, and the evening was just a confusing mess in his own mind. All he knew was that he had to wait for Marty. Dogger closed his eyes and listened to the traffic on I–80, counting the number of times he could hear the heavy roar of a semitruck pass by. Surely Marty would be there before he reached a count of fifty.

17

Marty stared into the blackness of the air to his left. He could feel the pain and pressure in his chest building rapidly and wondered if it was what a heart attack might feel like.

"Say something," Marty whispered. "Anything."

There was nothing. Marty held his breath to listen more closely. Suddenly, he could hear a sigh or perhaps the sound of someone taking a deep breath. Marty could feel his arms shake, and he tightly gripped the hood of the car.

"I heard you sigh," Marty said. "I know you are here."

"You are in trouble." The words came out slowly and with a breathy quality. At first, Marty thought he said the words himself.

"What did you say?" Marty asked, barely able to make the words come out. His eyes darted around the dark garage before returning to the black air beside him. "Hello?"

"You are in trouble, Marty." This time, the voice said the words more clearly and firmly. It was a male voice and had an eerie calmness.

"Do you know me?" Marty asked, squinting into the darkness. Marty was surprised to find that his hands relaxed and his arms stopped shaking. It was oddly reassuring to have his suspicions confirmed that he wasn't alone in the garage. "How do you know my name?"

"Yes, I know you," the voice said. The voice was coming from Marty's left side, where he had seen the movement before and felt the warmth.

"Why did she just leave me here?" Marty asked, directing his voice to his left and continuing to force an unnaturally casual tone.

There was silence. Marty once again thought the man was merely a hallucination until he realized that he could see the outline of a long and lean body standing nearby. If he looked directly at it, it disappeared. When he looked to the side, he could see the outline of a tall figure in his peripheral vision.

"Why did you run in front of her car?" the voice asked, in the same even cadence. It seemed calm and soothing only moments earlier, but now the same tone of voice sounded demented and unnerving.

"I didn't," Marty said.

"I saw you," the voice said. "You ran right in front of her car. Intentionally, almost."

"I was running away," Marty said. His voice was weak and cracking. "I was being chased."

"I guess it's a matter of perspective," the man said. "What I saw as running toward something, you saw as running away from something."

"I guess so," Marty said.

"What was chasing you?" the man asked.

The word *what* was especially disturbing to Marty. A normal person would ask *who* was chasing you, but this young man seemed to assume it was a *what*. A demon or monster, perhaps. Marty suddenly decided he didn't want to continue this line of conversation.

"You must have been in the backseat," Marty said.

"I was," the voice said. The voice once again sounded breathy, as if the words were being sighed out.

"Why didn't you go inside with Sonya?" Marty asked.

"I wanted to stay out here with you," the voice said.

Marty wheezed and felt ill. He swallowed hard, hoping to not throw up. He didn't even realize he said Sonya until well after the words came out. It seemed impossible that the woman driving the car was Sonya, and yet the man responded as if her name really were Sonya.

"That woman is named Sonya?" Marty asked.

"Yes," the young man said. "Who else would you expect her to be?"

"That's an abnormal answer," Marty said. Either it was a coincidence that the woman driving the car was named Sonya, or something was terribly wrong. The pain in Marty's stomach intensified.

"Abnormal? I'm sorry," the man said without a hint of humor or regret.

"Are you really here?" Marty asked. If this man was a spawn of Marty's own imagination, it somehow made his breathy and calm voice even more terrifying. "Or am I just losing my damn mind?"

"A little bit of both," the man said.

Marty threw up suddenly and violently. He could hear the vomit hit the car and the floor. The force tore his body from the car slightly, and he could feel the warmth of fresh blood from his chest. The air now smelled strongly like Slim Jims and whiskey.

"Feel better?" the man said.

Marty closed his eyes tightly. He could still feel the warmth of someone standing near him. Maybe it was someone messing with him.

Maybe it was an amazing hallucination, but Marty never thought his mind was this powerful.

"You can't be here," Marty said, opening his eyes and staring into the darkness. The longer he stared, the more the long and thin figure seemed to materialize.

"I'm sorry you feel that way," the man said.

"I just have to make it until dawn," Marty whispered. "Once the sun comes up and people in the neighborhood started waking up, then maybe someone will hear me."

"Nobody can hear you right now," the man said. "Not even Sonya."

Marty stared into the black of the garage, praying to see brighter cracks of light shine through, indicating dawn. With light, hopefully this human mirage would break apart and prove to be nothing more than a fear-induced hallucination. For now, Marty had no choice but to accept the strange feeling of the tall man watching him.

18

The bed was empty when Samantha woke up. Her eyes felt painfully dry and her body ached, almost as if she had a hangover from the fight with Doug. The words replayed in her mind, and she pulled the sheets up over her head. Doug slept on the couch, pouting and angry, precisely as predicted.

The front door of the apartment closed loudly.

"Hello?" Samantha called, quickly pulling the sheets off her face. "Doug?" There was no answer. The sound of the door closing must have been someone leaving, not coming in.

Samantha stared at the empty pillow next to her. The green polka-dot pillow case was perfectly fluffed and placed and clearly not recently slept on. Doug didn't even come in the bedroom to get his pillow. There was no doubt that he woke up with a sore neck if he tried to sleep on the stiff and unforgiving decorative couch pillows. He probably left drool stains on the fabric, Samantha thought, rolling her eyes.

Samantha looked at the digital alarm clock next to the queen size bed: 6:52 AM. Doug must have just left for work, and he must have left angry. Usually, even after a fight night, he would at least wake her up to kiss her good-bye.

It was Tuesday morning, which was always a busy morning at Super T's Truck Stop. She couldn't be late to relieve Chuck from the overnight shift like she was last Tuesday. She'd have to skip the shower today.

Samantha swung her feet out of bed. She took off the T-shirt she slept in, dropped it on the floor, and grabbed the aerosol bottle of deodorant off the dresser. She sprayed herself from head to toe with it before getting dressed. She shuffled into the kitchen and saw a note sitting on the kitchen counter.

Sam—I'm tired of having this same fight over and over again. I'm tired of sleeping on the couch when I'd rather share the bed with you. In fact, I'm tired of sharing you, period. I won't apologize for what I said last night. You need to make a choice. Let someone else step up and do the charity work for a while so you can focus on the rest of your life. I need you. I love you, and I don't want to lose you. Love, Doug.

Samantha folded the note and placed it in the pocket of her jeans. She and Doug would have to make up, or break up, later.

Dogger's head throbbed painfully, a sensation that was only minimized when he felt the pain in his shoulders. He wasn't sure where he was, but it felt as if someone had just kicked him in the side.

"Hey," a low voice said. "Wake up."

Dogger felt another kick to his side before he was sufficiently motivated to open his eyes. The bright light of the rising sun was intense and made his headache even more pronounced.

"Stop," Dogger tried to say, although no sound came out of his mouth. He cleared his throat and on the second try succeeded in barking out a rough "Stop!"

"Wake up," the voice said again. He didn't recognize it, and he hoped it wasn't the voice of a police officer.

Dogger looked around. He was lying on the incline of the embankment under Berler Bridge. He must have fallen asleep while resting with his weight on his elbows and shoulders behind him. A tall man in blue jeans and a gray T-shirt was standing next to him. The man gave a small kick to Dogger's side again.

"Stop it," Dogger said hoarsely. This time, Dogger sat up. At first, his vision blacked out when he sat up, but then it slowly returned, and he could see that he and this man were alone under Berler Bridge.

"I'm sleeping—what do you want?" Dogger asked. He looked up at the man, but the bright sunlight made it impossible to see the man's face.

"You got any booze?" the man asked.

"No," Dogger said. "Leave me alone. I need to sleep."

As Dogger began to lie back down, the man kicked Dogger in the side again—this time, harder than before.

"Why are you lying?" the man asked.

"I'm not lying," Dogger said, sitting up once more. His side now ached nearly as much as his head and shoulders. "What's your problem?"

"I don't have a problem," the man said. "Unless you're lying, in which case we both have a problem."

"I don't have any booze, any food, or any money," Dogger said. The truth was that he did have some food hidden in their secret stash, and he had some change in his pocket. There was no way this man could know that, though.

"You know how I know you're lying?" the man asked.

Dogger slowly forced himself up to his feet. He had to see who he was talking to, and he was beginning to feel too vulnerable staying down on the ground.

"I'm not lying," Dogger said. When he saw the man's face, he knew he had never seen him before. He had reddish blond hair with streaks of gray and deep lines in his sunburned face. He must be a traveler, and hopefully not one that was planning to stick around Mason for long.

"I can smell it on you," the man said. He sniffed the air around Dogger. "I got a nose for booze, and it leads me right to you. So hand it over."

"I was drinking last night with my buddy," Dogger said. "But we don't have any left."

Dogger suddenly realized that Marty wasn't with him. He was alone with this man under Berler Bridge. It seemed unlikely that Marty would have abandoned Dogger if he saw this traveler approaching.

"We're all supposed to share," the man said. "That's the code."

"What code?" Dogger said. "You aren't from around here—what would you know about how we do things?"

"I know what's right," the man said. "Why don't you just hand it over now, and we'll call it even?"

Dogger scanned the street below. It was vacant. While he couldn't remember anything specific about what happened last night, he did remember that he and Marty got separated. Marty was supposed to meet him under Berler Bridge, like he always did when they were separated. He remembered Otto was sleeping under the bridge last night, but when he turned he saw that even Otto was gone. It was as if everyone had abandoned Dogger to deal with this traveler.

"I'm a patient man," the traveler said. "But I have to be honest with you—my patience is wearing thin."

"I don't have any booze," Dogger said.

"You've got a stash somewhere," the traveler said. Dogger grimaced. He remembered going to the apartment last night. Maybe the traveler had been hiding in the apartment and saw him looking up at the vent where they keep the stash.

"No stash," Dogger said. He held out his arms and turned around. "Everything I have, you're looking at it."

When Dogger finished spinning around, he barely registered the look of violence on the traveler's face before he felt the hard blow to his right temple. He passed out moments after hitting the pavement.

✱ ✱ ✱

Angela woke up on the couch. She was lying on her stomach, arms tucked under her body and head turned toward the TV. The Weather Channel was airing old footage of Hurricane Katrina while local weather forecasts scrolled along the bottom of the screen. A booming voice with a perfected non-regional dialect provided commentary on the hurricane's destructive forces.

Angela grabbed the remote off the floor and turned off the TV. She listened carefully. She could hear *The Price is Right* seeping through the walls from her neighbor's TV. Bob Barker was up. She continued to listen, straining to hear anything unusual in between the sounds of cheers and contestants loudly announcing their hometowns. She heard nothing from downstairs. Maybe that man left. She didn't hear the garage door open during the night, but the TV was turned up pretty loud. She would know soon enough.

Angela got up and walked to her bedroom. She was still wearing her work clothes from the night before. Everything in her house looked normal. Everything looked like it had always looked. Nothing was out of place. Her dirty clothes were just where she had left them two nights ago at the foot of her bed. Her collection of cat figurines, which she never really wanted but her sister decided she should collect, stared blankly off the small shelf next to the window. They looked as they always had—their forced adorability was depressing.

Angela looked out the bedroom window. There were no police cars outside, no Channel 8 news crews. An overweight woman walked her black mutt down the middle of the street. The woman was smiling a little bit to herself and listening to something through headphones. Herbert Street was clean and tidy, the same as it always was. It almost seemed possible that last night never happened. She just needed to believe it.

The phone rang, and Angela answered. Her voice cracked tiredly. "hello?"

"Angela," the voice said. It was her sister, Christine. "How did it work out last night?"

"How did what work out?" Angela said. Her heart started pumping as she quickly attempted to remember what her sister knew about last night.

"Jeez," Christine said. "You got over that crisis fast. The hundred dollars you wanted to borrow? Did you file the incident report for the missing money?"

"No," Angela said. She had nearly forgotten about the missing one hundred dollars. She couldn't lose her job. With her mortgage, she couldn't afford to be out of work for more than two weeks. "I was going to go in early today to talk to Natasha in person."

"You didn't do the report?" Christine asked. "I thought—"

"I know," Angela interrupted. "But I thought it was best to talk to Natasha in person first."

"I hope you don't get fired," Christine said. A discreet tone in her voice reminded Angela that her sister would very much like to see her get fired. Christine had always been the good daughter, the wanted daughter. Angela being fired would nicely reinforce her superior status.

"Think you could use an assistant teacher?" Angela said with a small laugh.

"No," Christine said. "You need to fix this situation. The last thing you need is to be a suspect for stealing from the store."

"Yes, I realize that," Angela said, feeling impatient. "But I didn't take the one hundred dollars. Why would I have called you if I took it myself?"

"I'm not saying I think you did it. I'm just saying the truth doesn't always matter," Christine said. "You'll be the most likely suspect, and they'll fire you."

"I think you're wrong," Angela said.

"I've seen it happen," Christine said. "Someone has to be blamed."

"It doesn't have to be me."

"It doesn't have to be, but you are the most convenient person to blame."

"Why?"

"You were the one closing the store, and you were using the register. Plus, it would be cheaper to train your replacement than to train a replacement for the store manager."

"Thanks, Christine."

"And firing you is just the beginning," Christine said. "They can also sue you or have you arrested."

"I don't think they'd have enough evidence to arrest me," Angela said.

"They'd find it," Christine said. "They'd probably interview your friends and family, search your car and house for stolen merchandise … it could get really ugly really fast."

"How can they search my property?" Angela asked. She knew her sister was just trying to upset her. It was a bizarre dynamic, but her sister seemed to love her best when she was down.

"If they have evidence that you were stealing from the company and reason to believe you have company property in your car or house, they could conduct a search," Christine said. Angela didn't think her sister was correct, but she said it with such authority that it seemed plausible.

"I'll talk to Natasha this morning," Angela said. She didn't want to argue with Christine and prolong the conversation. "Mistakes happen. I'm sure it'll be fine."

"All right," Christine said. She sounded uncertain, or maybe just disappointed. "Call me with an update after you talk to Natasha."

"I will," Angela said.

"Hey, I e-mailed you some names," Christine said. "Friends of the family that I wanted to invite to Mom and Dad's anniversary party. I need for you to tell me if you have their addresses."

"Fine," Angela said. "I gotta get going."

"Jeez," Christine said. "Would it kill you to help me out a bit? They are your parents, too."

"Sure, they're my parents, too, but you're their only daughter." Angela intentionally mumbled her words.

"What?" Christine asked.

"I said I'll help, no problem," Angela said. "I gotta go. Talk to you later."

Angela hung up. She walked out to the living room and lay down on the floor. She pressed her ear to the floor. She could hear nothing from the garage directly below.

"Thanks for holding up your end of the bargain," Angela whispered through the floor. "I guess I'd better take the car into the shop. I hit a deer last night."

She got up off the floor and got ready for work. As she dressed, she visualized hitting a deer and replayed the image in her mind several times until it seemed like a real memory and not just her imagination. She'd have to wait until the next payday to take her car in, but it was important to get her story straight right now. She couldn't say she hit a deer in town, because people might wonder why they never saw a dead deer on the road. She could say she was taking a long drive in the country to clear her mind when it happened. She could say she didn't even know exactly where it happened, that it was just some dirt road in the middle of miles and miles of cornfields.

"The local farmer will find the deer and call in for someone to remove it, or take care of it himself," Angela said. "Fortunately, I was able to keep driving, and I made it home safely."

It sounded so real and believable. It was as good as true.

Angela ran down the stairs and out her front door. As soon as she rounded the corner of her walkway to her driveway, she could see that the garage door was closed. Closed? Angela froze momentarily, and then forced herself to continue walking as naturally as she could. The neighbors could be watching.

"He must have managed to close the garage door behind himself," Angela whispered. She believed it. After all, if she were leaving someone's garage, she would try to close the garage door behind herself. It would be rude to leave it open.

As Angela walked down her driveway, she studied the pavement. The driveway and the sidewalk looked no different than they usually looked. There were no long trails of blood or other incriminating remnants of the accident. She began to feel reassured, almost confident that nothing out of the ordinary had happened last night. Just a little accident with a deer.

"I'll have to call the repair shop as soon as I get my next paycheck," Angela said to herself quietly. "They see these deer collisions all the time. They'll know what to do."

As Angela began her long walk to work, there was simply no need to investigate who or what might still be in the garage. Besides, she didn't have time. She needed to focus on developing a good story for the missing hundred dollars.

19

The figure had not dissipated as sunlight seeped under the garage door, illuminating the small and mostly bare garage. In the dim light, Marty could now see the man clearly. He was tall and well dressed in a button-down white shirt with a stiff-looking collar and gray slacks. He was standing four feet away from Marty, leaning against the bare white wall of the garage. The man was watching Marty intently, just as he had all night long.

"You're still here," Marty said.

"Yes," the man said. He seemed to study Marty's face.

"Why are you still here?" Marty asked. "Why didn't you go with Sonya into the house last night?"

"With all the commotion of the accident, she must have not realized I was here," the man said.

"How could she forget a passenger in her car?"

"Is that a reasonable question to ask of a woman who hit you with her car and left you in her garage all night?"

"I guess not," Marty said.

"Besides, I told you. I wanted to stay here with you."

"Why?"

"Are you asking me to leave?"

"No," Marty said, and then added absently, "I'm sorry." The man was a stranger, and yet the fear and upset that his presence triggered was familiar.

"You remind me of someone," Marty said.

"Who?" the man asked.

"I don't know," Marty said. "I can't place it."

"Why not?" the man asked, smiling slightly. His voice was calm and even and had less of a breathy quality than it did the night before. The young man sounded more real, but just as jarring.

Marty replayed every minute he had been in the garage up until the time he first sensed this man's presence. He realized he never heard the sound of the car door open or close. Once again, he felt the prickling sensation of his hairs standing on his arms and neck.

"You didn't come out of the backseat of that car," Marty said, his voice still a whisper.

"Oh?" the young man said.

"I didn't hear the car door close," Marty said. "How could you come out of the car if not through a door?"

"You are right," the man said, nodding his head slowly.

"Are you a hallucination?"

"That depends," the man said. "Do you believe what you see, or see what you believe?"

"Whoever you are," Marty said, "I need your help. Get Sonya to call for help."

The young man leaned against the wall, shook his head, and stared at Marty. "Trust me. She won't listen to me."

20

Samantha hurriedly pressed the button to authorize Pump Five just as it looked like the driver was about to storm up to the cashier's box. Her Tuesday morning shift at Super T's Truck Stop was always busy and always stressful. It always reminded her of how grateful she was to usually work in the evenings.

"Hey!" the young man standing in the back of the line yelled. "Can't you get someone else up here? I'm in a hurry."

"There isn't anyone else!" Samantha yelled back as she gave change to the customer in front of her. She never even had a chance to look most people in the face. She always thought if the store were robbed during the morning rush, she'd never be able to identify the criminals.

"You're doing just fine, Samantha," Mark said, surprising Samantha. Mark had been a regular customer throughout the ten years Samantha had worked at Super T's. She always saw him on Tuesday mornings. "Pump Three and a pack of Camel Lights, hard pack."

"How are you doing this morning?" Samantha asked as she quickly rang up Mark's order.

"I can't complain," Mark said and handed Samantha a crisp one-hundred-dollar bill. "My morning is certainly better than yours."

"It's not so bad," Samantha said, taking the bill. She was supposed to always double-check any bill over a twenty to make sure it wasn't counterfeit, but she could never bring herself to do it. It'd be like accusing her customers of lying. Besides, she'd never heard of a counterfeit bill passing through Super T's.

Samantha forced a smile as she counted Mark's change. "Being busy makes the day go by quickly."

It was a phrase she used so often she wondered if her regulars had caught on that she was just repeating the same conversations over and over. She hoped they weren't insulted. As Samantha handed Mark his change, he leaned over the counter slightly.

"Not to make your day any worse," he said. "But someone threw up in the men's room and didn't exactly make it to the toilet."

"Really?" Samantha said. "That's great …"

As Mark turned to walk away, the next customer dropped his keys on the counter and said, "Number eight" dully.

"Bye, Mark," Samantha said.

Despite the promise made in small talk, the hectic pace did not allow the morning to pass by quickly. Three more customers told Samantha about the mess in the bathroom before there was a large enough break in the crowd for her to leave the register and clean it.

The only real benefit to being so busy was that she couldn't reflect too much on the fight she had with Doug the night before. There were a few quiet moments, though, when she couldn't escape thinking about him or cringing over the things that were said. In the short period of time between customers, she found her mind rereading the note he had left and wondering if this was the beginning of the end.

⚡ ⚡ ⚡

"You're early," Natasha said, looking up from straightening a rack of white, pink, and green blouses. Natasha was a tall black woman with wire-framed glasses and bobbed hair. She didn't appear upset or angry. She must not have reviewed the sales reports and compared them with the bank drops yet.

"Good morning," Angela said. "I wanted to see if you needed any help. I know I left a bit of a mess last night."

"Are you here on overtime?" Natasha asked. She looked Angela up and down, and then quickly returned to straightening the rack. "We don't have any money for overtime this month."

"No," Angela said. "I'm here voluntarily."

"All right," Natasha said. She seemed to like this answer. "I heard the alarm had to be reset last night," she said, laughing and revealing her crooked front tooth.

"It was pretty crazy yesterday," Angela said. She took in a deep breath, a windup for the long and well-planned story she had decided upon on the walk to work. "Mrs. Barnes came in, and she was very upset."

"Really?" Natasha said.

"Yeah," Angela said. "I've never seen her so angry."

"That's funny," Natasha said. "I just saw her this morning. She was in a great mood."

"Oh, that's good," Angela said. The story of Mrs. Barnes angrily insisting on an undocumented hundred-dollar refund would seem too far-fetched now. Angela felt a chill travel through her body as her mind quickly searched for Plan B. "She must've just been having a bad day yesterday. I wonder why she came in. She never comes in on Tuesdays."

"Why was she upset? What happened with her yesterday?" Natasha asked.

"Oh, nothing," Angela said. She'd have to rely on a bank error as the reason for the missing money. "She must have just been having a bad day."

"OK," Natasha said. "Did we meet our quota?"

"I don't think so," Angela said. She began absentmindedly straightening the racks, distributing the hangers equally around the circular rack and turning around shirts that were facing the wrong way. "I think we were almost a thousand dollars short of the quota."

"Dang it," Natasha said. "Did you know they closed two more stores this week?"

"Where at?" Angela said.

"Both in Ohio, I guess," Natasha said. "So at least they weren't around us. But if we keep falling so short of our daily sales quotas, they'll be shutting us down for sure, too."

Natasha had been worried about the store shutting down ever since Angela had started working at Fashionable Finds four years ago. Natasha had probably been worried about the store shutting down since she'd walked in the door as store manager at the grand opening seven years ago.

"Then I'd be the unemployed black woman in Mason. People would love that," Natasha muttered.

"You aren't going to lose your job," Angela said.

"The quota for today is $3,900. How are we supposed to make $3,900 today?" Natasha asked. "It's like corporate is setting us up for failure. What, do they expect a bus full of tourists to come off of I–80 to make a pit stop for nasty fifteen-dollar pink blouses and three-for-ten-dollar itchy nylon panties?"

It was unlike Natasha to make fun of the merchandise. Everyone knew that most of the stuff they sold was unattractive and of poor quality, but when you were surrounded by it every day, you grew to appreciate it. You even found yourself thinking it was fashionable.

"This stuff isn't that nasty," Angela said. It was the power of persistence. These things were staring at you every day, and you had to convince strangers that they were great. You eventually began to believe it yourself.

"Whatever you say, Angela," Natasha said, without a smile.

"Don't worry. Sales are always really slow in the morning," Angela said. "It'll pick up later today. I bet you get a lot of people in over the lunch hour."

"I don't know," Natasha said. She was shaking her head at the receipt.

"Are you able to work late nights this upcoming weekend?" Natasha asked. Then she looked at Angela over her glasses. "It won't be for overtime pay. We'll just have to juggle your hours around a bit."

"Sure," Angela said. "Why?"

"Inventory," Natasha said. She finished straightening the rack of white, pink, and green blouses.

"I can't believe it's that time of year again," Angela said. In her mind, the image of the drawer filled with evidence of "borrowed" barrettes, earrings, and bracelets suddenly seemed like an equal threat to her job as the missing one hundred dollars. They were all Kelly's fault. It didn't matter, though. Angela was the senior sales associate, and Angela knew about them. Angela would get fired.

The phone rang. Angela walked to the registers and picked up. "Thank you for calling Fashionable Finds, where the best deals in fashions find you. This week we are featuring buy two, get one half-off socks. How may I help you?"

"Natasha Warner, please," the female voice on the other end said.

"It's for you," Angela said, holding out the receiver. As Natasha picked up the phone, a sudden image flashed into Angela's mind with startling brilliance. That man clinging to the hood of her car. She had to force him out of her mind and focus on her breathing to calm down.

"Thank you for the call," Natasha said. "We'll look into it right away."

"Who was that?" Angela asked.

"First Bank," Natasha said. "Do you have something to tell me?"

"No," Angela said. She could feel the warmth of her cheeks flushing and hoped Natasha wouldn't notice. "Should I?"

"The bank drop you did last night was short $100.23 from the submitted register report," Natasha said.

"That must be a bank error," Angela said quickly. Natasha was standing behind the register, typing in something. The registers were on a raised platform, and Angela realized how much the customers must feel like defendants approaching a judge's bench when they approached the registers to pay for their cheap clothes. Natasha finished punching in numbers, and the register whirred as it printed a receipt. Natasha pulled it out and looked at it, shaking her head.

"Geesh," Natasha said. She pushed herself back from the register and rolled her head back. She sighed again, so loudly you'd think her body would start decompressing. "Banks don't make errors like that. Not according to anyone who matters. So why don't you tell me. How did that happen?"

"I'm not sure," Angela said. "Maybe a hundred-dollar bill was mistaken for a one-dollar bill. Maybe a bill fell out of the register, and a customer swiped it. Maybe there was a hundred-dollar sale that was refunded but not canceled off the system …"

Angela stopped listing possibilities when she saw Natasha staring at the air above her head. Her face had turned an unhealthy, unnatural shade of gray. It was probably the shade of a manager about to fire an employee.

21

Dogger was barely able to open his eyes. They felt heavy, and seeing the sunlight just made his head throb even worse. He could feel dampness on the side of his mouth and slowly realized that his face was pressed down on cement and he had been drooling in his sleep.

He reached up with his hand to wipe the side of his mouth, but when he lifted his head he immediately had to put it back down on the warm cement. It was just too painful.

As he slowly became more aware of his surroundings, Dogger realized that his body was resting on an incline. He must be on the concrete embankment under the bridge. He forced his eyes open and could see that someone was sitting next to him. He only momentarily thought it was Marty, but he quickly realized that the light jeans and long, thick legs didn't look like they belonged to Marty. In a flash, Dogger realized he was sitting next to the man that had punched him.

Dogger wasn't sure if he should sit up and alert the man that he was awake, or if he should just pretend that he was still passed out. He couldn't see past the man's legs to know if there was anyone else around, but he couldn't hear any voices. Had everyone just abandoned Dogger to deal with this hostile traveler on his own? Would they have done that if Marty were there?

A painful stiffness in his neck began to necessitate that Dogger change positions. He tried to slowly and discretely turn his head, lifting his face off the cement.

"Hey," the traveler whispered. "You awake?"

Dogger slowly forced himself up into a sitting position before he looked the traveler in the face. The traveler had messy reddish blond and gray hair that fell down into his eyes but was trimmed short on the sides. He looked as if he had spent the entire summer outside and had the unhealthy reddish tan hue to his skin that looked like layers of sunburn built up on fair skin. There was a well-worn and frayed red backpack sitting beside him.

"Listen, man," the traveler said. "I am really sorry for losing my temper. That wasn't right."

"It's all right," Dogger said. He felt his right temple, and then looked at his fingers, expecting to see blood. There wasn't any. "I guess."

"No," the traveler said. He shook his head vigorously. "I was way out of line. I've just had a bad week, I guess."

"OK," Dogger said. He started to stand up.

"Hey," the traveler said, grabbing Dogger's shoulder and stopping him from standing up. "Why don't you take a shot at me? Even things up?"

"That's all right," Dogger said. He shrugged off the traveler's hand on his shoulder and stood up. Looking around the Dead Zone, the only person he could see was Richie. Richie was sitting out in front of the old Whatta Dish Diner, like he often was, and appeared to be reading a book.

"Come on." The traveler stood up, too, and Dogger realized how much taller the man was than he had realized. The traveler pointed to his right temple. "A clean shot, right here. That's fair, right?"

"Really, no," Dogger said. He started walking down the embankment. "Call it even. Let's just forget about it."

"Fine," the traveler said. "Forgotten."

Dogger turned and looked under the overpass, just to make sure Marty hadn't tucked himself away and fallen asleep when he wasn't looking. But there was no one. The only people under the bridge were Dogger and the traveler.

"You looking for someone?" the traveler asked, picking up his red backpack and slinging it over his shoulder.

"No," Dogger said. He really wanted to ask the traveler if he had seen Marty, but it seemed wiser to just ignore him.

"I'm pretty good at keeping tabs on people," the traveler said. "If you're looking for someone, that is."

"I'm just waiting for someone," Dogger said. "I'm not looking."

"Someone supposed to meet you here?" the traveler asked. He had a strange smile on his face.

"Yeah," Dogger said. He walked down to the street level and leaned against one of the concrete beams that supported the bridge.

"Who is it?" the traveler asked. He, too, walked down the embankment and leaned against the concrete beam opposite Dogger.

"Just a friend," Dogger said. He wanted to walk away and end the conversation, but he was hesitant to leave just in case Marty showed up. If Marty was half as drunk as Dogger was last night, there was a good chance that he passed out somewhere on the way home. He could wake up at any time and come looking for Dogger at their meeting spot.

"I see," the traveler said. He seemed satisfied with this, and there was silence for several minutes before he asked, "When is he supposed to show up?"

"Any time now," Dogger said. He tried to sound casual and calm, but he knew his voice sounded anything but confident.

"Does your friend live around here?" the traveler asked.

"Yep," Dogger said. "Born and raised in Mason."

"I mean," the traveler asked, folding his arms, "does he live around *here?*"

"In the Dead Zone?" Dogger said. "Why?"

"Oh, nothing," the traveler said. "Were you guys hanging out together last night?"

"Yes," Dogger said.

"I knew I had seen you before," the traveler said, smiling. "I saw you guys last night."

"Oh," Dogger said. He wanted to ask more. Dogger couldn't even remember himself exactly where they were last night.

There were several more minutes of silence. Dogger could see out of the corner of his eye that the traveler kept glancing over at him. He tried to replay the events of last night in his mind, but it was frustratingly futile. He knew they had been drinking because he felt hungover. He vaguely remembered they stole money from a restaurant to pay for the booze, but even that seemed more like a dream than reality.

"It looked like you guys were drinking last night," the traveler said.

"Did you see us drinking?" Dogger asked.

"Yeah," the traveler said. "Like I said, I saw both you and your friend last night."

"Did … you …" Dogger stuttered and stumbled. He wanted desperately to ask the traveler more questions, but he knew this guy wasn't trustworthy. But if he saw what happened to Marty, he had to know. "Did you see Marty, then?"

"Your friend Marty?" the traveler asked. He unfolded his arms and walked toward Dogger. "I saw him."

"Did you see where he went?" Dogger said.

"I happen to know exactly where your friend is right now," the traveler said, smiling.

"Where is he?" Dogger said, straightening himself up as if he were ready to run in any direction the traveler suggested.

"Now slow down," the traveler said. "I can't just give away information for free."

"Hey, you punched me out," Dogger said. He could feel his fists clenching involuntarily. "You owe me one."

"You're wrong," the traveler said. "You don't have a very good memory, do you? You said we were even. We agreed it was forgotten. I don't owe you a thing."

"Why don't you just help me out, then?" Dogger suggested. He folded his arms tightly across his chest, squeezing his hands tightly to his body so they couldn't escape and throw a punch.

"Hey," the traveler said, shrugging his shoulders. "I've got to make a living somehow."

"What do you want?" Dogger asked.

"Ten bucks," the traveler said flatly.

"Ten bucks?" Dogger said, unable to hold back a laugh. "Do you seriously think it looks like I have ten bucks on me?"

"You're right. I'd reckon you have more," the traveler said, scrutinizing Dogger up and down. "Make it twenty."

"Twenty," Dogger said. "Forget it."

"Fine," the traveler said. He turned and began to walk away, taking only a few steps before turning back toward Dogger. "But I will tell you this for free. There's no point of waiting around here for him. He's not going to meet you under this bridge."

The traveler spun on his heel and began walking down Rochester Street. His red backpack bounced lightly as he walked. It was possible he was going to stay in Mason for a while, but it was also possible that he was heading toward the interstate to hitchhike. It was possible this man really had seen what happened to Marty last night.

"Wait," Dogger said. The traveler froze, and then turned to face Dogger. "What's your name?"

"Steve." The traveler began walking toward Dogger once again, sticking out his right hand as he walked.

"Dogger," Dogger said, taking Steve's hand and shaking it. His handshake felt firm and solid. "How do you know Marty isn't going to meet me under the bridge?"

"Because," Steve said with some exasperation. "Like I keep telling you, I know where he is."

"How do you know?" Dogger asked.

"Because I saw what happened last night," Steve said in a low whisper.

Dogger sighed and bit his lip as he thought.

"For twenty bucks, I'll tell you where he is," Steve said. "And trust me, you ain't gonna find him here."

"How long are you staying in Mason?" Dogger asked.

"I'll give you twelve hours to come up with the money." Steve laughed. "Then I have to leave."

"All right," Dogger said, sticking out his hand once more for Steve to shake. "I'll try to come up with it somehow. But you can't leave town until I find Marty."

Steve shook Dogger's hand again, this time squeezing it so tightly that Dogger had to strain to not register pain on his face. Steve pulled Dogger in closer to his face and said, "I don't think you are in a position to tell me what I can and can't do. Bring me the money by tonight, or forget about finding Marty."

22

"Sonny," Marty said. Marty didn't even know what Sonny looked like. As soon as he said his name, the strange feeling he had all night about this man unmistakably became the feeling of recognition. "You're Sonny."

"Yes." The figure moved toward Marty as he said this.

"You can't be here," Marty said. "It's just not possible."

Marty looked at the thin young man. His head was tilted down, looking at Marty with a mix of curiosity and concern. Perhaps Marty's own mind was altering the details of the young man's face as he studied it, but Marty suddenly saw a striking resemblance to himself in the young man.

"You have my nose," Marty said. "My nose exactly."

"You were hoping I'd get my mother's nose, weren't you?" Sonny said.

"Yes, I suppose I was," Marty said. "Sonny, I've missed you terribly. Just terribly."

Sonny said nothing.

"Have you missed me?" Marty said.

"I've never known you," Sonny said. "I couldn't miss someone I didn't know."

"I know," Marty said. He felt tears stinging in his eyes, almost more painful and much more embarrassing than his current state of being. "What did you expect me to be like?"

"I expected a monster," Sonny said flatly.

Marty said nothing but just stared at Sonny's nose.

"I mean, I expected a literal monster," Sonny continued. "Covered in slimy skin and gore. That's what I expected."

"I see," Marty said.

"Mom told me we were much better without you," Sonny said. "And I believed her."

Marty squeezed his eyes shut tightly and repeatedly before opening them again. He looked carefully at Sonny. He knew Sonny had to be a hallucination, but he looked real. He looked more real than hallucinations portrayed in the movies. He wasn't see-through or immersed in a foggy cloud. He was a very real young man standing in the garage. The details were all there. His body heat when he stepped close, the small shadow he cast from the light coming from under the garage door, the small wrinkle in the corner of his mouth when he smiled. He was real.

"I hope you didn't believe everything Sonya said about me," Marty said.

"I made my own stories about you," Sonny said. "When I was small, I told my friends you were an astronaut. In junior high, I told my friends you were in the Peace Corps. And you remained in the Peace Corps until I got to college."

"Then what happened?" Marty asked.

"Tragic accident."

"What?"

"You were killed by a tiger," Sonny said. "You were serving in the Peace Corps in Ghana when a tiger wandered into the village. It was injured and disoriented. It began chasing down a small child, but you distracted it and made it start chasing you. The kid was saved, but you were killed."

"People believed that?" Marty said.

"I mostly told the story to chicks," Sonny said. He laughed and seemed to relax for the first time in their conversation. "It was a very sympathetic and touching story."

"You killed me off so you could get laid in college," Marty said. He smiled broadly and let a small wheezing laugh escape. It was painful but unavoidable. "Wow."

"I didn't just kill you off," Sonny said. "You were the hero of the story. They still have a monument in a small village in Ghana in your honor."

"And you almost believe that, don't you?" Marty said.

"If you tell the story enough times," Sonny said, "you begin to believe your own lies."

"That's very true," Marty said.

"What did you tell people about me?" Sonny asked. He sat down on the garage floor and leaned against the wall. "Did you tell people the truth?"

"I said you were a doctor," Marty said. "You were very successful. I said that you loved me."

"So you didn't tell the truth," Sonny said. He suddenly seemed angry.

"And I believed my own lies," Marty said. "I had no choice."

"Of course you had a choice," Sonny said. "You could have admitted the truth."

"It's complicated," Marty said. "You were all the pride and shame I ever felt, wrapped up in one person. You had to be protected."

"You were right to feel shame," Sonny said. "You nearly killed my mom."

"I wasn't trying to hurt anyone," Marty said. "When a man loses his job, he loses everything that defines him. That job was my world. I was good at what I did, and I was recognized for it."

"What exactly did you do?" Sonny said. "Mom said you were just a factory worker."

"We made executive armchairs," Marty said.

"Executive?" Sonny said with a snort.

"Do you know the kind I am talking about?" Marty said. "I'm talking the finest leather, the finest craftsmanship."

"So you worked in a factory," Sonny said. "Just like mom said."

"These chairs cost hundreds and hundreds of dollars and were bought by CEOs and company presidents across the country," Marty said. "I wasn't just a factory worker pushing buttons or pulling knobs. My job was the most delicate skilled work of all. I had to shave the excess molding off the armrests. It took the steady hands and skills of a surgeon. One slip and the chair was ruined. I made a good salary, and I was respected."

"Why didn't you get another job when the factory closed?" Sonny asked.

"I tried," Marty said. "You've got to believe me that I tried. There just weren't any jobs to be had. There were a hundred other guys trying to get the same handful of jobs I was trying to get in Mason."

"Why didn't you move?" Sonny said. "You could have moved somewhere that had jobs."

"Moving cost money," Marty said. "And we didn't have money. Plus, Mason was our home. Why would we want to move to a town where we didn't know anyone and where I still didn't have a job?"

"So you stayed in Mason," Sonny said, shaking his head. "You started drinking …" In his voice, Marty could detect the distinct tone of Sonya. The disdain. The annoyance. It was unmistakable.

"Yes," Marty said. "I started drinking."

"Mm," Sonny said. It was all Sonya. That noncommittal grunt that was filled with judgment and superiority. It inevitably preceded or followed the question "Have you been drinking?"

It was as if Sonya had become obsessed with Marty's drinking. It was all she ever reacted to; it was all she ever asked about. The more she seemed to hate Marty for drinking, the lonelier Marty felt and the more he drank. He realized this even as it was happening, but he didn't have the strength to stop it. He just allowed himself to grow distant from Sonya. He allowed himself to drink every day. He allowed himself to self-destruct because that was the direction life was taking him. He didn't want to fight.

"I'm sorry," Marty said.

"Mom told me you've never said you were sorry," Sonny said. He stood up and walked toward Marty. Marty could feel the body heat radiate off Sonny. Even if this was a hallucination, it was more real than reality. "I don't think you mean it."

"I do mean it," Marty said.

"I don't think you're sorry about what you did to us," Sonny said. He crouched next to Marty. "I think you are sorry that you got hit by this car. I think you are sorry you have to confront me. I think you are sorry that you looked like a bad guy. But you have no remorse. You're incapable."

Sonny stood up and turned his back on Marty.

"I want to get out of here," Marty said.

"So you can go steal some whiskey from the grocery store?" Sonny said, turning around.

"That was a mistake, and I served my time," Marty said. "Why are you here tormenting me?"

"Because you want me here," Sonny said. His voice returned to that soothing, calm, even tone that had first greeted Marty in the garage.

"Help me," Marty said. "Can't you help me? Go call someone. Open the garage door. Do something."

"You know I can't do that," Sonny said. Marty did know. He knew Sonny couldn't do anything but talk. Marty knew Sonny couldn't possibly be there in the garage with him, but yet somehow his spirit was.

"Are you dead?" Marty asked.

"Like a ghost?" Sonny laughed. "No."

"I need to get help in here," Marty said. "I need to let people outside know I am in here."

"What do you propose?" Sonny said.

"I need to make a lot of noise," Marty said. "I can't shout. This is as loud as I can talk, and even this hurts."

"OK, so screaming is out," Sonny said.

"I can't pound the hood," Marty said. "It causes horrible vibrations that could damn well kill me."

"And the lawn chair is out of reach," Sonny said.

"Right," Marty said. "So what am I left with?"

"You are looking right at it," Sonny said. "I know you've seen it before. That 2002 Chrysler Sebring has an alarm system. A vibration-sensitive alarm system."

23

After the morning traffic cleared, Samantha rang up a cappuccino and leaned against the counter behind the register. She surveyed the empty store. The coffee station was cluttered with crumpled napkins, empty sugar packets, and brightly colored miniature tubs of flavored creamer. The once tidy aisles of the convenience minimart were now skewed, the floor littered with fallen candy bars, car fresheners, and potato chip bags.

Samantha turned her back on the store and stared out the window. The mess could wait until just before the lunch rush when people exited off I–80 to grab a bite to eat and fill up. She watched the traffic on Route 1 coast by and allowed her mind to wander.

A man walking on the other side of the road caught Samantha's attention. She squinted at him, trying to make out the details of his face in the bright morning sunlight. It was Dogger, and it looked as if he were alone.

Samantha pounded on the thick glass window of Super T's, but Dogger kept walking. She put down her coffee and walked around the cashier booth. The front door chimed as she opened it and leaned out.

"Hey, Dogger!" she called. Dogger kept walking. His unstable, slightly insane-looking strides were a Dogger trademark. Samantha yelled again, "Hey, Dogger!"

Dogger seemed to be intentionally ignoring her. Something didn't seem right. Samantha quickly looked over her shoulder into the store, and seeing no customers, she allowed herself to step out of the store. She ran across the street and put her hand on Dogger's shoulder.

"Dogger," Samantha said. She was already nervous about leaving the store unattended, even though she was still standing right in front of it. "What's going on? Didn't you hear me?"

"Yeah," Dogger said. He stopped walking but didn't look at Samantha. "I heard you. I just didn't feel like walking across the street."

"Is everything OK?" Samantha asked. She glanced back at the store, although it appeared to still be empty and no one was at the pumps.

"Everything is just fine," Dogger said. He glanced at Samantha, and she saw his eyes were almost pure red, and it looked like he had taken a serious blow to his right temple. He looked ill.

"Chuck isn't in this morning," Samantha said. "Why don't you stop by for a cup of coffee?"

"No," Dogger said. "I'm busy. Plus, I can't be troubling you." He started walking, but Samantha gripped his shoulder. Something was wrong—he was sick or hurt or something.

"It's no trouble," Samantha said. She couldn't just let him walk on. In her mind, she could see him strutting with that crazy unbalanced strut right into traffic. She didn't care if this meant Doug was right and she did have a "hero complex."

"I don't know," Dogger said, shaking his head.

"I'd really like the company," Samantha said.

"Well," Dogger turned and looked at Samantha. He looked down at his feet, but Samantha could see a small smile on the corner of his lips. "If you want some company …"

"Come on," Samantha said. She almost wanted to grab his hand and pull him across the street, but she knew that would give him the wrong impression.

When she turned to return to Super T's, she saw that a vintage Volvo had pulled up to Pump Five. The young woman driving the car seemed to openly stare as Samantha and Dogger crossed the street together and entered the store. It wasn't until Samantha and Dogger entered the store that the woman stepped out of her car.

"I bet she's paying at the pump," Dogger said with a small, insincere-sounding laugh.

"Probably so," Samantha said. "Have a seat, and I'll bring you some coffee."

"Thanks," Dogger said, slumping down in one of the chairs by the coffee and soda machines. Something was really odd about this encounter, and Samantha couldn't put her finger on it.

"Are you sure you feel OK?" Samantha asked as the Styrofoam cup filled with aromatic coffee. "I bet you have a bad hangover. You were pretty out of it when I saw you running on Frontage Road."

"Frontage Road?" Dogger said, and then stared down at his hands, lost in thought.

"Are you feeling OK?" Samantha repeated the question.

"I was up all night," Dogger said with a heavy sigh. "I feel about as good as I can feel."

"Fair enough," Samantha said. She put the coffee cup down in front of Dogger. "Where is Marty? Didn't you meet up with him at Berler Bridge?"

24

"Explain to me again why you didn't file an incident report last night," Natasha said. She was leaning on the register counter, bent over with her head in her hands.

"I wasn't sure I had counted correctly. I wanted to talk to you first," Angela said.

"And you thought you could blame the bank," Natasha said, shaking her head. "This disappoints me."

"No, it's not like that," Angela said. Of course, it was exactly like that.

"You surprise me, Angela." Natasha stood up. "I am going to assume you know how to count, and you knew that Register One was one hundred dollars short." She stared down at Angela, looking at her as if she were a subordinate who would be expendable if necessary to save her own job. "I should have you tested for drugs."

"Why?" Angela said.

"Money is missing. I saw you had to reset the alarm," Natasha said. "You're either on drugs or stupid."

"I'm not on drugs," Angela said. "You know that. And I was stupid last night. I was so tired that I was completely stupid."

"I'll let you explain that to the big bosses," Natasha said, her eyes wide. "Do the incident report right now."

"No problem," Angela said. "I will. I'll do it right now."

"Get up here," Natasha said. "I'll go get the procedures from the back."

Angela stepped up onto the platform of registers. She was grateful that at least there weren't any customers in the store to see this.

"Use Register Three for the online report!" Natasha yelled from the back room. "I'll fill out the paper report myself."

"OK!" Angela yelled back. Unlike the other two registers, the third register was in pristine condition. The numbers were clear and unfaded on the keypad; the screen was unscuffed. Register Three didn't have the scattering of dots and dashes left by blue Fashionable Finds pens over the front. When Register Three was used, it meant something very unusual was happening. The last time Angela had used it was approximately one year ago to report inventory numbers to corporate.

Angela logged onto the third register using her employee ID number and pass code. Natasha had reemerged from the back room and dropped a two-inch-thick three-ring binder on the counter next to Angela.

"And do you know what the worst part is?" Natasha asked, as if she and Angela were in the middle of a conversation.

"What is that?" Angela said. She was afraid to stop typing the report for even a minute, but the distraction of Natasha was causing repeated typos that had to be deleted and retyped.

"You are making this report now, instead of last night when you should have made the report," Natasha said. "Now, you are officially on the clock. And I don't have any money to pay you."

"It's OK," Angela said, still trying to type and talk at the same time. "We can just move some hours, right?"

"No," Natasha said. "No, we can't do that because I already have minimal coverage as it is. When you are scheduled to work, I need you here."

"So we'll just clock me in for an hour this morning for the incident report," Angela said, surprised at how calm she was remaining. "And I'll work an hour off the clock for my evening shift tonight. No overtime necessary."

"But the store can't operate on paper without a manager or senior associate on duty," Natasha said, folding her arms.

"We'll just report you were here for that hour," Angela said. "You're salaried, right? No overtime pay necessary."

"Yeah, that will work." Natasha almost sounded disappointed that further drama wasn't going to develop. "You are damn lucky I am not firing you on the spot."

* * *

Marty's knowledge of cars was limited. He knew how to change the oil, he knew how to strip the best parts for resale, and he knew how to disable a car alarm. The impact of Marty's body had deformed the hood and partially lifted it up off the car. After what seemed like several hours of exhausting work, he was able to lift the hood just far enough to reach his left arm under to search for the dipstick.

"I really am sorry about how things turned out," Marty said as his left hand swept back and forth under the hood, feeling for the dipstick. "Everyone has skeletons in the closet, I guess."

"True enough," Sonny said. "But what people forget is that those skeletons have lives of their own. If you ever open the closet door, you might find an entirely different set of bones than you expected."

"What do you mean?" Marty said.

"I mean, you don't know me or anything about me," Sonny said. "The last you knew, I was in my mother's womb."

"That's true," Marty said. He stopped searching under the hood for a moment and looked at Sonny. Sonny didn't look angry or hurt; the look on his face was just as dull as the tone in his voice. Marty gave a small, wheezing laugh. "I realize you are no longer in your mother's womb."

"But in your mind, you have controlled my life ever since," Sonny said. "You seem to have forgotten that when you locked me away in that closet that I would still be living my own life, and it wasn't necessarily the life you wanted me to live or one that you were even capable of imagining."

"I know, Sonny," Marty said. He resumed searching under the hood for the dipstick. "I realize that you most likely are not a doctor."

"Most likely not," Sonny said.

"I suppose you'll say the same holds true for your mother," Marty said. "She isn't the evil woman that I've made her out to be since shutting her in the closet?"

"Exactly," Sonny said. "She's an entirely different set of bones than what you are expecting, too."

Marty sighed uncomfortably and continued to blindly search for the dipstick under the hood.

"I hope you realize," Sonny said, "that you are a skeleton in my closet, too. And in my mother's closet."

"Of course," Marty said. "I guess I always knew that I was probably just an embarrassing secret to you."

"And I suspect you have just become a skeleton in this women's closet," Sonny said, pointing to the ceiling.

"I suspect you're right," Marty said. "Otherwise, I think she would have already called for help, and I wouldn't still be stuck here."

"I think you might have the upper hand," Sonny said. "After all, you know something she doesn't know."

"What's that?"

"You know that skeletons in the closet have lives of their own," Sonny said with a small smile on his face. "She wants to just forget about you, maybe even rewrite history. But she doesn't realize that you are going to keep right on living, whether she likes it or not."

"So when she finally opens the door, I'll be an entirely different bag of bones than what she expects?"

"Exactly."

"That doesn't sound too promising," Marty said. "But I think I know what you mean."

Sonny leaned against the wall, looking satisfied that he had made his point.

Suddenly, Marty's fingertips grazed the top of the dipstick. He gripped it as firmly as he could.

"I've got it," Marty whispered. Sweat was stinging his eyes and dripping down his cheeks. He took a moment to breathe slowly.

"You know what to do with it, skeleton," Sonny said, his cadence even and smooth.

"I do?" Marty said. Sonny nodded and pointed under the car hood.

Marty painfully bowed his head down to follow Sonny's finger under the hood of the car to a small box on the driver's side of the car. A small red light flashed intermittently.

"The car alarm," Marty whispered.

Marty carefully brought his right hand under the hood of the car and transferred the dipstick from his left to his right hand. He couldn't see where his arm was going, but he knew the most important thing was to hold onto the dipstick. He slowly moved his right arm. The stick hit metal, and Marty stopped moving.

"How am I doing?" Marty asked.

"You aren't even close," Sonny said, squinting under the hood of the car. "Move your arm to the right."

Marty moved his arm to the right and immediately hit what felt like a metallic boulder with the back of his hand. The reverberation caused pain to shoot up through his arm and into his chest.

"Don't drop the dipstick," Sonny said, his eyes wide and looking at Marty. "Don't drop it."

"I won't," Marty said through clenched teeth. "Help guide me."

"You can lift your arm up about an inch," Sonny said. "You'll go over the engine but not hit the hood of the car."

Marty lifted his hand up and painfully rotated his arm to the right. He anticipated impact at any moment. He looked at Sonny, who was bent over, looking under the hood of the car and nodding. As crazy as

Marty knew it was, he had to trust Sonny. The end of the dipstick made a metallic scratching sound as it hit the right side of the car. He had made it.

"Great," Sonny said. "Now if you can bring your hand back toward you, and flex it out about forty-five degrees."

Marty followed the instructions. He imagined this was something like those games at fairs and arcades where you try to direct a mechanical claw to pick up stuffed animals and cheap plastic watches. The promise was always there, printed in bold purple letters: "You Grab It, You Keep It! Win Fabulous Prizes!" It looked very easy, and it was a popular game, but Marty had never seen anyone win.

The dipstick hit something with a plastic-sounding thunk. Marty gripped the small metal handle of the dipstick even tighter and looked at Sonny.

"That was it," Sonny said, grinning. "You just hit the outside of the car alarm unit."

Marty excitedly hit it a few more times, but the same plastic thud sounded and nothing else. Sonny looked carefully under the hood; his eyes studied the inside of the car.

"You might be able to trip it if you knock the wires on the far side of the box," Sonny said. "That should trigger the vibration sensors."

"How am I going to do that?" Marty said.

"It's a dipstick, remember?" Sonny said. "It has a small curve at the end. If you move your arm to the left and flex your hand and an extreme angle to the right, you should make contact."

Marty tried this, but his feeble swings weren't connecting with anything.

"You're missing everything," Sonny said. "Angle your wrist more."

With a burning pain in his shoulder and chest as he moved his body away, ever so slightly, from the locked metallic embrace of the car, Marty was able to bend his wrist a little more. This time, he hit something. Something plastic.

"That's it," Sonny said. "Now just hit it hard."

It was difficult to get much of a windup for a good solid swing, but Marty strained, and then flicked his wrist and fingers with as much force as he could. The light sound of metal hitting plastic was the only result.

"Again," Sonny said, looking under the hood. "You're so close."

Marty strained, and then swung again. Nothing. Just like the game at the fair—it looks so easy, but no one ever wins.

"This isn't working," Marty said.

"Keep trying," Sonny said. "You are so close. You only need to connect one time."

"I don't think I can hit it hard enough," Marty said.

"You don't have to hit it too hard," Sonny said. "You just have to hit it right. The vibrations should set it off."

Marty inhaled deeply, tensed his body, and flicked his wrist and fingers as hard as he could.

The car chirped loudly, like an electronic hiccup. The sound ricocheted around the small garage and was deafeningly loud. Marty and Sonny stared at each other, wide-eyed and grinning. It was the first sound he had made that was loud enough for someone outside the garage to hear.

"You hit the sweet spot," Sonny said.

25

"What is Marty up to today?" Samantha asked. Dogger seemed reluctant to talk about Marty, and Samantha suspected they had had a fight of some sort.

"I'm not sure," Dogger said. He eyed Samantha up and down, and then sighed loudly. "He didn't come around here, did he?"

"I haven't seen him," Samantha said.

"I'm sure I'll meet up with him later," Dogger said.

"Listen," Samantha said, quickly looking out the window to ensure no customers were heading into the gas station. "You look really beat. Why don't you take a little nap here?"

"Thanks, but I've got to get going," Dogger said, nodding his head toward the door.

"Please?" Samantha said. Dogger looked more than tired; he looked sick. "I insist. If you don't want to sleep too long, I can wake you up after just a short while."

Dogger pursed his lips and looked out the window. His eyes seemed to be searching, maybe watching to ensure Chuck wasn't heading in unexpectedly. Chuck was never too happy to see Dogger or Marty hanging around.

"I bet you'll feel much better with just a little sleep," Samantha said. "And things will be pretty quiet here until the lunch hour."

"All right," Dogger said. "A nap on one of your cots does sound pretty good."

Samantha grabbed a key from behind the counter and led Dogger down the hallway to open one of the private rooms that weary travelers could rent by the hour and sleep in. She wanted to know what happened the night before and why Marty wasn't around, but that could wait until after Dogger got some rest.

"Is Room Eight OK?" Samantha asked, unlocking the door.

"My favorite." Dogger smiled a toothless grin and walked past her. He immediately dropped down on the cot and rolled onto his back.

"Thanks, Samantha," Dogger said before Samantha closed the door.

"No problem," Samantha said. "Sleep well."

The customers continued to trickle in and out of Super T's. Most midmorning customers paid at the pump. In contrast to the morning rush, it felt like the truck stop was in slow motion.

As the morning progressed, Samantha became increasingly anxious to hear what Dogger had to say once he woke up. He was clearly inebriated last night, and he wasn't with Marty when she saw him running along Frontage Road. Maybe they had gotten into a drunken argument. She didn't remember seeing that shiner on his right temple last night, but it was dark. It didn't seem like Marty to be violent, but maybe the fight had gotten physical. The phone rang, jolting Samantha from her thoughts about Dogger.

"Super T's Truck Stop, this is Samantha."

"Hi, Sam." It was the familiar voice of the manager on the phone. "It's Chuck. I think I left my house keys there after my overnight shift."

Samantha opened the drawer under the register. There was a glowing orange coil keychain.

"Yep," Samantha said. "How did you get in your front door this morning?"

"My wife was home," Chuck said.

"You need to start keeping your car keys and your house keys in the same place," Samantha said. "Just have one keychain, like the rest of us."

"I know, I know," Chuck said. "I already got the lecture from my wife."

"Are you just going to pick them up on your shift tonight?" Samantha said.

"Today's my day off. I'm not coming in for work until tomorrow afternoon," Chuck said. "I'll stop over right now and get them. I just wanted to make sure they were where I thought I left them."

"OK," Samantha said as cheerfully as she could, but her stomach was sinking.

Chuck had this habit that any time he came to the store on business or pleasure he'd give it a quick inspection. She could envision Dogger getting up from his nap at just the wrong time, or Chuck wanting to see the driver's license she was supposed to be holding for the person who was checked in Room Eight. Plus, the fact that there were no cars or trucks parked would be a dead giveaway that something was amiss. Chuck was a nice enough guy, but he despised the "local hoodlums" who would try to "mooch off the good nature" of his associates.

"Thanks for checking," Chuck said. "I'll be right over."

"See you soon," Samantha said. Chuck only lived about two blocks away, so he could be over before she even finished hanging up the phone. Samantha could just imagine what would happen to her relationship with Doug if she got fired for housing homeless people in the truck stop.

Samantha hurried through the short aisles of the convenience store and down the back hallway toward the sleeping rooms. She pounded on the door to Room Eight. She pressed her ear to the door, but she couldn't hear anything.

"Dogger?" Samantha said. She knocked on the door again. This time, she could hear the sound of something moving. "Dogger, you have to get up."

Samantha pressed on the door handle, expecting it to be locked, but it opened. Samantha opened the door just far enough to put her head into the small room. She could smell beer and realized immediately she would need to clean the sheets and spray the room with Lysol.

"I'm sorry to wake you," Samantha said.

"Mmmm," Dogger grunted. He rolled to his side and sat up on the cot. He furrowed his brow as he looked at Samantha, probably not fully awake yet.

"Chuck is coming," Samantha said. Dogger's eyes suddenly appeared more alert, and he stood up. "You've got to go. I know he'd check to see if this room was checked in and paid for, but I didn't—"

"He's here now?" Dogger interrupted. He brushed past Samantha into the hallway.

"No," Samantha said. "He's on his sway."

Samantha followed Dogger. When he reached the end of the hall, he froze. He turned his head to Samantha.

"Isn't that his car?" Dogger asked. Samantha looked out the glass window. At first she only saw a red SUV at the pumps, which wasn't Chuck's car. Then she saw the black Jeep Grand Cherokee parked in front of the store.

"Oh, crap," Samantha whispered. She squinted and thought she could see a figure still in the car. It could be Chuck, or maybe it is his wife, waiting for him. It was hard to tell through the heavily tinted glass. "Hold on."

Samantha walked in front of Dogger and scanned for people. The store was empty. She looked at the Cherokee and saw the car door opening.

"OK, he's just getting out of the car now," Samantha said. "Just don't go out the front door. You can go out the side door."

Samantha pulled at Dogger's arm, leading him out of the hallway and toward the side door marked "Exit Only."

"Thanks for letting me sleep a bit," Dogger said. He seemed more coherent than he was just a couple hours before.

"Anytime," Samantha said. She saw Chuck walking up the sidewalk toward the store.

"Anytime except for when Chuck is here, right?" Dogger said. He opened the door.

"Wait," Samantha said. Dogger turned. "You have to tell me—why isn't Marty with you?"

"I don't know where he is," Dogger said. The front doors chimed. Samantha turned and saw the tall round figure of Chuck walking in.

"Do you think he's in trouble?" Samantha said as she pushed Dogger out the door.

"He might be," Dogger said.

"Samantha?" Chuck's low and naturally booming voice startled Samantha, and she turned. Chuck had his hands resting on his hips, making his already imposing figure appear even more intimidating. "Everything OK?" Chuck asked. "Is this guy giving you any trouble?"

"No. No trouble," Samantha said. "He was just leaving." Samantha turned to Dogger, who was already backing out the door. Dogger looked at Samantha with an expression that would haunt Samantha for the rest of the day.

"Marty's missing," Dogger said. "I have no idea what happened to him."

26

"Where is the rest of the alarm?" Marty said.

"That was just the warning chirp," Sonny said. "It's set off by loud noises or vibrations when the car is turned off. With your level of strength, the only way you can trigger enough vibration is to hit the sensors directly."

"A warning chirp," Marty repeated.

"Keep hitting it," Sonny said. "Try to hold your hand and wrist in the exact same position and swing the exact same way."

Marty tried to recreate his previous swing, but all he got was a dull plastic thud. Without waiting for prompting, he took a breath and swung again. Then on the fifth swing, he connected, and another piercing chirp filled the garage.

With maniac speed, Marty kept flicking his wrist. Despite the pain, he refused to let his wrist relax from the current position. It was imprecise, but on every ninth or tenth swing, he would connect, and the car would chirp.

"That's it," Sonny said.

Marty could focus on nothing other than carefully holding his hand and wrist in the exact position to recreate the exact same swing over and over again. Despite the exhaustion he quickly felt with the effort, every loud chirp of the alarm gave him a shot of energy to keep going.

Suddenly, the sound of deep and heavy banging shook the entire garage door and startled Marty. The sound was so loud and so sudden that it disoriented Marty, and at first he wasn't even sure of what he was hearing. It seemed as if he were caught in an earthquake and the entire garage was threatening to collapse.

"What was that?" Marty whispered. Sonny was silent and staring wide-eyed at the garage door. Marty resumed flicking the dipstick at the alarm sensor, but his aim was much worse now that his rhythm was off. Finally, after what must have been at least twenty swings, the car alarmed chirped.

Just seconds after the car alarm gave its warning chirp, the pounding and shaking of the garage door began again. This time, they continued much longer and sounded much louder. Marty looked over at Sonny, but he seemed just as bewildered.

The pounding stopped, and the shaking garage door shuttered to a stop. The sound of a man's voice could be heard yelling, "Hey! Take care of that, jerk!"

"Hey," Marty said back. He felt a tingling sensation spread throughout his body, accompanying the sudden realization of what was happening. A man was standing outside the garage door right now. It wasn't an earthquake—it was the sound of the man knocking on the garage door.

"You're bugging the whole neighborhood!" the man yelled, and then gave the garage door another reverberating pound.

"Hey," Marty said again. But his voice was barely above a whisper. He didn't realize how small he sounded until he compared his voice with the voice of the man at the door. "Help," Marty whispered.

"Keep setting off the alarm," Sonny said.

Marty flicked his wrist and solidly hit the alarm. It chirped in response. Marty paused, expecting to hear more pounding on the garage door. Instead, he heard nothing.

"Where did he go?" Marty asked.

"Maybe he's calling for help," Sonny said. His voice sounded hopeful, although the expression on his face was quite doubtful.

The chime of a doorbell could be heard, muffled but distinct. The man must have moved to the front door. Marty kept swinging his wrist; the alarm hiccupped loudly. As if in response, the doorbell rang several times in a row.

"I'd say you've definitely been heard," Sonny said, smiling.

27

Natasha leaned over Angela's shoulder like a vulture ready to pick apart the dead weight of an employee on the brink of termination.

"This report wouldn't be so difficult for you if you were more familiar with the standard procedures," Natasha said.

"I should review the manual more often," Angela said.

"I'd say so," Natasha said with a loud sigh. Although Angela didn't turn to look at Natasha, she knew she was shaking her head when she said this. That particular sigh always accompanied a slowly shaking head.

The phone rang at the end of the counter. Angela moved to answer it, relieved for any reason to duck away from the stream of hot breath hitting the back of her neck and filling the air with the odor of stale coffee.

"I'll get it," Natasha said, stepping away. "You keep writing."

"Thanks," Angela said.

"Thank you for calling Fashionable Finds, where the best deals in fashions find you. This week we are featuring buy one, get one half-off socks. This is Natasha. How may I help you?" Natasha said one of the corporate-approved greetings of the week into the phone without enthusiasm.

"She is kind of tied up right now," Natasha said, her tone irritated. "Can it wait?"

Angela continued typing the report's narrative. *Two associates were logged onto the register* ...

"Her car is what?" Natasha said. Angela froze. "I'll let her know. Good-bye."

"What was that all about?" Angela asked. She forced her voice to sound casual.

"Did you walk here today?" Natasha asked as she stepped off the register platform and looked through the glass front doors.

"Yeah," Angela said. "Who was calling about my car? What's going on?"

"I bet it's that weird neighbor of yours," Natasha said. "Bob Barker, or whatever you call him?"

"Yeah," Angela said. She hit send on the register without rereading the report. It would just have to be good enough for corporate. "Was that my neighbor on the phone?"

"No," Natasha said. She seemed to fold the panties with an excruciatingly slow pace and delivered her speech equally slowly. "It was your townhouse association president."

"What did he want?" Angela said. She logged herself off of Register Three and began inching away.

"That car alarm of yours is acting up again," Natasha said. "It's not going off, but it's chirping and annoying the neighbors. You gotta go take care of that, or they are going to enter your garage and take care of it for you."

"I guess I had better go take care of that," Angela said. "Right now."

"Wait," Natasha said. "Did you finish that report?"

"Yes," Angela said. She picked up her purse from behind the register. "I just sent it."

"All right," Natasha said. "Then get out of here."

Angela began walking to the door. She turned and said quickly, "I'll see you later this afternoon. I'm scheduled from three until close today."

"Why don't you just take care of your little car problem?" Natasha said. "I'll cover your shift tonight if need be."

"Thanks," Angela said as she turned and ran out the door. Somehow, exhausted and overworked Natasha was suddenly feeling up for a twelve-hour work day. Angela could easily read the subtext. Angela was now suspect, and Natasha wasn't sure she wanted her closing the store by herself again.

Within moments, Angela's strides elongated and quickened from a brisk walk to a sprint. Her legs pumped furiously, almost out of control, as she ran. She sensed a brief break in the traffic and ran across Route 1 and toward the residential ring of Mason. What felt like an unseasonably cool day this morning now felt like an inferno.

As Angela ran, she thought of all the reasons her car alarm could go off. She did just get into a car accident last night, after all, so it was quite possible that the accident somehow broke the car alarm. The car alarm was easily tripped. She was constantly sticking the remote on her keychain out the door at work to turn off the car alarm after it had been accidentally tripped. It would sometimes chirp a warning alarm before it would go into its full series of alarm sounds. Maybe it was chirping because it needed a new battery. Angela wasn't certain that car alarms did that, but it seemed like a reasonable possibility.

It took Angela about ten minutes to make it to Herbert Street. As she turned the corner to jog down her home street, she saw a man in a striped T-shirt pounding on her garage door and shaking his head.

"Hello, Bob Barker," Angela whispered. At least the garage door was still closed. Angela ran up behind the man and tapped him hard on the shoulder.

"Hey," Angela said. She was out of breath and barely able to speak. "What are you doing?"

"This jerk's car alarm is going off," the man said, looking Angela up and down. The frowning man was probably in his sixties. His round face and short, muscular build made him look like an aged high school wrestler. "It's driving me crazy."

"I'm sorry it's bothering you," Angela said. "I'm sure it can be fixed."

"This is your place?" the man said, clearly taken aback. "You're my neighbor?"

"Yes," Angela said. She wanted the conversation to end and for Bob Barker to go home as soon as possible. "Thanks for letting me know about the problem."

"You weren't answering your door," he said. "So I called the association president. The alarm kept going off, so I thought I'd try to get you to answer the door again. It's driving me crazy."

"I was at work," Angela said. Suddenly, a loud chirp came from the garage.

"See?" the man said, pointing at the garage door. "That's what I'm talking about. Let's turn that off right now. I can help you." The man started walking toward Angela's front door.

"Yes," Angela said. "I'll get it taken care of right now. You can go back home. Thanks for calling."

Angela walked past the man, pulling out her keys. He continued to stand next to the door. The car alarm chirped again in the garage.

"I know something about cars," the man said. "Let me help you disable your alarm. It might just be too sensitive."

"I can handle it," Angela said. "Thanks again for calling. It was nice meeting you."

"I was just offering to help," he said. He watched Angela put her keys in the door.

"I appreciate that," Angela said, "but no, thank you." She didn't want to even push open the door with Bob Barker standing there. He seemed like the type of guy that would take that as in invitation to come inside. Then he'd want to help fix the car.

"Well, get it fixed immediately," the man said. "I will call the association president again if I hear it going off. And this time, you won't get a courtesy call. He'll probably just come in and take care of it for you."

"What?" Angela said. She could feel herself shaking as this man brought her agitation level to a full boil.

"Next time your alarm gives you trouble, the president will just come in and take care of your car himself," Bob Barker said. "And, believe me, he probably won't be gentle with your car."

"Is that a threat?" Angela sputtered. "He can't do that. This is my private property."

"Yes, he can," he said. "Read your association bylaws book. You are disturbing the peace, and it is within the president's rights to enter your property if you are violating the association bylaws."

"Fine," Angela said through gritted teeth. It was the second time today she was accused of not reading a manual. "Good-bye."

"We won't be so nice next time," the man repeated. He watched Angela for a moment longer before turning and walking away. The car alarm chirped again. Angela watched as Bob Barker froze in his tracks, shook his head, and then continued walking.

As soon as Angela heard the front door of his neighboring townhouse close, she pushed open the door to her house. She quickly turned and locked her front door behind her, including the deadbolt.

Angela stared at the door to her garage for several moments, half-expecting to see the door handle slowly begin to turn. The house, and the garage, seemed still. Angela pressed her ear to the door, and she could immediately hear a small scraping and knocking sound. It was an eerie sound that made her stomach tense instantly.

What would make that sort of sound? Was there an animal in her garage? A raccoon scuttling on the floor? While she could think of a hundred plausible causes for the scraping sound, she couldn't shield her mind from the truth. She knew exactly what was making the sound. It was that man, that thing, that ran into her car last night. It was still alive, and it was still in her garage.

Angela held her breath and quickly opened the door to the garage. As soon as she saw what was in the garage, she gasped, and then began coughing and choking on the air.

Marty did not want to see that woman. He wanted the man that was pounding and yelling outside the garage door to finally break in. He'd even be happy to see Henry Gates coming into the garage. But not this woman. Her face looked even more like Sonya than before. She looked cold and repulsed. She looked as if she hated Marty. She didn't even respect him enough to feign kindness. She obviously felt nothing but hate for him. It was easy to believe that she was, in fact, Sonya.

When she walked into the garage, she looked at Marty for a few moments, and then suddenly began convulsing. Her back arched, and she bent over and coughed hard at the floor, her mouth wide open and spit dangling from her lower lip. She looked like a sick cat trying to cough up a hairball. After several moments she finally stopped coughing, and she slowly straightened up. Even in the dim light, she looked pale, and Marty could clearly see red splotches had appeared on her neck. The look of shock and sickness on her face told Marty that he must look pretty bad.

This realization led to an unexpected and bizarre feeling of pride. It was a badge of honor to be so grotesquely mangled. His pain and fear were justified. He wasn't just a coward this time, unable to handle the smallest discomfort. The fact that he was even alive must be a testament to some strength. Marty felt himself grin a little bit.

The woman stared at Marty for several long moments. She seemed unable to move.

"Hello, Sonya," Marty whispered hoarsely. His lungs filled with pain when he spoke. "You remember Sonny."

Marty nodded to his left. He watched as the woman's eyes, round with horror, slowly scanned to Marty's left. Her brows twitched and furrowed slightly, and then she returned her gaze to Marty. Marty looked to his left and saw the fallen lawn chair, smatterings of dried vomit, and nothing else except the wall. Sonny must have decided to hide. The woman continued to stare; she seemed unable to move.

"If you aren't going to help me," Marty whispered, "I'll just keep doing my thing."

Marty began flicking his wrist quickly and firmly. With practice he had greatly improved his accuracy and was now able to make contact with almost every fourth try. His wrist and arm burned furiously. The pain radiated first to his head, and then to his stomach as well. Marty's first swing missed, and he could hear the dull sound of metal hitting plastic.

Sonya's frown deepened. Her eyes narrowed at Marty, but she still didn't move. Marty flicked his wrist again. This time, he connected, and the car chirped loudly. The sound seemed to send a shock through the woman, and she suddenly began charging toward the car. Marty braced himself.

The woman looked under the hood. As she leaned, her fragrance met Marty's nose. The scent was sweet and clean. It was only in contrast to her smell that Marty realized his own odor was so foul and almost death-like.

The woman grunted as she lifted the hood slightly and reached in. Her head and upper body were squeezed under the car as she reached for the dipstick in Marty's right hand. Marty realized in that second that if he had the strength, he could shove the hood down on her and probably hurt her, if not kill her, right now.

Instead, Marty dropped the dipstick. It rattled its way down the inner workings of the car before the sound of it hitting the cement garage floor signaled the end of its fall.

The woman carefully backed herself out from under the hood. She dropped the hood, and its weight pressed down heavily on Marty's arms and scraped his chest. Marty moaned, and the woman appeared satisfied with this.

"Get help, Sonya," Marty said. He wished he hadn't played with her. He wasn't in the position of power; Sonya was in the position of power. "I need help."

The woman walked around the car, inching between the car's back bumper and the closed garage door. She kept her eyes on Marty as she moved. She walked up the driver's side of the car, and then ducked down.

When Sonya straightened up again, she was holding the dipstick in her hand. It was even longer than Marty had imagined as he was blindly trying to hit the sweet spot on the car alarm. She seemed to sneer at Marty as she held it up for him to see. She was reveling in this small victory.

"Call for help, Sonya," Marty said. He knew it was fruitless. He knew that if she hadn't called for help yet, she wasn't going to call for help. But he had to ask. She was his only connection to the outside world. She was the only one who could help.

"Wait, Sonya," Marty said. "Olive shoe! Do you remember? Olive shoe."

Sonya walked around the trunk and toward the door. After giving Marty one last troubled and cold look, she dropped the dipstick in the garbage can and walked out, slamming the door behind her. Sonya hadn't changed in the last thirty years.

28

Samantha had driven the length of Route 1 so slowly that she had already received the finger twice since leaving work at Super T's Truck Stop. She pulled into parking lots to look behind buildings. She had gotten out of her car three times to look around promising shrubbery. That last look on Dogger's face had haunted her all day, that look he had when he said "Marty's missing." It nagged at her. She had to find Dogger to learn what happened. Better yet, she might find Marty and get the story from him.

She tried to assure herself that she was being overly dramatic. Marty was, after all, a homeless man, and probably an alcoholic and possibly a drug addict. It was easy to calculate the high probability that he was simply passed out somewhere. Or maybe Dogger and Marty had gotten into an argument, and Marty just wanted to be alone for a while. That look Dogger gave Samantha told her something bad had happened. Dogger probably knew more than he was letting on.

Samantha turned onto 1st Street. It contained a few businesses— an auto shop, hair salon, consignment store—and a few residential homes. Samantha scanned the street, sidewalks, and small alleys, prepared to see the napping body of Marty curled up against any one of these buildings. With the exception of a young man sweeping outside the auto shop, the street was empty.

Samantha reached into her purse and pulled out her cell phone. She knew she might regret this phone call, but she had to make it. She dialed as she continued to drive slowly down 1st Street.

"Hello?" Doug answered.

"Hi, honey," Samantha said. She forced herself to sound cheerful and happy. Maybe the argument from the night before could just be forgotten. "It's me."

"Hey," he said. His voice sounded light, as if he were playing the same deception game of pretending the fight never happened. "When are you coming home?"

"Coming home? I know it's been months, but it still sounds weird to hear you say that," Samantha said with a little laugh. "I guess I still think of it as my apartment."

"Well, get used to it," Doug said. "You've got a lifetime of this to look forward to."

"Hopefully not a lifetime in my tiny little place," Samantha said. If they were always going to have arguments like the one last night, they needed more space to get away from each other.

"Hey," Doug said. "It's *our* tiny little place. Have you left work yet?"

"Yes," Samantha said. She relaxed. Doug definitely wasn't angry anymore. Maybe writing the note had gotten everything out of his system. Of course, that happy-to-love-you tone in his voice would likely disappear as soon as he found out what she was up to. "I just needed to run a couple of errands before I come home."

"Anything I can help with?" Doug said. Samantha thought he was probably asking because he wanted to know what she was doing, not because he really wanted to help.

"Actually, yes. I am calling to ask one little favor," Samantha said. "I need Wendy's number. I don't have it on my cell phone, but it's written on a Post-it note by the calendar on the side of the fridge."

"Wendy from the soup kitchen?" Doug asked. His voice sounded a little bit annoyed.

"Yes," Samantha said. "I need to call her."

"Are you volunteering tonight?" Doug said. He sounded as if he were trying to stay calm. His voice was about two notes higher whenever he was forcing himself to act calm. "I thought you only did that on Sundays and Wednesdays. Are you going to start saving the world with soup on Tuesday nights now, too?"

"That's cute," Samantha said. She turned the car off of 1st Street and entered a residential neighborhood. "Do you see the number?"

"Hold on, I'm looking," Doug said. "Why are you calling her?"

"I wanted to ask her if a certain person had come in to the soup kitchen today," Samantha said.

"Who?" Doug said. His voice was still too high.

"A guy named Marty," Samantha said. She scanned the street of small ranch-style homes as she drove.

"Should I be jealous?" Doug said. "That name is familiar."

"You've probably heard me talk about Marty and Dogger," Samantha said.

"Right," Doug said. "Why are you looking for Marty? Did he leave his Blackberry behind at the truck stop?"

"He's missing," Samantha said.

"According to who?" Doug asked quickly. He sounded a little bit impatient.

"According to Dogger," Samantha said. "And I have a bad feeling."

"Maybe that is your instinct telling you to stay out of this," Doug said. "Why don't you just come home? I can tell the guys at the station to look out for him tomorrow."

"Do you really think the police would care?" Samantha asked. "Are they going to drop everything and look for a homeless man because the file clerk's fiancée has a suspicion that something bad happened?"

"It's better if they look for him than you, sweetie." Doug's voice softened. He was clearly making an effort to avoid another fight. "That's all I'm saying."

"I'm just going to drive around a little more, talk to Wendy at the soup kitchen, and then I'll be home," Samantha said. She could hear Doug sigh loudly through the phone. "I'm not trying to be antagonistic."

"OK," Doug said, followed by another heavy sigh that whistled through the phone.

"If I don't look for Marty, who will?" Samantha said.

"OK, I get it," Doug said. "But for the record, I think you need to stay out of this. Getting involved in their world is a good way to get yourself killed."

⁘

Dogger found himself sweating profusely, even as the sun was drifting low in the sky. It wasn't just the summer heat; it was the cold and sick-feeling sweat he often got the day after drinking a case of beer.

He couldn't believe the day was almost over, and Marty had never shown up. Even though it seemed more unrealistic with each passing moment, Dogger hoped Marty would come running up to him from out of the shadows, excitedly telling some fantastic story about what happened to him over the last eighteen hours.

Dogger's feet dragged along the sidewalk of Main Street. All the businesses had already closed for the day, and the street was vacant. How was he supposed to get twenty dollars? He knew he had to. Marty would most definitely do the same for him if their roles were reversed. He might have to go back to Frontage Road and walk to the restaurants off the I–80 exit ramp. For some reason, stealing tips was the only idea he could come up with. He had no weapon to hold up a store. He couldn't expect to get more than some loose change if he begged for money. Plus, begging for money also quickly led to an unpleasant encounter with Henry Gates.

Dogger's eyes widened when he saw the answer in front of him. He was walking by a row of four parking meters. They were the only parking meters in town. They were old and tired-looking; two of them listed to the side slightly. The parking meters were a source of great controversy for the town when they were put in thirty years ago. They were to be used to raise money for pothole repairs. The four spots they occupied were probably the best parking spots in town, as they sat in the middle of Main Street, right in front of a popular drug store and a few other businesses.

Dogger approached the meters, quickly looking around him before extending his hand to touch the warm metal casing at the top. Each of the four meters read "Expired." Dogger turned the knob on one of the meters, and it ticked as he turned it, moving the "Expired" flag out of view. Once he let go of the knob, the word "Expired" quickly sprang back up into place.

It seemed unlikely that they contained much money. Dogger scanned the street and noted several large potholes that had been in need of repair for years. Plus, there was plenty of parking available throughout Mason. People didn't need to use the meters very often. On a rare Saturday, if they were having an event like a parade or sidewalk sale, all the available spots would be taken, and people would be forced to park at the metered parking. On every other day, these were the least used parking spots in town.

Dogger quickly looked around again. He appeared to be alone. He gripped the top of the parking meter and shook it back and forth quickly. It made a rattling sound, but it was hard to tell if that was money rattling around on the inside or just the mechanics of the parking meter.

Quickly, Dogger searched his pockets. He didn't have any tools with him. He had a hammer back in their stash at the apartment, but he never carried the thing with him in the summer. In his right side pocket, he felt the metal tips of his fork. He pulled it out. The fork might work.

Attempting to look casual in case someone happened to see him, Dogger approached each meter and gave it a small shake. He found the third meter had the loudest and heaviest rattle, so he concluded it must have the most money inside.

Dogger examined the parking meter carefully. He knew he was fortunate that the meter was so old. Most modern meters were extremely difficult to break into. As far as he knew, no one had broken into these meters for at least fifteen years. Fifteen years ago, some kid sawed off the meters at the base and took them home. His mom found them in the kid's room and made the kid call the police himself. When it first happened, everyone in town assumed it was one of the homeless or a traveler that did it. Turned out to be the mayor's nephew.

It was amazing the parking meters hadn't been harvested before. Part of Dogger realized that was because everyone knew that there was almost no payoff inside. There was an extremely good chance that he was about to risk arrest for only sixty cents in dimes and nickels.

Dogger shook the third meter one more time, carefully listening to the rattling sound. Surely there was more than sixty cents inside. It sounded like there were several dollars, and maybe even the full twenty he needed.

The sound of a car approaching shot Dogger upright from his inspection. It was a small blue Buick. It was a car Dogger had seen before in town, but he didn't know the people who owned it. As it approached, Dogger began walking down the sidewalk, keeping an eye on the driver.

The driver was a middle-aged woman, her hands tightly gripping the steering wheel at ten and two. She was staring stoically ahead. It was a look that told Dogger that she had spotted him and was making every effort to not make eye contact. As the car drove slowly past, Dogger slowly kept walking until he could no longer hear the car behind him. He turned and looked down the street, and the blue Buick was nowhere in sight.

Dogger half-ran back to the third parking meter. His hand slid around the contours of the warm metal casing, feeling for a place where he could try to pry the casing apart.

The meters looked to be more than fifteen years old. Maybe after the police recovered the stolen meters they just put them back in place. Dogger couldn't remember if the young boy managed to get them open or not.

Looking around once more to ensure no one was in sight, Dogger shoved the fork into the side of the meter where a seam ran around the periphery. With one forceful push, the casing popped open. Dogger's fork was bent backward onto itself, but he could hopefully fix that later.

The sound of change clinking on the ground gave Dogger a rush, and he couldn't believe how easy it had been.

"Yes," Dogger hissed under his breath, and he could feel a wide smile involuntarily cover his face. But the sound of money falling was short-lived, and Dogger looked down to see a single quarter and dime on the ground. He quickly bent down to pick them up, feeling embarrassed at his preemptive celebration. They must have just been stuck in the coin slots.

Inside the meter was a black box. Dogger reached in to take it, but it wouldn't move. It was firmly bolted into place. There was a keyhole and coin slots, but the rest of the box was solid.

Frustrated, Dogger grabbed the pole of the parking meter and shook it vigorously. That same rattle sounded, but this time, it wasn't dampened by the outer casing. This time, it was louder, and it was clearly coming from the coin box. Dogger quickly realized that he hadn't really gotten any closer to the money. The meter was meant to open the way Dogger had just pried it open. Then the police or city official would have a key to open the small armored box of change.

Dogger could feel defeat already wrapping around him, but he gripped the small black box with his fingers and pulled. He leaned back, using both his body weight and muscles in an attempt to remove the box. Soon, his fingertips burned with the effort.

With a heavy sigh, Dogger closed the casing on the meter box. It appeared exactly as it did before, showing no signs of Dogger's efforts.

Dogger scanned the row of closed businesses. He might be able to break in and take money from a register. Of course, in all likelihood, the registers would have been emptied at the end of the day. Walking along Main Street, staring into the shop windows, Dogger tried to avoid seeing his own reflection. He knew he must look disheveled and ill today because that was exactly how he felt. He didn't need his reflection to tell him that.

Walking past the last business on Main Street, Dogger found himself walking back to Frontage Road. The sun was already setting, and he had to be sure to stop Steve before he left town. Maybe he could reason with the traveler. Between the money that came out of the meter and the extra change he already had in his pocket, maybe he could buy a dollar's worth of information. Even just the slightest hint of Marty's whereabouts was better than nothing.

29

The idea that she had hit a deer seemed more difficult to believe. Angela's townhouse no longer felt safe. The walls of the house on the only genteel street in Mason had once been protective insulation. Now that crazy man was still in the garage. It was like having an intruder in the house. Angela's teeth clenched painfully tight, her molars grinding together. The line between being angry and being afraid was indistinguishable.

Bob Barker was a confirmed jerk. He was unlikely to help Angela if that man in the garage came up and attacked her. He'd probably just pound the walls and tell her to keep it down as she screamed through her death throes.

As the sun set, the one-bedroom home seemed even smaller, and she was slowly surrounded by an overwhelming darkness. She contemplated going back to work, but she couldn't leave. She couldn't walk all the way to work only to get another phone call. This time, the call would probably be from the president of the townhouse association, telling her they were breaking in. She wasn't even sure who the president was, but she imagined he was just like another Bob Barker. He was probably nosy and forceful and would only be too happy to break into her garage if the alarm acted up again.

Angela sat on her couch and stared into the air in front of her for what might have been several hours. Only the sound of her phone ringing jolted her from her semiconscious trance.

"Hello?" Angela answered. She glanced at the caller ID and instantly wished she hadn't picked up.

"Hey," her sister, Christine, said. "How did things go today at work?"

"Fine," Angela said, realizing how much her jaw ached. "I filed the incident report."

"Was Natasha mad?" Christine asked. "Are you in trouble?"

"No," Angela said.

"Interesting," Christine said. She sounded disappointed. She probably didn't believe Angela. "Well, I'm calling to check on those addresses I asked about."

"What addresses?" Angela asked.

"I need the addresses of a few of Mom and Dad's friends," Christine said, sighing loudly. "God, Angela. We talked about this last night."

"I have no idea what you are talking about," Angela said.

"The list I e-mailed to you," Christine said.

"I haven't checked my e-mail," Angela said. She could hear Christine mutter something indistinguishable through the phone. "My computer is broken."

"Why didn't you tell me that last night?" Christine said.

"It only just broke," Angela said. She walked into her bedroom and stared at her computer. The screensaver streaked geometric shapes across the monitor. "I couldn't even turn it on this morning when I was checking for that e-mail from you."

"You know what, Angela," Christine said. "If you aren't going to help me at all with this anniversary party, just say so. But I think Mom and Dad would be pretty disappointed if they found out that I had to do all the work."

"I'll help," Angela said, walking back into the kitchen. "I'm helping."

"How exactly are you helping? You haven't lifted a finger yet," Christine said.

"Listen, I really can't have this conversation right now," Angela said. "I've had a hard day, and I just want to go to bed."

"Oh, yeah," Christine said. "Your life is so hard, isn't it? You don't have a husband to worry about, or kids, or even a real job. But you are stressed out, and you don't have time to help me with this party?"

"That sounds about right," Angela said. Suddenly, a loud moan could be heard through the floor. Angela froze. "I have to go."

Angela quickly hung up the phone on the wall, without even waiting to hear her sister's response. She walked carefully and light-footed into the living room. She slowly lowered her body to the carpet and pressed her ear to the floor. She couldn't hear anything.

The image of that mangled man holding onto the hood of her car swept through her mind, igniting goose bumps up both her arms. She felt an unexpected surge of anger at the man. There was no question as to whether this feeling was fear or anger—it was rage.

"Why didn't you leave last night?" Angela shouted at the floor. "You should have just left; that was the master plan. We agreed. You were going to leave, and I was going to tell everyone I hit a deer in the country."

Angela pressed her ear to the carpet. She heard nothing.

"Do you want me to suffer? Is that it?" Angela said, straightening up. She pounded the floor with her fist. "Did you want to torment me before going on your way? You sick bastard. Just leave." The image flashed in her mind again, and she knew that man was not going to leave. In fact, she knew that man could not leave. He was barely alive.

Angela pressed her ear deep into the carpet, straining to hear anything that might come through the ceiling of the garage and into the floor of the living room. She could hear nothing. Perhaps that moan was just a product of her paranoia and imagination.

If she drove her car to a hospital and left it there, clearly the authorities would be able to find her, and she'd most certainly be in trouble. Perhaps she could detach him from the car and just drop him off at the hospital. Or detach him from the car and drop him off in the Dead Zone and let the other homeless deal with him. Angela didn't want to touch the man, though.

What if she changed the time of the accident? What if she drove the car to a hospital, and then told the doctors that she had just hit this man moments earlier? The man could tell them he had been trapped in a garage for an entire night and day, but he sounded drunk and crazy so they might not believe him. Hopefully, the doctors wouldn't be able to tell how old his wounds were. That might be the only option. The best thing, though, would be for him to just leave.

"Just go away," Angela whispered into the carpet. "And we can put this whole thing behind us. Leave."

Angela put her ear back to the carpet and listened. At first, she heard nothing. Then, suddenly, she could hear the murmurs of a raspy voice, but she couldn't tell what was being said. Angela quickly lifted herself up off the floor, shaking. She turned on the television and increased the volume to the maximum level.

30

Dogger jingled the change in his pocket as he walked. There was no way Steve, who was obviously prone to violence, was going to be happy with a dollar in change when he wanted twenty dollars.

As Dogger walked, he occasionally slowed his pace and even stopped several times. Maybe he should try to rob a gas station. He could pretend to have a gun. The closest he had to a weapon on him was a bent fork, but he knew he looked like a dangerous man to most people. Of course, Dogger also knew the likely outcome of trying to rob the gas station. He'd end up in jail and without any hope of finding Marty … unless Marty happened to be in jail, too.

As the pavement below his feet slowly devolved into broken pieces of concrete with long blades of grass and weeds growing between the cracks, he knew he had nearly reached the Dead Zone.

Steve had told him he needed the money tonight, otherwise he was leaving town. But maybe Dogger could convince him to stay just one more day. Maybe Dogger could get his hammer and try those parking meters again in the middle of the night.

"Dogger!" a voice called. It was a voice Dogger didn't recognize at first, but when he looked up he realized it was too late to turn back. Steve was walking toward him, his thumbs hooked under the shoulder straps on his backpack. He was smiling, showing his yellow but straight row of front teeth.

"Hey, Steve," Dogger said. He quickly glanced around, hoping to at least see Richie sitting out in front of the former Whatta Dish Diner. The Dead Zone was quiet. It was as if everyone was hiding from this red-haired traveler and just waiting for him to leave town.

"You got the money?" Steve asked as he stepped up off the street and onto the sidewalk. He quickly moved in close to Dogger, so close that Dogger could smell the acrid stink of his breath.

"I managed to get some money," Dogger said. He found he wasn't even able to look at Steve. It was as if making eye contact would result in another brutal punch to the face.

"How much?" Steve asked, folding his arms.

"Not much," Dogger said, digging into his pocket. He didn't even want to pull the change out.

"How much?" Steve repeated.

"If you could stay just one more day," Dogger said. He looked up at Steve for the first time. Steve was squinting at Dogger, already looking as if he was in disbelief about Dogger's failure to do what he needed to do to save his best friend. "Just one more day, and I'm sure I could come up with the full twenty dollars."

"I'm a straightforward guy," Steve said, stepping back from Dogger a few feet and looking around. "I said I am leaving tonight, and I'm leaving tonight. I don't have time for this."

"Couldn't you just give me a clue?" Dogger said. He could hear a shake in his voice that he hoped wasn't audible to Steve. "Marty's my best friend. I'm worried about him."

"How much you got?" Steve said, nodding toward the hand Dogger still had stuck in the pocket of his jeans.

"It's hard to come across real money around here," Dogger said. He felt if he admitted that he only had a dollar, Steve would knock him out right on the sidewalk and leave town.

"That's not my problem," Steve said. He walked past Dogger, continuing down Rochester Street and toward Frontage Road and the interstate. Dogger found himself unable to say anything. Suddenly, Steve stopped, and turned toward Dogger, and said, "Apparently, you aren't that worried about Marty. Although you should be."

"Please," Dogger said, stumbling to catch up to Steve. "I only have dollar, but I'll give it to you. Just tell me something, anything."

"A dollar?" Steve scoffed. "You can't even get a cup of coffee for a dollar. Why would I sell valuable information for a dollar?"

"The information does you no good after you leave town," Dogger said. "You can't sell it to anyone but me."

"Do I look like I'm stupid?" Steve asked, furrowing his brow.

"No," Dogger said. "You obviously aren't."

"Exactly," Steve said. He turned and continued walking.

"What's a dollar's worth of information?" Dogger said. Once again, Steve stopped walking. Dogger held his breath as Steve quickly turned and looked at him, appearing as if he were ready to swing at any moment.

"Give me the dollar first," Steve said. He was frowning as he held out his hand.

Dogger quickly dug in his pockets and pulled out all the change he had. He didn't even count it as he put it in Steve's open hand.

"That's all?" Steve said.

"That's everything I have," Dogger said. "You can search me if you want."

Steve sighed loudly as he jostled the coins in his hand before putting them in his pocket. It felt as if several minutes passed before Steve said anything, and Dogger was preparing himself mentally to take another blow to his temple.

"I saw Marty with someone last night who was not you," Steve said.

"Who?" Dogger asked. Steve shrugged but said nothing. "Was Marty OK?"

"Let's just say he was a bit compromised," Steve said. He turned away from Dogger once again and resumed walking.

"Was he with the police?" Dogger asked, walking quickly alongside Steve.

"I already gave you more than a dollar's worth of information," Steve said. "I told you way more than you paid for."

"Was he hurt?" Dogger asked.

"What did I just say?" Steve said. He was clenching his teeth in a way that told Dogger he was pressing his luck.

"I can get twenty dollars," Dogger said. "I swear it."

"How?" Steve asked flatly.

"I have a way," Dogger said. "But I just need one more night. I can have it to you by tomorrow."

Steve walked several more paces before stopping. Dogger noticed the back of his neck was red and blotchy, as if he were angry and about to finally lay Dogger out.

"If I stay another day," Steve said, turning to look at Dogger, "and you tell me tomorrow night that you still don't have the money ..."

"I'll have it," Dogger said. He didn't want Steve to make a threat that he would feel obligated to carry out.

"If you don't," Steve began, walking toward Dogger and pointing a finger in his face, "I'll be very, very angry."

"I'll have twenty dollars for you by tomorrow night," Dogger said.

"Fifty," Steve said. "You'll have fifty before midnight tomorrow, or there will be hell to pay for wasting my time."

"Fifty?" Dogger said. He heart was racing uncontrollably. He tried to sound calm, but he wore his nerves on his sleeve.

"For fifty, I'll take you to where I last saw Marty myself," Steve said, flashing a yellow smile.

"It's a deal," Dogger said quickly. He wasn't sure what he was going to do, but he knew he'd have to wait until nightfall before he tried anything too daring. "You'll have fifty dollars by midnight tomorrow."

31

As night came, Samantha was driving closer to the outermost part of Mason. She hated the term "Dead Zone," but it seemed that everyone in town referred to the area by that name. The closed businesses and empty cardboard-window houses looked foreboding in the early evening light. Samantha had been to the Dead Zone before, but only a few times. Most people in town simply stayed away from it, and many mentally erased it from the map altogether.

Samantha knew her search would end up there. Her careful drive through the residential neighborhoods had been fruitless. Wendy said neither Marty nor Dogger had been to the soup kitchen today. That wasn't terribly unusual since they frequently missed days when the soup kitchen was open.

Samantha fought herself momentarily before deciding against calling Doug again. He would be upset that she had driven this far looking for Marty. As comforting as it would be to hear Doug's voice right now, nothing good would come from the phone call. It would just provoke another argument about Samantha's hero complex.

Samantha scanned the empty lots as she drove by. A large sign reading "John's Grocery" towered through the tall wild grass that grew between cracks in ancient asphalt. John's Grocery was torn down over fifteen years ago, leaving behind little but the rectangular footprint of a building and empty space. Four people, all facing in and huddled close together, stood in the middle of the crumbled cement lot. Samantha imagined they were sharing a pipe or a bottle. She quickly evaluated the stature and clothing of the four men and didn't think any looked like Marty. She kept driving.

Ahead, she could see Berler Bridge. It was the favored summertime hangout for Dead Zone residents. If Marty wasn't there, Samantha decided, she'd go back home and make a plan for tomorrow.

As she approached the overpass, the forms of almost a dozen people became visible through the dim evening light. Their bodies were stretched out at the top of the overpass, on the concrete hill, or standing at the base of the overpass. Her tires crunched loudly over the broken pavement. Some people turned and looked at her suspiciously, but most ignored her. Squinting at one of the sleeping figures, Samantha realized it was Dogger. He was curled into a fetal position at the top of the overpass.

Samantha rolled down her passenger side window and yelled, "Dogger!"

Nearly everyone looked at Samantha, and a few chuckled, but Dogger didn't move. Samantha hesitated, and then before she could think about it any further, she got out of the car and started walking toward the curled-up body. As she walked quickly and rhythmically, in her mind she heard *thisiscrazythisiscrazy* with every footstep.

She brushed past the men, many of whom smiled and nodded at her in recognition. Most, mercifully, ignored her. As she walked up the concrete incline under the bridge, she had to duck lower and lower as she approached Dogger. *Thisiscrazythisiscrazy.*

"Hey, Dogger," Samantha said, reaching out and gently pushing him. Dogger snorted and opened his eyes.

"Samantha?" he said. He grimaced; he looked both embarrassed and filled with disbelief. "What are you doing here?"

"I want to help you find Marty," Samantha said.

"Nobody here has seen him," Dogger said. "At least, no one who is willing to talk."

"Could you at least get up and help me look for him?" Samantha asked.

Dogger grunted and rolled out of the concrete and metal cubbyhole. Samantha caught a glimpse of what appeared to be a hammer tucked into his pocket. As Dogger sat up, he pulled his T-shirt down and covered the metal tool. Samantha began walking to the bottom of the overpass. *Thisiscrazythisiscrazy.* She couldn't imagine why Dogger would have a hammer. Maybe he always slept with one for protection. She didn't want to know and struggled to push the image of the hammer out of her mind.

"Who's your girlfriend, Dogger?" a young-looking man chided Dogger. Samantha turned to see Dogger turn, red-faced. He was blushing.

"Just ignore him," Dogger said to Samantha, as if she had been insulted. "That kid's always saying stupid stuff."

Samantha got into her car, and Dogger followed. As soon as he sat down, Samantha could once again smell the odor of alcohol. It was hard to tell if he had recently been drinking, or if the smell was still lingering from the night before.

"Your shiner's looking purple," Samantha said as she started the car.

"Oh." Dogger shot his hand up and gingerly touched his temple. "It'll fade with time. It doesn't hurt."

"How about some coffee?" Samantha asked.

"There isn't any place around here," Dogger said.

"Do you mind if I drive us back toward I–80?" Samantha asked as she turned the car around and began driving back down Rochester Street toward Frontage Road. Looking in the rearview mirror, it seemed as if every single person had lined up to watch them leave. She hoped this spectacle wasn't going to cause problems for Dogger later.

"That's a long walk back here," Dogger said as he turned around in his seat and looked out the back window. Since when was Dogger worried about having to walk across town?

"Don't worry," Samantha said. "I'll drive you back."

"All right," Dogger said. He turned back around in his seat and sighed heavily. "Just don't take me to the County Inn."

"I won't even ask why," Samantha said.

"That's probably best," Dogger said flatly.

✱ ✱ ✱

The Silver Spoon Diner was full, as it typically was. It was one of the first businesses off the exit ramp in Mason, and open twenty-four hours a day. Samantha's coffee was bitter, but it still tasted good.

"Does Doug know we are going out on a date?" Dogger said.

"Very funny," Samantha said. "Actually, I don't think Doug approves of my actions tonight."

"Really?" Dogger said, sounding enlivened to receive such personal gossip. He stared at his coffee cup and swirled the creamer slowly with his spoon. "Why not?"

"I guess he thinks I should mind my own business," Samantha said. "But I just can't. I am really worried. When did you last see Marty?"

"Last night," Dogger said, he voice once again sounding grim.

"Well, what happened?" Samantha said.

"I don't remember much," Dogger said. "If I did, I'd probably know where Marty is right now."

"Do you remember where you were when you last saw him?" Samantha asked.

"Not exactly," Dogger said, his eyes darting back and forth nervously. "But the more I have thought about it today, the more I am pretty sure that we were at the park." Dogger paused, lowered his voice to a whisper, and added, "We were drinking at the park."

"Which park?" Samantha said. She figured it could only be Hillside Park but had to be sure that "park" wasn't slang she didn't understand.

"At Hillside Park," Dogger said. "But I don't remember much, like I said."

"Did you guys have an argument?" Samantha asked.

"No," Dogger said. "Not that I remember, anyway."

"How'd you get the black eye?" Samantha asked. A waitress stopped in front of them and refilled both of their cups. Both Samantha and Dogger were silent as the coffee trickled loudly into their cups.

"Thanks," Dogger muttered as the waitress walked away.

"How'd you get the black eye?" Samantha asked again. She looked at Dogger's face, trying to gauge if he was hiding something. He just looked tired.

"Some jerk traveler," Dogger said. "He said … well, he's just a jerk."

"OK," Samantha said. She sat back in her chair. She was beginning to feel like the conversation was fruitless.

"I hate to ask you this, Samantha," Dogger said. He glanced quickly at Samantha before returning his gaze to his cup of coffee. "But is there any way I could borrow some money?"

Samantha thought for a moment. She had always made it her policy to not give out cash or even lend money to friends. It has been years since Dogger had asked to borrow money, but she suspected that when she caved in last time and gave him ten dollars, he just bought booze with it.

"What do you need it for?" Samantha said. She didn't want to sound judgmental, but she could hear a hint of it in her voice.

"I'm sorry to bother you with it," Dogger said, still staring at his coffee cup.

"To be honest, Dogger," Samantha said. "I think I only have enough money on me to cover our coffees. If you really needed money, I'd have to go home first to get it." The truth was that Samantha would have to borrow money from Doug to give to Dogger. She didn't even want to imagine how that conversation would go down.

"Never mind," Dogger said. "I have a feeling the money wouldn't do me any good, anyway."

"OK," Samantha said. Maybe Dogger did just want to buy himself more booze, after all. "Do you remember what happened in the park?"

"I remember we were running," Dogger said quickly. "The police showed up, so we had to run."

"So you lost track of him when you were both running from the police?" Samantha asked.

"Yes," Dogger said. "It's so hazy, but I remember Marty took off sprinting. You wouldn't believe how fast that guy can run. I was far behind him, so far behind him that I lost him."

"Maybe the police caught him," Samantha said. She set her empty coffee mug at the edge of the table, hoping the waitress would see it and refill it again.

"Or maybe he's still running," Dogger said.

"Did you hear anything?" Samantha asked. "Did you hear him yelling? Did you hear sirens? Anything?"

"Not really," Dogger said. He was speaking slowly and thoughtfully. "I was wasted. That night was confusing at the time, and it is even more confusing to recall. All I know is that when I finally stopped running, I realized Marty was nowhere around me. I called his name a few times, but he didn't respond. So I just kept running all the way back to the Dead Zone. That's when you saw me running on Frontage Road. I was going to meet Marty under Berler Bridge."

"You guys weren't arguing when the police showed up, were you?" Samantha asked.

"No," Dogger said. "I'm telling you, we weren't arguing. We were just having a good time."

"What makes you think something bad happened?" Samantha said.

"I just know it," Dogger said. "Marty and me have been best friends for over twenty years. We've never spent more than a couple hours apart. The few times we have been separated, for whatever reason, we always meet again under the Berler overpass at first opportunity. It was like a procedure that we always followed."

"How do you know he wasn't picked up by the police?" Samantha asked.

"Because the police were well behind us," Dogger said. "I was even able to stay ahead of them. To catch Marty, they'd have to catch him on foot."

"They might have picked him up, but you either forgot or didn't see it happen," Samantha said.

"No," Dogger said, shaking his head. "One of them was Henry Gates. He would have been gloating about picking up Marty when I saw him late last night. Besides, there was just no way they could have caught him. Marty was way too fast and way too far ahead of them. They would have caught me before they caught him."

"If Marty is missing, we need to contact the police," Samantha said.

"What's the point of that?" Dogger asked.

"I can go with you to the police station and help you file the report," Samantha said. "It won't take long."

"You don't understand," Dogger said, folding his arms over his chest. "They never help people like us. As far as they are concerned, guys like Marty are already dead."

"What do you mean?" Samantha said. "If he's missing, he's missing. The police should know."

"A man without property," Dogger said, counting on his fingers as he spoke, "a man without a job, without a car, no driver's license, he doesn't pay taxes, he doesn't vote, he doesn't give anything to this community. He's just taking up space, like a corpse. He's already dead. The police don't care about him."

32

"Did you say 'olive shoe'?" Sonny asked. He was still watching Marty, leaning against the wall of the garage casually.

"Yes," Marty said.

"What does that mean?" Sonny said.

"It was the code words Sonya and I used to use to say 'I love you'," Marty said. "See, the first time I told her that I loved her, she thought I said 'olive shoe' instead of 'I love you'."

"Cute," Sonny said.

"Yes," Marty said with a sigh. "It was very sweet, actually."

"So did she always say 'olive shoe' to you," Sonny asked, "or did she also say 'I love you'?"

Marty thought for a moment. He had never reflected on this before.

"I think she usually said 'olive shoe'," Marty said. "It was our little joke, and she seemed to always find it funny."

"It's certainly easier to say than 'I love you'," Sonny said.

"I guess so," Marty said.

"Maybe she never meant anything more than 'olive shoe' when she said it," Sonny said. "Maybe she never loved you. Maybe she just liked your company, liked the things you did together, and liked the idea of getting married."

It suddenly felt as if Sonny were being antagonistic, like he really wanted Marty to get upset. But Marty was years past being hurt over their failed marriage. The pain was just a dull ache, and the sharp sting of even the worst memories had faded.

"Maybe," Marty said. "But I think you are being too optimistic. I don't think she ever liked me."

"Well, she definitely isn't going to help you now," Sonny said, his voice calm and even. He knelt next to Marty. It felt warm and soothing when Sonny put a hand on Marty's forehead. Marty closed his eyes. "You've got to help yourself."

"I know," Marty whispered. He opened his eyes to find Sonny gone. He could still feel the warm handprint pressing gently on his forehead, but that, too, soon dissipated.

"Sonny?" Marty said. Only silence. Marty swallowed hard and took a deep, painful breath and said, "Sonny? Don't leave, I want to talk more."

The garage was intensely, and cruelly, silent. The silence pushed on Marty's ears, ensuring he was aware of how alone he was in the garage. Marty knew Sonny's last words to him were nothing but pure truth. He had to help himself.

Marty looked down, forcing his eyes to focus on the image he had been intentionally avoiding. The garage was dark, but enough dim light crept under the door to allow Marty to see everything with a grainy clarity. His chest was embedded into the car. His shirt was ripped and stained.

Marty squinted and craned his neck down for a closer look. In a few places, he could see through holes and rips in his shirt to his chest. The car and his chest were connected. In several places it appeared that his wounds had started clotting and healing around the metal of the car.

He was some horrible Frankenstein creation—part man, part metal. It could be the beginning of a superhero. Just like some superheroes are created in a nuclear explosion or by falling into toxic chemicals, Marty would become a superhero by colliding with a car. Marty smiled, and then laughed.

His mind began to swirl around the fantasy of becoming the next DC Comic Superhero. His humble beginnings, the dramatic accident, the bizarre transformation including instant muscles and spandex, and then the explosion of Technicolor two-dimensional heroics … Marty struggled to keep his thoughts lucid. He was just cognizant enough to know he was slipping. Death could come at any time.

Marty knew that if someone ever discovered his body in there, they would find him slumped pitifully over the car. It would appear that his final act was to simply allow death to overcome him without a fight. He might as well be holding a white flag. This would be final confirmation that everything Sonya had said was right, and Marty was just a passive shell of a man who let life happen to him rather than taking responsibility for anything.

"I'm a better man than you think I am, Sonny," Marty whispered. "A better bag of bones."

He returned his gaze to his wounds. He knew he had lost a lot of blood, and if he managed to pull himself free of the grill, he would lose more blood as he reopened the crusted gashes. It could very well be fatal. But at least he could try to get free. He would just need to make it to the door and to the outside world. Then someone, someone more compassionate than Sonya, would see him and call an ambulance.

Marty's arms were stiff as he retracted them, slowing bringing them out from under the hood and back toward his body. The sound of wheezing filled the garage as Marty placed both hands on the grill in front of him and pushed. His legs, painless and helpless, remained hidden underneath the car. Marty knew that if he was able to free himself, he'd have to walk out on his hands.

Marty pushed. A disturbing crunching sound joined his wheezing. It was his flesh breaking away from the car. The pain was almost unbearable, and it went against every instinct to continue, but Marty pushed harder.

Marty's back, which was previously lightly grazing the wall, suddenly hit the wall solidly as his upper body become upright. His body narrowly and slowly slid down the wall until he was on the floor and staring at the undercarriage of the car. The pain ripped through his chest and into his stomach, but Marty smiled. He was free.

Marty could see the dark outline of his legs in front of him. They were twisted unnaturally and looked torn apart. Marty knew it was a blessing that he couldn't feel anything below his waist. It was all part of the superhero transformation. He'd be in his heroic spandex soon.

He threw both his arms to his left side, and his hands landed in a still-damp puddle of vomit. The smell overwhelmed him momentarily, but he closed his eyes and paused until the queasy feeling subsided. He could feel warm blood trickling down his stomach as he began inching himself sideways until he was no longer in front of the car. He moved his legs to the side and allowed both of his arms to fall forward. Then, straining under the weight of his body, he began crawling forward toward the door.

His body was sliding on concrete that was becoming increasingly slick with blood. Marty realized he was dying. He could literally feel the life drain out of him, and the dark garage became pitch black. At least when someone found his body and when they told his son what had happened there, Sonny would know that he tried. He tried to live. He didn't let life and death just happen to him; he struggled against both.

Marty could feel his body slip. He landed facedown on the concrete.

33

Dogger ran. He decided it was better to go back to the Dead Zone on his own rather than have Samantha drive him. Samantha was well meaning, but Dogger knew she wouldn't be able to find Marty. Especially if she really believed that filing a police report would result in any sort of action. The sooner Dogger got some money, though, the sooner he could find Marty and make Steve leave town. Steve had become more than a nuisance already in his short stay in Mason. Most everyone just avoided him altogether.

He ran toward Main Street, only slowing down when he felt he had to catch his breath. It had become dark enough to try to get some money, and Dogger tried to focus his mind on what needed to get done. His body still ached from the strain of retrieving the hammer from the stash earlier today. Everything was so much easier when Marty was there. Soon, though, he'd have the money, and Marty would be back. Dogger had to believe that.

As soon as he rounded the corner, his eyes fell on the row of four parking meters. The third meter was listing lazily to the side, as if it couldn't stand straight under the weight of the money inside. It seemed impossible that it would hold fifty dollars, but Dogger had no choice but to hope that it did. He looked up and down the street. The entire street looked vacant. The only sounds were the distant rushing flow of traffic from I–80 and the soft chirp of crickets.

Dogger ran toward the third meter. Using the claw end of the hammer, he quickly popped the face of the meter open. That was the easy part, he knew. The armored box inside would pose the greater challenge. Dogger ran his fingers around the black box inside the parking meter. It felt cool, heavy, and impenetrable. There was a very thin seam where the box, when unlocked, would open and allow its contents to be emptied into the waiting bag of a city official.

Dogger angled the hammer, trying to set the point of the claw on the seam. It wouldn't fit. He tried to push and pull the hammer anyway, just in case it grabbed some leverage and could pop open the box. But it was useless. He would have to try another approach.

Taking his bent fork out of his pocket, Dogger bent the tines so that only one stuck out straight. He pushed the tine into the lock of the armored box as far as it would go. When he let go, he was pleased to find that the fork remained in place, sticking out of the lock. After a quick glance over his shoulder to ensure he was still alone, Dogger swung the hammer at the fork. The fork bent up, partially folding around the form of the armored box. Dogger reached and tried to open the box, but it was still locked. Gripping the fork by its bent handle, he tried to twist the tine inside the lock. The fork came out of the lock into his hands, but the one tine was broken off and remained in the lock.

Dogger dropped both the fork and the hammer and gripped the parking meter with both hands. He shook it back and forth vigorously; the heavy sound of change sloshing from side to side in the box compounded his anger tenfold. How could a teenage kid rip off all of these parking meter years ago, but Dogger couldn't even open one?

Dogger picked up his hammer and began swinging at the box. At first he was aiming at the armored box, but soon his swing was aimed at anything that could get broken. The dial, the knob people turned after inserting money, the metal stem that held the parking meter to the ground. Sounds of metal hitting metal loudly ricocheted off the row of brick buildings. Dogger could feel tears stinging his eyes, blurring his vision and causing him to throw a few missed swings with his hammer.

"Dammit," Dogger grunted as his arms burned with exhaustion. He wiped his eyes and quickly looked around to ensure no one was watching his embarrassing losing battle with the parking meter. Dogger kicked the broken fork off the sidewalk, and it lightly clattered into the street. He put his hammer back in his pocket and sat down on the curb. With his head in his hands, his mind reeled as he tried to imagine ways that he could get fifty dollars.

"I've got a gun," Dogger said. "Give me all your money."

He pulled the hammer out of his pocket and turned it over in his hands. "I'll bash your head in," Dogger said. "Give me all your money."

Dogger sighed and dropped his head down onto his bent knees.

34

Angela was still awake when the sun rose, filling her living room with soft light. She stared at the ceiling from her couch for only a moment before grabbing the TV remote off the floor and turning off the television. She listened carefully. She could hear Bob Barker's TV next door, but that was all.

Angela rolled off the couch and onto the floor, pressing her ear to the carpet. She couldn't hear anything. Perhaps the voice she heard last night had been imagined. Angela pressed her ear more tightly to the floor. The silence was reassuring. He probably left last night. Finally.

Angela got up and walked to her bedroom. She started to look through her clothes to find something to wear to work. Not only was it possible that she didn't hear a voice coming from the garage last night, she also could have imagined seeing that deranged thing in the garage last night. What she saw in there was nothing more than an image—nothing more than an image she might have seen on television. The phone rang, causing Angela to drop a clothing hanger and white blouse to the floor. She ran into the kitchen and looked at the caller ID box. It was her sister again. She picked up the phone anyway.

"Yes?" Angela said.

"Good morning to you, too," Christine said. "Listen, I'm sorry if I was a little harsh with you last night. I'm just feeling frustrated because no one is helping me with this party for Mom and Dad. Jack doesn't help."

"Jack never helps," Angela said. It was better to have no husband than to have a husband as useless as Jack. "Why does that even surprise you?"

"Parties just aren't his thing," Christine said. "I know your relationship with Mom and Dad has been strained lately. Maybe this could help bring you closer to them?"

"Don't try to make it sound like you have my best interests at heart," Angela said. "Just say you need my help."

"I need your help," Christine said. "Why is this like pulling teeth to get you to help?"

"I've been really busy lately," Angela said. "I'm under a lot of stress."

"Well," Christine said, "I won't repeat what I said last night."

.

"I'll help you as soon as I can," Angela said. "I promise. Please just don't tell Mom and Dad that I didn't want to help you plan this party."

"I wasn't calling to argue again," Christine said. "But if you are serious about helping, maybe we can get together tonight?"

"I don't know," Angela said. "At my place?"

"Well, I think it would have to be," Christine said. "I want to get some planning done; I don't want to have to listen to you and Jack fighting all evening."

"I have to work," Angela said quickly.

"Really? Did they change your regular schedule?" Christine asked.

"Mandatory overtime," Angela said.

"OK." Christine sounded uncertain. "But I need to come over soon."

"Just please call first," Angela said before saying good-bye to her sister. It was eight o'clock, so she had to hurry to get to the store by ten.

✗ ✗ ✗

"You look terrible" was the first thing Angela heard when she walked through the front door at Fashionable Finds.

"Thanks, Kelly," Angela said.

"And you're late," Kelly said. "I had to open the store all by myself. I'm not sure if that's legal."

"Don't worry about it," Angela said as she walked to the back room and dropped her purse on the table. She reached into the basket of Fashionable Finds nametags. She thought momentarily that destroying her nametag might be a dramatic way for Natasha to say "You're fired." She was a little relieved when she found the one labeled *Angela.*

"Don't worry about it?" Kelly said. She was practically shouting from the registers at Angela. "I think you are the one who needs to worry about it."

"Lower your voice," Angela said, walking out of the back room and toward the registers. "What are you talking about?"

"Natasha called me at home last night," Kelly said. "She wanted me to come in at five o'clock yesterday because you couldn't cover your shift."

"Thanks for coming in," Angela said. Natasha must have decided she didn't want to close alone, but she had never called Angela at home and asked her to come in. She wondered if Kelly and Natasha were chatty on the phone, or if it was brief and businesslike.

"Did that put you into overtime hours?" Angela said.

"Yeah," Kelly said. "Cha-ching! I can use the extra bucks, for sure."

"I thought we didn't have any money for overtime," Angela said.

"Natasha didn't say anything about not having money," Kelly said. "She told me I'd get paid overtime."

"Interesting," Angela said. She could feel herself frowning but tried to keep her voice light.

"So, anyway, you were in hot water for missing work last night," Kelly said dramatically. "And Natasha was also pissed because you didn't follow procedures for filing an incident report."

"Well, it got filed," Angela said. Natasha evidently was chatty with Kelly—chatty enough to complain about Angela. "Did she tell you what the incident was?"

"No," Kelly said. "We were busy with a lot of customers. I assume it was because the register was short the other night."

"You were in the report, you know."

"What? Why?"

"Register One was short a hundred dollars," Angela said. Kelly was supposed to be her ally at Fashionable Finds, but she seemed to turn on Angela so quickly. "And only three people were on Register One: Natasha, me, and you."

"Wow," Kelly said. "Fine, I'm not worried about it."

"By the way," Angela said. "Did you bring back that barrette?"

"I forgot it today," Kelly said. "But I will soon. You should have come to the club Monday night instead of screwing up the closing. It was awesome. Jason was there."

"Did Natasha tell you we are about to start the annual inventory?" Angela asked.

Kelly frowned. "I think she mentioned it."

"How are we going to account for this?" Angela said. She pulled open the drawer under the register, revealing dozens of empty barrette, earring, necklace, and ring holders.

"Shoplifters," Kelly said. She shrugged and smiled. "Every store has shoplifters."

"Really?" Angela said. "Did you know an incident report is supposed to be filed every time there is a shoplifting incident?"

"No," Kelly said. "That's not true. It's only if the value is over a certain threshold. Like twenty dollars or something."

"Wrong," Angela said. "Look it up in the manual. Every time there is a shoplifting incident, associates must create an incident report—regardless of the value of stolen merchandise."

"But it's not stolen," Kelly said. She looked like she might start crying, which gave Angela unexpected satisfaction. "It's just borrowed."

"Then bring it back," Angela said. "Otherwise, we'll both lose our jobs. By the way, did you also happen to borrow one hundred dollars out of Register One?"

"Why are you being such a bitch?" Kelly asked.

"Well, I'm sorry," Angela said, although she wasn't at all sorry. She wanted to see how much she could say before Kelly called her on it. It was a method that Angela often employed. If she concentrated her bad attitude in a small time frame, it could be dismissed as a bad day and not greatly impact her reputation as a good friend and employee.

"You look terrible," Kelly said. "Is everything all right?"

"It's just been a bad couple of days," Angela said as she leaned back against the wall and stared at the racks of clothing. "I'm tired. Plus, I kind of feel like crap."

"Do you have the flu or something?" Kelly said. She closed the drawer under the register and stood in front of it as if she were guarding her kleptomania.

"Maybe," Angela said.

Kelly joined Angela and leaned against the wall. The two women stared at the empty store, wordless for several minutes.

"Where's your car?" Kelly said. Her eyes were squinting toward the parking lot. "You didn't walk here, did you?"

"Yes, I walked here," Angela said. "I took a drive in the country to clear my head Monday night, and I hit a deer."

35

The men looked angry, dangerous, sad, and lost. It gave Samantha a sick feeling to look at some of these pictures. She recognized a few mug shots as regulars at the truck stop. She really didn't want to know the criminal records of her customers. Her eyes fell on a picture of Mark Richards, the handsome local truck driver who she saw every Tuesday morning buying coffee and gas. He was arrested last year for domestic violence. Samantha supposed that explained his recent divorce.

"Do you see Marty in there?" Doug said.

"No, but I've found a lot of guys I didn't want to see in here. Work is trying enough when I imagine my customers are stellar citizens and loving spouses," Samantha said. "I haven't seen Marty yet. Is this the only book you guys have?"

"We have older books," Doug said. "If he's been picked up in the last three years, though, he'll be in this book."

"I'm sure he's been picked up in the last three years," Samantha said with a sigh.

"And you're sure you don't know his last name?" Doug said. "I couldn't find anything under 'Marty' on our database."

"I guess I've never asked his last name, or even his first," Samantha said. She felt embarrassed that she had dehumanized Marty by never bothering to learn his full name. "Everyone just calls him Marty."

"Why isn't Dogger helping you?" Doug said. "Didn't you say he and Marty are best friends?"

"He couldn't bring himself to come to the police station," Samantha said. "It's my day off. I don't mind."

"You have a big heart," Doug said. "I'm a lucky man."

"Thanks," Samantha said, although she knew Doug disapproved of her involvement. Sometimes the more he disapproved of something, the more indirect he was. Saying Samantha had a big heart was just Doug's justification for this otherwise unjustifiable behavior. It was, at least, a more pleasant approach than yelling. And at least he wasn't talking in that falsetto voice of feigned calmness.

"There he is," Samantha said as her eyes landed on Marty. She pointed to a photograph on one of the pages of the photo book. The man in the picture was dressed in a plaid flannel shirt and green army jacket. His beard and hair were greasy and unkempt. His eyes were dark and empty; his lips curled into a sneer that looked more confused than aggressive. He looked a bit different now, but that picture was definitely Marty. "I recognize that shirt."

"Let's see." Doug took the book and turned it around. "This was taken two years ago. Martin Freeman."

"Martin Freeman," Samantha repeated. "Now what?"

"When was he last seen?" Doug asked. He turned to his computer that sat on his desk and began to type.

"Dogger said he was with him on Monday night," Samantha said.

"Monday night?" Doug said. "What time?"

"Pretty late," Samantha said. "Dogger thought it was after midnight. Maybe even one o'clock in the morning."

"Oh, really?" Doug said. He stopped typing. "Unless foul play is suspected, the police really don't start investigating until a person is missing for at least forty-eight hours."

"That's crazy," Samantha said. "Marty is missing. We know he is missing. Why wouldn't the police look for him?"

"That's just the standard," Doug said. "I'll get this report started, but I can't file it until late tonight."

"Come on," Samantha said. "Dogger thought something may have happened to Marty."

"He's probably just passed out somewhere," Doug said. "It happens all the time. Especially with these homeless guys. They are hard to keep track of."

"Doug," Samantha said. "I am asking you, begging you, as your future wife. Please get someone to look for Marty."

"What is the evidence of foul play?" Doug said.

"It isn't like Marty to be gone this long," Samantha said.

"Being out of character is not evidence of foul play," Doug said. "That's what husbands with runaway wives say, and it never works. The police never look until forty-eight hours have passed. The woman usually shows up within forty-eight hours, either with an apology or with another man."

"Marty and Dogger have been best friends for over twenty years," Samantha said. "They've never been apart for more than a few hours. Something is really wrong."

"I cannot submit this report yet, honey. I'm sorry," Doug said.

"Dogger was right," Samantha said. She was almost sorry for saying it before the words came out, but she couldn't stop them. "You guys don't care about the people living in the Dead Zone. They are just as much a part of Mason as you or I. They are your citizens to protect."

"Of course we care," Doug said. "But we have to follow protocol."

Samantha could feel her eyes stinging, threatening tears. Doug's eyes softened as he looked at her face.

"OK, listen," Doug said gently. "I will talk to Jake. He's a good guy. He's doing traffic patrol today, and I'll ask him to be on the lookout for Marty. Sort of off the record. That is all we can do right now."

36

Angela paused as she Windexed the dressing-room mirrors. Her reflection looked distorted and almost monstrous as the glass cleaner slowly dripped down the mirror in long tears. A terrible feeling of uneasiness overwhelmed her, the image of that thing in the garage flashing in her mind. She forced herself to ignore it. It was just an image, a scary image, but just an image. No more powerful or real than an image on television. She wiped the mirror clean, avoiding eye contact with herself in the mirror.

"Angela," Kelly whispered, surprising Angela from behind. "Customer."

Angela turned and stepped out of the dressing room just in time to see an obese woman pull open the store's glass front doors. She was dressed in black. A massive black purse was slung over her shoulder; it was overstuffed and bulky-looking and seemed to be the perfect reflection of its owner. The woman's lips were turned down into an exaggerated frown that was probably more just how her face naturally fell than an intentional scowl.

"Welcome to Fashionable Finds," Angela chirped as brightly as she could. The woman in black smiled and looked around.

"Thanks," the woman said to no one in particular. She obviously couldn't tell where the voice that greeted her came from. Kelly began giggling. Angela pushed Kelly to the side and walked past her toward the customer so she could see. The woman made eye contact with Angela and smiled, and then began looking through the clothing racks.

"Don't be so mean," Angela whispered to Kelly. "Go do something productive."

"There's nothing to do," Kelly whispered back. "The store is clean."

Angela glanced at the customer, who looked back down at the clothing rack as soon as Angela made eye contact. She probably thought they were whispering about her.

"Go ask the guest if she needs any assistance," Angela said. Kelly rolled her eyes but walked away. She slowly strolled to the front of the store, where the customer was continuing to look carefully though the clothing racks.

"Welcome to Fashionable Finds," Kelly said as she neared the woman. "My name is Kelly. Can I help you find anything?"

"No, thank you," the woman said. She only quickly glanced at Kelly, and her hands never stopped moving through the racks of clothing. "I'm just looking right now."

"OK," Kelly turned and began to walk back toward Angela. She stopped and turned back to the customer. "Plus sizes are in the back of the store."

"Thank you," the woman said. Her neck immediately turned red, followed by her entire face. "I'm just looking."

Kelly gave Angela an exaggerated shrug as she walked back toward the dressing rooms. Angela shook her head. Before Kelly even reached the dressing-room doors, the first customer of the day had already left the store.

"You are a terrible salesgirl," Angela said.

"You told me go help her," Kelly said. "I was trying to help her."

"You didn't have to tell her plus sizes are in the back," Angela said.

"But they *are* in the back," Kelly said. She almost sounded genuinely confused.

"That's insulting to her," Angela said. "She didn't ask you where the plus sizes were located."

"She said she was just looking," Kelly said. "I thought I was being helpful by telling her where her size could be found."

"I'm not having this conversation," Angela said. She moved to the next dressing-room stall and resumed cleaning the mirrors.

Kelly was finally silent. When Angela looked over her shoulder, she saw Kelly had walked to the area near the registers and was trying on hair accessories.

"That isn't sanitary!" Angela shouted across the empty store. "Plus, we can't afford any more empty accessory cards." Kelly rolled her eyes and returned the hair clips to the plastic holder, which she hung back on the spinner. She stepped up onto the register platform and leaned against the back wall.

Angela finished cleaning the fitting-room mirrors. Stepping back to admire her work, she realized they looked about the same as they did before. At least the physical work kept her mind away from the image of the thing in the garage. She put the Windex away in the back room and joined Kelly at the registers.

"There is no way we are making quota today," Angela said, staring at the empty sidewalk in front of the store.

"Natasha will be pissed," Kelly said. She didn't sound like she really cared. "Did I tell you I saw Jason at the club the other night?"

"I think you mentioned it," Angela said. "Was he there with anyone?"

"No," Kelly said. Angela was surprised to feel herself breathe a sigh of relief. "He was alone, like usual. Alone. Cute. And looking for you, I think."

"Why do you say that?" Angela asked.

"Because he asked me where you were."

"Well, yes, then I guess he was looking for me."

"Why don't you call him?"

"It's too early," Angela said. "He's probably still sleeping."

"It's almost ten-thirty," Kelly said. "If he's not awake by now, he should be. Call him. Tell him you're sorry you missed him the other night."

"My cell battery is low, and I hate to use the store phone," Angela said.

"You can say you were on your lunch break," Kelly said. "Even Natasha uses the store phone for personal calls during her lunch break."

"It would be nice to just say hi to him," Angela said. "I don't know, though."

"Wait a minute," Kelly said slowly. She was looking at Angela with a tilted head. "Have you ever called him before?"

"No," Angela said. She could feel her cheeks growing hot. "I don't know what to say to people on the phone. I'm just not a phone person."

"You have to call him," Kelly said. "He probably thinks you hate him because you've never even called him."

"He has given me his number about five times now," Angela said.

"See?" Kelly said. "He wants you to call him. Just acknowledge the poor guy. You don't have to talk for very long. Just say hi and tell him you hope to see him at the club this weekend. How hard is that?"

"Painfully hard," Angela said.

Kelly stared at Angela for a few minutes, and then ran to the back room. When she came back out, she had an odd smile on her face as she trotted back to the registers.

"What are you doing?" Angela said. She noticed Kelly was clutching a small piece of paper. "Did you get that out of my purse?"

"You stay here," Kelly said. She picked up the phone, looked at the scrap of paper, and began dialing. She handed Angela the phone. Angela shook her head.

"It's just Jason," Kelly said. "Come on. Do you want to be a boyfriendless loser forever?"

"Thanks," Angela said. She took the receiver and pressed it to her ear. "It's ringing." Kelly nodded excitedly.

The phone line clicked, and Angela could feel her eyes grow wide. Then, much to her surprise, a woman's voice answered. "Hello?" Angela slammed the receiver back down in the cradle.

"What was that all about?" Kelly said.

"A woman answered," Angela said.

"That jerk," Kelly said. "I bet he's married."

"But he wasn't wearing a ring," Angela said.

"If a married man is going to a nightclub like Hysteria without his wife," Kelly said, "he isn't going to wear his wedding ring."

"So that was what was so weird about him," Angela said. "I knew there was something weird."

"What's really weird is that the idiot gave you his home phone number," Kelly said. "Now that's weird."

"I shouldn't have called him," Angela said, shaking her head.

"And here I thought he was an axe murderer, or a pedophile," Kelly said, staring into the air thoughtfully. "And it turns out he's married. What an asshole."

"I knew something was really wrong," Angela said. "Why did you make me call him?"

The phone began ringing. Angela looked down at the phone and saw the familiar number in the caller ID box.

"She's calling back," Angela said. "I don't want her to think I'm the other woman."

Kelly gently pushed Angela aside and picked up the phone.

"Thank you for calling Fashionable Finds, where great deals on great clothes are always in fashion. This week we are featuring buy two, get one free capris. This is Kelly. How may I help you?" Kelly finished her greeting, and then squinted as she listened to the other end of the phone. Angela's stomach ached as she waited.

"We were trying to call a customer back who left a credit card here," Kelly said. Angela smiled. "No, it was me. I hung up as soon as I realized I misdialed. I didn't realize you had already picked up when I was hanging up. I am sorry to have troubled you."

Angela studied the expression on Kelly's face. She seemed to be growing impatient. "No, I didn't mean to call this phone. I apologize. It was just a mistake. Good-bye." Kelly hung up and rolled her eyes dramatically.

"She was not happy," Kelly said with a small smile. "She must know her man is a cheating, lying jerk-off."

"Why do you say that?" Angela said.

"She said this was her fiancé's cell phone," Kelly said.

"Wow," Angela said.

"Look," Kelly said. She was pointing over Angela's shoulders. "The police are here."

Angela spun around. A police car was parked directly in front of the store, and two officers were still sitting inside.

"Do you think that crazy bitch called the cops?" Kelly said.

"I don't know," Angela said.

"I mean, it did take her a few seconds to call us back. Maybe she called the police first," Kelly said. Both police officers got out of the car. "And she did have caller ID. Maybe she was calling the cops and saying we were harassing her."

"Could be," Angela said. She watched as the police officers pulled open the door to the store. "But I doubt it."

37

A soft light glowed under the garage door. Marty realized he had passed out and slept through the night and into the next day. Or perhaps he had slept for two days. His head lay heavily on the concrete floor. His lips, mouth, and throat were parched. As he tried to lift his head he could feel pressure in his right temple where his head had hit the concrete when he collapsed.

Disoriented, Marty scanned the garage to get his bearings. He had traveled at least three feet away from the car. As he painfully craned his neck around, he could see a disturbing trail of smeared blood indicating his path. He looked down, arching his back slightly, trying to see the wounds that caused this terrible mess. Marty's shirt was blackened with blood, and a wide pool of dark liquid filled the concrete around his torso.

Marty once again felt that strange pride. Maybe it was a sign that he was deranged from the blood loss, but looking at the mess and his wrecked torso gave him a good feeling. Marty knew guys that would have crumbled and panicked in this situation. But Martin Freeman was keeping it together. Sure, he was a little scared, and he felt pain, but seeing the blood justified his fear.

Marty rested his head back down on the concrete. He needed to think. As he put his head down, he could feel the weakness in his body. The pain was there, but it was dull. It was overrun by partial numbness and a slight tingling sensation. Deep inside his body he felt cold, but heat was radiating, making his skin and fingertips hot. It was unlike any sensation he had ever felt before. Marty could only conclude it was the feeling of his body dying.

Marty forced his eyes back open. He couldn't allow himself to just lie there and die. Dogger must be frantic by now, wondering what happened. Marty wondered if he saw the accident. If he did, it would seem that he would have called for help. Even though Dogger had a terrible fear of the police, surely his best friend wouldn't abandon him.

Marty let his eyes fall shut again. He knew his time was running out.

38

"So do you often pick up strange, dirty old men and drive them around town?" Dogger asked. He looked better than he did the day before, but the sadness in his voice was easy to detect.

"Only the ones I like," Samantha said. "You OK?"

"I had a long night," Dogger said. "I really don't want to talk about it."

"All right," Samantha said.

"Where are we going?" Dogger asked, looking out the window as they drove out of the Dead Zone.

"I have an idea," Samantha said. "I thought maybe we could try to recreate the last time you saw Marty. It may jog your memory."

"And Doug knows about this," Dogger said. He seemed genuinely concerned about the state of Samantha's relationship with her fiancé.

"He knows I am worried about Marty," Samantha said. "After we left the diner last night, I went back home and couldn't sleep. This morning I went to the police station. I think Doug only let me come to work with him and look for pictures of Marty because he felt sorry for me."

"You didn't answer the question," Dogger said. His persistence reminded Samantha that her life was probably a soap opera to Dogger. "Does Doug know you are driving me around town today?"

"I guess I didn't specifically tell him I was doing this," Samantha said. She had a sudden urge to call Doug right now and tell him what she was doing, but the urge was easy to fight off.

"Why not?" Dogger asked.

"He would worry about me," Samantha said. "He doesn't really know you."

"You don't really know me, either," Dogger said.

"I've known you for over ten years," Samantha said. "How many times have I fed you and given you a place to sleep? I feel like I know you pretty well."

"Ten years, really?" Dogger said. He looked at Samantha, and then looked out the window of the car. "I'm not as nice as you might think I am."

"I think you're plenty nice," Samantha said.

"Yeah, but ..." Dogger said. He gave Samantha a quick sideways glance, and then returned his gaze to the window. "If you knew everything about me, I don't think you'd want to help me. You'd kick me out of the car and call the police."

"You are nice enough to want to find your friend," Samantha said. "That's good enough for me."

"All right." Dogger seemed to like this response to his semi-confession. He leaned back in the car seat and sighed loudly.

"Let's find Marty, OK?" Samantha said as brightly as she could manage. Dogger nodded.

The car pulled in front of Hillside Park and parked on the street. Dogger and Samantha got out.

"This is where you last saw Marty, right?" Samantha said.

"We were drinking on the merry-go-round," Dogger said.

Samantha scanned the landscape. She saw a pavilion with two picnic tables and an outdoor grill. She saw a slide with a tree-house top, a swing set, and a large sandbox, but no merry-go-round.

"Are you sure it was this park?" Samantha said. "I don't see a merry-go-round."

"I'm sure." Dogger laughed. "That's part of the beauty of it. You can't see the merry-go-round from the road. It's just on the other side of the swing set. There is a little valley it sits in."

Dogger and Samantha walked toward the swing set. Samantha was relieved that the park was empty. She was most worried about seeing the kids that lived on the first floor of their apartment building. They had a gift for asking embarrassing questions at just the wrong time and in front of just the wrong people.

Samantha scanned the ground, and she looked around the trees as they walked. She still expected to find Marty passed out somewhere. Although it seemed unlikely that he could still be in a drunken state two days later, she had read that alcoholics could go on multi-day benders and end up in bizarre places.

As they trekked up the slight incline toward the swing set, the landscape beyond it slowly came into view, including a rusted and skewed merry-go-round. The merry-go-round was a grim image that combined child's play with decay.

"I guess we left this behind," Dogger said. He was a few steps ahead of Samantha and bent over to pick up an empty beer can. A Black and White brand whiskey bottle lay in the center of the merry-go-round.

"Yeah," Samantha said. "It looks like you guys were definitely here."

"Sorry about the mess," Dogger said. "We don't usually leave trash behind like this."

"So tell me how this happened," Samantha said. "You and Marty were here drinking. And then the police came from which direction?"

"Over there," Dogger said, pointing over the small hill toward the swing set. He seemed to be remembering more than he did the day before. "I didn't see the cop car, but I think it was probably parked about where you parked your car just now."

"So when you saw the cops coming into the park," Samantha asked, "which way did you run?"

"I ran that way," Dogger said. He pointed in the direction exactly opposite the direction he had pointed previously. "I ran down that hill. It really is a blur, though."

"Let's check it out," Samantha said and began walking down the slope of the hill. "As you were running down this hill, where was Marty?"

"He was ahead of me," Dogger said. "Way ahead. Marty can run like a cheetah, especially if he is running from the police."

"Could you see him running?" Samantha asked.

"I saw him take off running," Dogger said. "He was running in this direction, but he quickly disappeared. It was dark, and I was loaded. I'm sorry I can't be more specific, but I know he was ahead of me."

Samantha and Dogger walked to the bottom of the hill, where a sidewalk ran the length of a residential neighborhood. It was Bethel Street. Samantha looked to the right and saw a turn from Bethel Street onto Herbert Street. Looking to the left, there was a turn on the road from Bethel Street onto Jewel Street. Bethel Street continued and curved out of eyesight to the left and curled into a cul-de-sac on the right.

"When you reached the bottom of the hill," Samantha asked, "did you see Marty down here?"

"No," Dogger said. "He wasn't anywhere in sight. I was calling for him and everything. But those cops weren't too far behind, so I had to keep running."

"Which way did you go?" Samantha asked.

Dogger looked down the street to the right, then to the left, and then right again. He grimaced. "To the right. Down toward that cul-de-sac."

"How far did you run?" Samantha said.

"I hid in someone's yard," Dogger said. "They had a dog."

"Did you ever see the police?" Samantha said.

"Yeah," Dogger said. "It was Henry Gates and some other guy, some smaller guy."

"That might have been Jake," Samantha said. "He's sort of new. Doug knows him, and he was going to ask Jake to be on the lookout for Marty today."

"Why would he do that?" Dogger asked, and he looked at Samantha with a furrowed brow. "He wanted to arrest Marty the other night. If he finds Marty, he'll just arrest him. Or rough him up a bit for giving him a hard time."

"No," Samantha said. "Doug knows Jake. I don't think Jake would rough Marty up."

"Right," Dogger said, letting out a long sigh and shaking his head.

"So you were hiding in their yard, and then what happened?" Samantha asked.

"I ran all the way to Frontage Road, which was where you saw me. Then I ran all the way to the Dead Zone," Dogger said. "I waited, but Marty never showed."

39

Angela held her breath as the two police officers walked through the doors at Fashionable Finds. The image of that thing, bloody and deranged in her garage, flashed into her mind. Angela stared at the back of her hand, studying the light blue streaks of veins that showed through her pale skin. She had to replace that terrible thing in her mind with something else, anything else. She concentrated on the light brown freckle below the knuckle of her index finger. The image in her mind dissipated.

"Welcome to Fashionable Finds," Kelly chirped brightly, surprising Angela and causing her to snap her head up. "How may I help you?"

"Don't be an idiot," Angela said under her breath and lightly pushed Kelly in the arm. "Act normal."

"You act normal," Kelly said. Her eyes looked Angela up and down with a furrowed brow. Then she shook her head.

The cops could be there for any number of reasons, not just that thing in the garage. It could be about the incident report she filed with corporate, Natasha might have discovered the "borrowed" inventory drawer and decided to call the police, Jason's fiancée might have traced their phone call and accused them of harassment, or it could be just a friendly visit. The cops weren't necessarily there about that thing in the garage.

"Good morning, ladies," the taller of the two male police officers said. His tone seemed casual, and Angela tried to smile in response to his greeting. "How is everything here this morning?"

"Good," Angela said. Her voice cracked a little when she said this. She cleared her throat. "Just fine. Thank you."

"Are we being arrested?" Kelly said. Her question was punctuated with a high-pitched, squealing laugh. The two officers looked at each other, and the shorter one smiled, and then instantly repressed his smile. Men always loved Kelly.

"No," the tall police officer said. He appeared to force a smile, as if to show he was just as much fun as his partner. "Unless there is something we need to know about."

"Shut up, Kelly," Angela said. She looked at the officers, who now simply looked unamused. "She was just joking."

"They know that," Kelly said, and then smiled at the two men.

"Is there anything we can help you with?" Angela said. As she fidgeted, she could feel how sweaty her palms and fingers had become in the last ten seconds. She hoped the officers wouldn't want to shake her hand at some point.

"Maybe," the shorter of the two officers said. He took off his hat and inspected the inside casually. His dark brown hair was matted and sweaty. "I'm Officer Jake Russell, and this is Kevin Coyne. We are visiting all the local businesses, checking in about a missing person."

"Do either of you ladies know Martin Freeman?" the tall officer, Kevin, asked.

"Is he an actor?" Kelly said and giggled. "Didn't he win an award for *Driving Miss Daisy* or something?"

"No, he's from Mason," Officer Kevin said humorlessly.

"She was kidding, Kevin," the shorter officer, Jake, said while hitting his partner's shoulder with the back of his hand. Then he looked at Kelly and smiled. "That was funny."

"Thanks, I sorta thought so," Kelly said.

"So neither of you know a Martin Freeman?" Officer Jake replaced his hat and looked at Angela.

"I don't think so," Angela said. She refused to allow her mind to imagine that Martin Freeman was the name of that man in her garage. There was no man in her garage. She had to believe it. Angela looked at Kelly, who was shaking her head.

"Sorry, I don't know him," Kelly said.

"We wouldn't know him," Angela said. "We sell ladies' clothing only, so he wouldn't be a customer here." She realized that was a stupid comment as soon as she made it. She knew she was trying too hard.

"Would you mind just glancing at this photo?" Officer Kevin said. He pulled a folded piece of paper out of his back pocket. "Sorry the photocopy has gotten a little beaten up."

Kelly took the picture from the officer and looked at it. "Yikes," she said. "He looks like a bum. Why are you looking for him again?"

"He's missing," Officer Jake said. He removed his hat again and began to fan himself with it. "We are showing this picture to people as we make our rounds today. Just to see if anyone has seen him in the last two days."

"He looks dangerous," Kelly said. "I hope you find him."

Kelly handed the photocopy paper to Angela. Angela held the paper in front of her. She studied the white space between the photograph and the edge of the paper. She squinted to examine the T-shaped creases where the paper had been folded and refolded. She handed the paper back to the tall officer.

"I've never seen this man," Angela said.

40

Marty stared at the garage door, his vision blurring, then returning into focus, and then blurring again. Suddenly, a figure appeared, leaning against the garage door. Marty stared at it. It could be a rake, or a broom, but as his vision refocused once more, it was clearly a man leaning against the garage door, looking down at Marty.

"Sonny?" Marty whispered.

"Your time is running out," the familiar voice with the even cadence said.

"Sonny," Marty said. "Please help."

"You'd better do something, skeleton," Sonny said.

"Sonny," Marty whispered again, loudly and painfully. As he stared at the tall, lean figure, it became grainy in appearance, and then disappeared altogether.

"Wait, please," Marty said. He stared at where Sonny had been standing. He closed his eyes and reopened them several times, each time expecting Sonny to be back. Instead, he saw nothing but the cold blank wall of the garage.

Marty knew, logically, that the figure was merely a hallucination. In the real world, people didn't just materialize and then disappear. But this garage wasn't the real world. It was some other realm where his past life had collided with his present life. Marty knew Sonny was a hallucination, yet he was also very real. Marty found comfort in his company. He didn't want to be alone in this bizarre realm.

Marty forced his mind to focus on the immediate and on his surroundings. He could too easily get lost in the hallucination and get stuck in this strange world forever.

Marty knew he couldn't simply get up and walk out the door. The door to the house seemed much taller and out of reach from the perspective of the concrete floor than it appeared when Marty was still on the hood of the car. He knew from a couple of experiments that he could only raise his upper body off the ground by about six inches. He wouldn't be able to reach up high enough to touch the handle.

The conclusion was obvious. He couldn't get out of this garage on his own. The only way out was to get help. The only way to get help was to make noise.

He remembered the lawn chair, which made a loud clatter when it fell out of his reach before. The chair was several feet behind him, and it would require turning his body around and backtracking. Marty couldn't stand the idea of dragging himself back toward the car. That would mean moving himself further away from freedom and closer to the problem that landed him there in the first place. He just couldn't do it. Besides, he imagined the chair would be extremely awkward, if not impossible, to wield. The only way to go was forward.

Marty's body was facing the garage door. It was about five or six feet away. He knew he wouldn't be able to open it, but he might be able to knock loudly enough on it to be heard. The neighbor had pounded so loudly on the garage door it seemed as if the entire door, and this entire strange world, would collapse. The material must be thin, so even a weak knock could create a loud sound.

"I need to keep moving," Marty whispered. "I'm not giving up, Sonny."

Marty placed both his hands under his body and pushed up. A raspy grunt escaped through his clenched teeth as he lifted himself up. Then he moved one shaking hand in front of the other and dragged his heavy and twisted body forward, millimeter by millimeter.

41

"Marty isn't officially a missing person yet," Samantha said. "We have to wait forty-eight hours for that to happen."

"When will it be forty-eight hours?" Dogger asked. He seemed uncomfortable as they sat on the hill that sloped down the back of the park. He shifted around into several positions before settling on sitting stiffly cross-legged.

"Tonight," Samantha said. "Actually, tomorrow morning at around 1:00 AM."

"Is that based on my story?" Dogger said. He seemed surprised.

"Yes," Samantha said. "And you are lucky that Doug was willing to take an official police statement from me. He had to get permission. You really should have been the one giving the statement."

"I just don't like the police," Dogger said. "That uniform just does something to me."

"If Doug hadn't taken my statement, we'd have nothing," Samantha said. "Now at least the police know he is missing. Jake was going to keep his eye out for him today."

"I still don't think you should have the police looking for him," Dogger muttered under his breath.

Samantha watched a car drive slowly through the residential neighborhood at the bottom of the hill. She looked at Dogger. He was slumped down into a terrible posture. His arms were folded tightly over his chest. He was staring down at his crossed legs, frowning.

"We'll find him, Dogger," Samantha said. "Don't worry. I won't give up until we find him."

"I know you won't give up," Dogger said. He smiled a little. "Marty used to tell me you were the only person in Mason with a genuine heart."

"That's sweet," Samantha said, and she could feel herself blush. "But that's not necessarily true. There are a lot of good people in Mason."

"Not people that are good to us," Dogger said. He returned his gaze to the residential neighborhood in front of them.

"Some people are just more comfortable ignoring people whose lives seem radically different from their own," Samantha said. "They just can't relate; they think there is no common ground. It doesn't mean they are bad people."

"I'm glad they are comfortable," Dogger said.

"It's more complicated than I made it sound," Samantha said. "It isn't just a comfort thing; it's small-town pride. Acknowledging the homeless is acknowledging that Mason is failing, possibly dying."

"Mason has failed every single guy living in the Dead Zone," Dogger said. "By that measure, it is a failed town."

"Exactly," Samantha said.

"Just because most people never visit the Dead Zone doesn't mean it doesn't exist," Dogger said.

"I know," Samantha said. "But if you had a choice, do you think you'd be hanging around the Dead Zone?"

"Maybe," Dogger said. "Marty always says he likes the freedom of living like this."

"So he's homeless by choice?" Samantha said.

"Yeah," Dogger said. "He's a good salesman for living on the streets. He can make you believe it was good luck and not misfortune that brought him to the Dead Zone."

"He does seem pretty happy," Samantha said.

"He seems happy, but I know him well enough not to believe him," Dogger said. "There's no freedom in getting chased by the cops and hated by an entire community."

An awkward silence followed. Samantha had always prided herself on not thinking in terms of "them versus us," but the distinction felt heavy and apparent between her and Dogger right now. Maybe she did feel an ironic superiority because she told herself she *wasn't* better than anyone else.

"I was back there," Dogger said abruptly, jolting Samantha from her thoughts. His neck was craning around to look behind him. "Or maybe I was closer to about right here where we are sitting."

"OK, so you were at the top of this hill," Samantha said. She knew alcoholics sometimes had windows to their inebriated memories open, but they could shut as quickly as they opened. "Do you remember where Marty was at that point?"

"He was ahead of me," Dogger said. He was now pointing ahead, down the hill. "He was really far ahead of me. I remember now that I heard something. I didn't see anything, but I heard something."

"What did you hear?" Samantha said, hoping he wasn't about to say gunshots.

"It was really loud," Dogger said. He was staring down the street thoughtfully. "I remember it surprised me."

"Should we go and take a closer look down there?" Samantha asked. She was hoping that by reenacting his walk down to the residential neighborhoods, he might remember what his mind was blocking out. She couldn't shake the feeling that they would find shells from a discharged shotgun. She stood up.

"OK, let's go," Dogger said. He looked uncertain, but he stood up anyway.

Dogger and Samantha walked to the bottom of the hill in silence. Samantha was carefully, systematically scanning the ground as they walked.

When they reached the bottom of the hill, Bethel Street continued to both the left and the right. To the right, Bethel ended in a cul-de-sac, where Dogger said he hid from the police. There were two nearby neighborhood streets that intersected with Bethel Street: Jewel and Herbert. They were an interesting juxtaposition.

Jewel Street was more typical of the residential neighborhoods in Mason. The middle- and lower-middle-class houses varied in size and quality. Samantha always loved that every house looked different. It wasn't like the cookie-cutter homes on treeless lots that seemed to plague larger and richer towns.

Herbert Street was one of the few newer neighborhoods in town. The rows of townhouses that curved around the bend in the street seemed almost cosmopolitan when they were constructed ten years ago. The street looked tidier than other streets; the townhouses and single-family houses all had neutral-colored siding that defied aging. The homes were inexpensive and small but clean. Herbert Street stood out from the surrounding neighborhoods, and people in Mason either loved it or hated it. There was no in-between.

"Let's look on the ground around the base of this hill for any clues," Samantha said. "Anything that might tell us what happened to Marty, and what that loud sound was that you heard."

Samantha and Dogger started by scanning the sidewalk, then the grass between the sidewalk and the street, and finally the street. It seemed they had been searching for an hour before Samantha finally saw something of consequence. It wasn't a gunshot shell, but it was just as ominous.

"Dogger!" Samantha called. Dogger was up the street, several yards in front of her. "Come here and look at this."

Samantha knelt down and examined the small bits of broken plastic.

"It looks like part of a headlight," Samantha said. She scanned the immediate surrounding street.

"I wonder if I could have heard a car accident," Dogger said slowly. He knelt down next to Samantha and picked up bits of plastic and dropped them back down on the pavement.

"I'm going to call Doug," Samantha said. She reached into her pocket and pulled out her cell phone. "The police should know about this. At the very least, they need to clean this up before it pops someone's tire."

"So someone may have hit Marty?" Dogger said. His eyes looked wide with disbelief.

"I'm not sure," Samantha said. "It's hard to say how long this has been here. But this appears to be an unreported accident. If it were reported, they would have cleaned it up."

"The loud sound might have been a crash," Dogger said, sounding unconvinced and staring at the small pieces of clear plastic scattered on the pavement.

"I don't know. It still doesn't make sense," Samantha said. "If that were the case, where is he? Why didn't you see the aftermath of the car accident when you reached the bottom of the hill?"

"Oh, God," Dogger whispered. "Poor Marty."

⚡ ⚡ ⚡

Angela focused on the rhythmic sound of her shoes hitting the concrete. She was willing herself to focus on anything other than the cops that visited Fashionable Finds with a picture of a man named Martin Freeman.

She stared at her feet so she didn't stare into the air, which she figured made her look crazy. She just needed to put this day behind her.

Like a well-trained dog that always walks the same route, Angela knew where to turn without looking up. When she found she was walking on grass, she knew she'd made it to the park. She was only a minute from being home. Quickly, Angela glanced up to see if there were any people in the park. It was empty, which meant she could shuffle through as slowly as she wanted. The park had always been a comforting place. It was so close to home, but it wasn't home.

As Angela walked down the small slope to the merry-go-round, her eyes caught something sparkling in the afternoon sunlight. It was an empty Black and White brand whiskey bottle sitting in the middle of the merry-go-round. Angela was filled instantly with disgust. Who would drink liquor at a children's park? Especially the cheapest, most vile type of liquor? Why wouldn't they go to a bar or a club if they wanted to drink? Or just stay home? It was undoubtedly teenagers that needed a place to drink secretly.

Walking by the merry-go-round, Angela was suddenly hit with the scent of stale liquor. She couldn't tell if the odor was real or imagined, but it was a smell she associated with only negative things. The smell transformed Angela, and she suddenly found her mind flashing to the image of that man and her car. This was what he smelled like when she hit him.

Angela walked more quickly now, her legs half-walking and half-trotting down the hill past the merry-go-round. She wanted her mind to focus on other things. Her sister, the party, her job, all the ways she might be about to lose her job, the incident report, the impending inventory. Even as she listed out these alternatives in her mind, the image always came back. That man, who was probably Martin Freeman, was in her garage. He was deranged and bloody, and in her garage.

Angela neared the bottom of the hill, and looking up, she saw a forty-something woman with blonde hair and a man wearing a dirty T-shirt and jeans looking closely at the road. Angela froze. They seemed an odd and unlikely pair, and the sight of them was unsettling. It appeared that they were looking for something on the street.

Angela walked in a large arc to go around them, and they seemed too intent on searching the street to notice her. Angela knew, as much as she tried to push the thought out of her mind, that they were searching the spot where the accident happened.

Once Angela reached the sidewalk on the other side of Bethel Street, she walked briskly toward Herbert. She made a sharp left turn onto Herbert and tried to force a casual gait, but she knew she ended up walking even more stiffly. Maybe the woman was an undercover cop. Maybe she was a relative. But the man looked like he could be homeless. He was probably a friend of the man in her garage. In Angela's paranoia, his connection to this neighborhood seemed painfully obvious. So obvious, she wondered if everyone who saw him would know that the missing homeless man was dead or dying in Angela's garage.

Angela continued walking stiffly and briskly until she reached her front door. She fumbled with her keys for what seemed like several minutes before managing to unlock the door and step inside.

As soon as Angela walked into her home, she could smell it. There was an almost solid wall of odor in the archway of her front door. She quickly closed and locked the door behind her, as if the smell itself could escape and tap that woman and homeless man on the shoulders and tell them to look in Angela's garage.

Angela covered her mouth and nose, but the result was negligible. It had been a hot and humid day, and as usual, she had turned her air-conditioning off before she left for work. The result was a suffocating mixture of urine, vomit, and decay. While it was difficult to tell where the odor came from, Angela knew it could only come from one place: the garage.

Angela ran up the stairs to the main floor of her townhouse. She opened the linen closet door in the hallway next to her bedroom and began pulling out bottles, knocking papers, books, a mop, and countless miscellaneous items onto the floor until she pulled out a large aluminum spray can of Lysol.

The Lysol led the way as Angela sprayed the air in front of her. The lemon-scented mist felt damp on her skin as she walked down the short hallway and slowly descended the steps toward the landing. She choked on the artificial scent, and her eyes burned from the chemicals, but she kept spraying. She wondered if that thing in the garage died. It looked dead the last time she went in, but she thought its chest was moving.

Angela reached the base of the stairs. The moment she stopped spraying, that odor of death and sickness reemerged from the lemon-scented air. Angela held the can close to the garage door and sprayed the outline of the door. The Lysol hissed as she moved it around the periphery of the garage door, spraying into the small cracks between the door and the frame.

42

Marty heard a hissing sound and realized it was emanating from the door to the house. Sonya was spraying something around the door. Short blasts of a foggy-looking spray shot through the door next to the frame. Drops of liquid rolled out and streaked down the frame, as if the door were crying.

For a moment, Marty thought she might be trying to poison him. She was trying to turn the garage into a gas chamber. Then the aroma of artificial lemons descended upon Marty, and he knew she was trying to cover up his presence. She was trying to hide Marty from the outside world and keep him trapped in this bizarre realm. Although Marty could no longer smell himself or most of the odors that had gathered in the garage over the course of the last two days, he imagined they were quite strong.

Marty had slowly pulled himself several feet, and he was now within striking distance of the garage door. The temptation to reach out and begin banging on it was overwhelming. But he'd have to wait, at least until she wasn't standing right outside the door. The last time she caught him making noise, she came in and took away the dipstick that was making the noise. If he were caught knocking on the garage door, she might take away his arm. The thought seemed at once ludicrous and real.

There was a knock at a door, and the hissing sound of the spray can stopped and was followed by a loud clatter, as if something had been dropped. A visitor. This was the time for Marty to knock on the garage door.

Marty strained forward, reaching his arm out. He threw his fist in front of him but ended up hitting only the air. He was not as close to the garage door as he had previously estimated.

Marty could hear the knocking sound once again, this time louder. Why wasn't Sonya opening the door? Marty strained to pull himself forward; he had to make it to the door before this visitor left. Marty pulled himself, his arms burning with exhaustion. He collapsed facedown onto the cold concrete.

"Help," Marty wheezed. "I'm in here."

His voice sounded small, and he knew no one could hear him. Marty breathed slowly, listening to the wheezing sound of his lungs expelling air. Two words kept coming to mind: death rattle.

43

Samantha continued to scan the ground as she walked. Her steps were in perfect sync with Dogger. The sidewalks on Herbert Street were exceptionally clean, which just added to the artificial feel of the street that many in Mason said lacked character. Herbert Street didn't fit in with Mason, but the people who lived on this street were very proud of it.

"We aren't going to find Marty here," Dogger said, taking Samantha out of her thoughts. "Marty wouldn't hang around this neighborhood."

Of course it was an unlikely hangout for the town's poorest population, and that was the way it tried to portray itself. It was a lower-middle-class neighborhood attempting to mimic an upper-class neighborhood in another town—a town without poverty and astronomical unemployment rates.

"He may not be hanging around by choice," Samantha said. "He could be hurt."

"Marty's tough," Dogger said as they continued walking slowly along the sidewalk. "Even if he was in a car accident, he'd have enough sense to get out of this neighborhood. These people wouldn't help him."

Samantha looked at Dogger's face and realized he was terribly uncomfortable there. He wasn't scanning the ground, looking for clues. He was looking around him, looking like this neighborhood was about to swallow him up.

"I've already checked with the hospital," Samantha said. "They don't have a Martin Freeman—or a John Doe."

"Marty wouldn't have gone to the hospital if he were hurt," Dogger said. "He'd go back to the Dead Zone."

"We've looked there," Samantha said. "You waited for him there two nights ago; we searched there just last night. Marty isn't in the Dead Zone."

"I don't know," Dogger said. He stopped walking. "This just doesn't feel right."

"What do you mean?" Samantha said.

"Marty and I had this pact. If we ever got separated, we'd meet under Berler Bridge," Dogger said. "And right now, we are separated.

I'm wandering around this hoity-toity neighborhood, and Marty may be waiting for me right now."

"But he isn't there," Samantha said. "If he didn't make it there within forty-eight hours of your separation, doesn't that tell you that something is wrong? There is a reason why he isn't there."

"I just don't want him to think I forgot our pact," Dogger said. "I don't want him to think I abandoned him. He's my best friend, my only friend."

"You haven't abandoned him," Samantha said. "You're helping me look for him."

"Respectfully, Samantha," Dogger said. His head was lowered as he looked up at Samantha. "I know Marty better than you, and I know what he would do. We made a pact."

"I know you made a pact," Samantha said. She was struggling to keep her voice calm. "But Marty may not be in a condition to keep the pact."

"I need to meet him under the bridge," Dogger said, and he began walking toward the far end of Herbert Street. "I'm sorry, Samantha. But I know Marty, and I know exactly where he would go in a situation like this. I just can't bear the thought of him waiting there all alone. I really need to wait for him."

"All right, Dogger," Samantha said.

"Will you be OK out here?" Dogger asked over his shoulder as he continued to walk away. "All by yourself?"

"I'll be able to find my way back to the car," Samantha said.

Samantha turned and stared at the length of Herbert Street. It was quiet. She stepped into the street and began walking back toward the car. She would have to walk back down Herbert Street, across Bethel, and then through the park.

She studied the concrete in the street as she walked, hoping to see something that might provide an answer. Dogger's behavior was abrupt but also sort of predictable. He was always worried about being loyal to Marty, and abandoning his promised post was clearly making him uncomfortable. No amount of logic could keep Dogger away from Berler Bridge for too long, given the circumstances.

It seemed clear to Samantha that Marty would not be waiting for Dogger under the bridge. It was hard to believe that something terrible might have happened to him, but that was beginning to seem like a real possibility.

"Hang in there, Marty," Samantha whispered. "I won't give up."

44

"My refrigerator broke, and some food has been rotting all day," Angela whispered to herself. "I just hit a deer."

Angela nervously pulled open the front door, praying it wasn't the police pounding on the other side. To her surprise, it was Bob Barker, and he looked apologetic.

"My name is Dave." Bob Barker stuck out his hand. Angela stepped through the doorway to block "Dave" from entering.

"Angela," she said, reaching for his hand.

Dave retracted from the handshake before Angela had barely even gripped it. He started coughing in short, loud bursts.

"Were you just cleaning?" Dave said. He waved his hand in front of him. "That is toxic."

"Thanks," Angela said, suddenly feeling even more nervous. What if Dave had an extremely sensitive sense of smell? What if he could smell what she was trying to cover up? She adopted a casual tone to her voice. "I was just cleaning."

"Wow," Dave said, still coughing.

"My refrigerator broke," Angela said quickly. "The food spoiled while I was at work. Sorry about the smell."

"You've been having bad luck lately," Dave said. A positive result of the strong odor was that it forced Dave to step back a few feet, and he didn't seem interested in entering the house.

"Is there a problem?" Angela said.

"In a way, yes," Dave said with an odd laugh. "I called our association president when your car alarm was going off. Then I came over here and sort of lost my head."

"Yes," Angela said, reaching back and pulling the front door partly closed behind her. "I remember, but thanks for the recap."

"I realized that wasn't too neighborly of me," Dave said. "I guess I have a short fuse. I am very sensitive to noise, and that car alarm was just driving me nuts."

"You listen to your TV rather loudly for someone sensitive to sound," Angela said, but she immediately regretted it. "I'm just kidding."

"I know I do," Dave said. "I like to block out the entire outside world sometimes. So I turn the TV up to the highest setting. I find it very relaxing. I guess I shouldn't, if it bothers you."

"No," Angela said. She quickly realized that Dave blocking out any outside sounds was the best thing he could do right now. "Your TV doesn't bother me at all."

"The truth is," Dave said, "I got so upset about the car alarm because I usually take a late morning nap. So any other time of day it wouldn't have been such a big deal, but it was cutting into my nap time."

"I understand," Angela said. "I'm glad you let me know. Thanks for stopping by."

"I know it isn't your fault that it was going off during my nap time," Dave continued. "It's not like the car could have known that."

"Right," Angela said. "Well, it's fixed now, so that shouldn't happen again."

"You've really been a good neighbor otherwise," Dave said. "I've had no complaints."

Standing outside, the warm breeze felt soothing and made a gentle sound as it rustled the leaves in the short bushes that lined the front of the townhouses. But Angela's ear detected another sound. It wasn't the gentle swish of leaves—it was a heavier sound. The sound of something dragging. It was barely detectable, but it was there. She could feel her arms prickle with goose bumps.

"And then I realized that I'd never even introduced myself to you," Dave continued.

"Yes," Angela said quickly. "Thanks again for coming over to introduce yourself."

"I realized I didn't even know your name," Dave said. "That didn't seem right."

Angela realized the dragging sound would stop and start. A raspy wheezing sound, also barely detectable, seemed to be a constant, dim background noise. It was a strange sound. A brilliant image flashed in her mind of that thing in the garage, wheezing as it clung to the edge of her car. Angela needed to get Dave out of there.

"So you do like living here?" Dave asked. He looked at Angela with a plastic look of feigned interest.

"Yes, I like it just fine," Angela said. "It's a very pretty neighborhood. Everyone is nice."

Dave cocked his head in a strange way, as if he were listening to the air.

"Thanks again for coming over," Angela said. "It was good to meet you, Dave."

Angela stuck out her hand and noticed it was shaking. She pulled her hand back before Dave even noticed it was offered.

"Sure," Dave said. He looked uncertain about something. Angela didn't know if he was offended by her lack of small talk, or if he was hearing strange sounds from the garage. He was, after all, very sensitive to sound.

"I'm glad to be able to put a name to a face," Angela said.

"Me, too," Dave said. He was walking away but seemed to eye the garage door. "We should organize a neighborhood potluck sometime. Really get to know everyone."

"Great idea," Angela said. She stepped back and pushed open the front door behind her. "Good-bye."

Angela watched as Dave turned and walked past the garage before disappearing from eyesight. Angela closed and locked the front door.

She leaned on the door, realizing she was breathing hard. Her body was shaking as she reanalyzed in her mind the looks Dave seemed to be giving to the garage door. As if he heard something, too.

There was light tapping at the door. Dave had come back. Angela's stomach felt as if it dropped. She knew she couldn't act like she wasn't home. She'd just poke her head through the door and get rid of him as quickly as possible. Angela unlocked the front door and looked through the crack between the door and the doorframe before pulling the door open further. No one was there. Angela stuck her head out. She craned her neck to see the pavement in front of the garage door was also empty.

Then another knock sounded, this one more distinct. It was coming from the garage.

45

Dogger walked briskly to Frontage Road and toward the Dead Zone. He couldn't stand to waste time searching the streets when there was one man who knew the answer. Steve only promised to stay for one more day, and as the sun was setting, it was becoming more and more likely that he would leave town before telling Dogger what he knew about Marty.

Dogger debated telling Samantha about Steve but was afraid she'd want to call the police or, even worse, come with him to the Dead Zone. Dogger had to handle Steve himself.

Dogger reached into his pockets, feeling for change or forgotten folded money. He had none. Last night had been a total failure. He couldn't afford any negotiations, trying to buy whatever small pieces of information Steve wanted to give him. He placed his hand on the hammer that weighed down the right side of his jeans but remained concealed under his long T-shirt. The hammer was the only negotiating power he had. He didn't want to use it, but he had to.

As Dogger approached Berler Bridge, he quickly scanned the overpass for Marty. The only people he saw were Tommy and Joe, sitting under the bridge. As he approached, he could hear a few whispers and chuckles. In the dim early evening light, he could just make out the half-grins they both had on their faces as he approached.

"Have a nice date last night?" Tommy said with a snort.

"That was the chick from the soup kitchen, right?" Joe said. "She's pretty hot."

"What are you talking about?" Dogger said.

"We saw her picking you up last night," Tommy said. "What was that all about?"

"Nothing," Dogger sighed.

"So did you have a nice date?" Tommy repeated with a laugh. He was talking fast and had a wide-eyed expression that told Dogger he was probably high.

"Yes," Dogger said flatly. Tommy and Joe both looked at each other with furrowed brows, and then spontaneously began laughing.

"Have you guys seen Steve?" Dogger asked, scanning the dark area under the bridge for any signs of someone lurking in the shadows.

"Steve?" Joe said shaking his head. "Steve who?"

"That redheaded traveler," Dogger said.

"No," Joe said. "Why you need him?"

"Personal business," Dogger said.

"I've seen him," Tommy said. He was still laughing a bit but seemed to be trying to compose himself. "That guy's a jerk."

"I know," Dogger said. "Where is he?"

"I think he's hanging out in the apartment," Tommy said.

"Anyone else in there with him?" Dogger said.

"How the hell should I know?" Tommy said with another laugh.

Dogger ran his fingers over the head of the hammer sticking out of the pocket of his jeans. It was a small hammer, but it had a sharp claw.

"Thanks, guys," Dogger said, spinning on his heel.

Dogger couldn't allow himself to think too much about what he was about to do. If he did, he would change his mind. He quickly walked toward the boarded-up thrift shop. As he walked, he let his fingers run over the head of the hammer, inspecting the pointed claw with his fingertips.

The once promising parking meters proved impossible to break into. The only way to get money, enough money, would be to hold up a gas station. No one in town thought that Dogger really had a gun, so he'd have to hold up the gas station with the hammer. He could already imagine the bemused looked on a gas station clerk's face if he pulled out a hammer and demanded money. Most likely, the clerk would pull a shotgun out from behind the counter, and Dogger would have to either run for it or just wait for the cops to show up and arrest him. As he played out the scenarios in his head, it seemed like he had a 10 percent chance of successfully robbing a gas station with a hammer. The odds just weren't good enough.

Dogger came to the thrift shop and quickly glanced around to ensure no one was watching. The sun was setting, and the streetlights had just turned on, casting an oval pool of light in front of the entrance to the old thrift store. The street looked empty, except for Tommy and Joe, who looked like two small, dark shadows under Berler Bridge at the end of the street.

Dogger began inching his way through the dark alley, holding his arms out in front of him like Frankenstein's monster to feel for any roadblocks. He was nervous but was surprised that he also felt bold and confident. Maybe it was actually the extreme helplessness that made him feel as if he had nothing to lose. Dogger didn't even want to imagine living life in the Dead Zone without Marty, so any measure that might help him find Marty was worth taking.

He felt guilt for not coming up with the fifty dollars. It felt as if that were the price placed on Marty's head, and Dogger had been unable to pay it to save him. Part of Dogger knew, though, that even if he were successful and had been able to get the fifty dollars Steve wanted, there was no guarantee that Steve would give him any useful information. Steve would still be the one in control—he'd still be the one with power. He could give him what he considered to be fifty dollars' worth of information, and then demand more money. Dogger was already too close to becoming Steve's patsy. He had to end it now.

When Dogger emerged from the alley, there was a figure of a man standing behind the building. It was too dark to see who the man was as the building shadowed the backyard from the benefit of the streetlights. Dogger felt a chill go through his body and he gripped the hammer head tightly through his T-shirt. He couldn't pull it out yet, but it was reassuring to feel its presence.

"Hey," Dogger said to the tall figure.

"Hey yourself." The glowing orange ember of a cigarette bounced up and down as the man spoke. The man didn't seem to recognize Dogger, either.

Dogger slowly walked toward the man and noticed a small pile of something sitting by his feet.

"Hot night," the man said. The ember of his cigarette seemed to dance eerily in the air.

"Brutal," Dogger said. The air behind the apartment did seem especially humid and almost suffocating. As Dogger stepped closer, keeping his eye on the cigarette, he could begin to make out the man's face. "Richie?"

"Yeah," Richie said. With a small laugh, he added, "I couldn't tell that was you, Dogger."

"What are you doing back here?" Dogger said.

"I stepped out to have a cigarette," Richie said. He lowered his voice to a whisper to continue. "I was hanging out in the apartment and went to light a cigarette, and this asshole told me I had to take it outside."

"Who was that?" Dogger asked, his stomach tightening. He knew exactly who it was.

"Some guy named Steve," Richie said. "I've never seen him before today. He's a real asshole, like I said."

"So he's up there right now?" Dogger asked.

"Yep," Richie said. "I was going to sleep there tonight, but now I'm thinking it ain't worth it. Where you headed?"

"To the apartment," Dogger said. "I need to talk to Steve."

"You guys friends?" Richie said as he carefully put out his cigarette between two wetted fingertips.

"Not exactly," Dogger said. "Would you do me a favor and make sure no one else comes up there? Steve and I need to have a private conversation."

"Sure, I guess," Richie said. He stuck the extinguished half-smoked cigarette behind his ear. "So long as you share with me the next time you're holding."

"Fine," Dogger said. He looked up the fire escape. All he could see around the doors and windows to the apartment was darkness. Hopefully, Steve couldn't hear their conversation. "Just stay here until either I leave or Steve leaves. And don't talk to him."

46

Marty didn't know if the visitor was still outside or if Sonya had ever even responded to the knock at the front door. He reached out, placing his weight on his right arm and reaching for the garage door with his left. This caused an alarming and excruciating pain to radiate from his right shoulder down his back. The pain seemed to penetrate into the core of his body and spike his heart.

Marty strained, and his left hand reached the garage door. He flicked his wrist and tapped the door with his fingertips. His right arm buckled, and his upper body fell slowly to the floor.

Attempting to once again arch his back up and support his weight on his arms resulted in immediate failure. Marty was splayed on the concrete floor; it felt cool and soothing on his cheek. It would be so easy to just close his eyes and drift off to sleep, or to oblivion.

Marty wondered what Sonya planned to do with the soon-to-be dead man in the garage. Based on her actions so far, it seemed possible she would ignore the body. She'd leave town and leave the corpse behind to deteriorate. Maybe once the smell became great enough to alert the neighbors, the police would break in and find his greasy and bloated remains. By then, Sonya would be long gone.

Another possibility, but one that would require more bravery on her part, would be for her to retrieve his body and bury it in her backyard under the cover of night. She would have a hard time lifting his body, Marty imagined, so she'd probably need to get someone to help her. Maybe a boyfriend or a female friend that also had a hatred for unemployed drunk ex-husbands. Sonya was always good at making friends with women that had big chips on their shoulders.

Marty could see the image of Sonya hosing out her garage, with that terrible look of judgment and disgust on her face. Even in death, Marty couldn't please her. He couldn't die neatly enough. He didn't take charge of his life or his death, like a real man would. He just let the world happen to him. In Sonya's look of judgment and disgust, there was some satisfaction. The satisfaction of being right. This is exactly how Sonya knew Marty's life would end. Alone and without courage.

Marty lifted his head off the concrete and looked at the garage door ahead of him. His left arm was still extended toward the door, his fingertips lightly touching the surface. If he could move his body and left arm forward just one more inch, he could be close enough to give the door a solid knock without lifting his entire body up.

Instinctually, Marty attempted to push his body forward with his toes. No feeling or motion resulted. His legs were completely dead, a fact he had too easily forgotten. If it wasn't for the distinct weight of dragging them behind his torso, Marty would suspect his legs were completely severed and still dangling from the car.

He rolled his upper body slightly from left to right. With each roll, he used his shoulder to push his body forward. Slowly, his left hand was touching the garage door with not just his fingertips, but his entire palm. Marty smiled.

Curling his fingers into a fist, he flexed his wrist back, and then pushed it forward with all his strength. A definite and strong knock sounded, and simultaneous pain traveled up Marty's left arm. It was sharp and oppressive pain that made Marty think that either he had ignited a heart attack or the reverberation was mimicking one with fierce intensity. The pain mercifully subsided as quickly as it started, and Marty reeled his wrist back for another knock.

A blast of air-conditioned wind hit Marty as the door to the house flung open. Marty froze. He knew without looking that it was Sonya. Marty's face was turned; the back of his head was to the door. Marty had a chance to play dead. It was the only thing he had the strength or ability to do at this point. He closed his eyes.

He could hear a gasp and heavy breathing. While labored, it sounded light and feminine. It was most certainly Sonya who was standing in the doorway behind Marty. Marty heard footsteps slowly approach him. The breathing grew heavier and more intense. He could feel the warmth of someone bending over his body, perhaps looking at him. The breathing stopped for what seemed like several seconds, and then he heard a gasp.

The warmth quickly disappeared, and the footsteps rapidly followed. The door slammed so hard, the garage door shuddered under Marty's fingertips.

✱ ✱ ✱

That thing in the garage was dead. Angela slammed the door and ran up the steps and into her bedroom. She knew it would die, but yet it was still a shock to see it actually dead. She sat on the bed, staring straight ahead, trying to calm herself down. She had to think rationally.

Maybe it had exhausted itself making its way to the garage door. But now, it wasn't moving or breathing. It couldn't be saved. Feeling sorry for it or trying to get help now was pointless. It was dead. The only purpose it now served was damning Angela.

All the things she should have done differently tortuously played in Angela's mind. Maybe she should have stopped and called 911 right away. Maybe she should have forced that man to leave her garage. If only she hadn't had to work late that night, the accident never would have happened. It was all because of that missing one hundred dollars that Kelly probably stole. Now her job was on the line, and she had a corpse in her garage. The facade of living a good and successful life was threatening to collapse.

Soon, her sister, Jack, her mom and dad, Kelly, Natasha, and the whole town would know what a failure Angela Johnson had been at life. This would be perfect confirmation that her life was a mistake, an accident. The world would be a better place if she were never born. That thing in the garage would denigrate Angela's status from being ignored and unloved to being locked away and hated. The thing in the garage was evidence. It was nothing more and nothing less than damning evidence. It had to be destroyed.

The solution hit Angela with sudden force. Fire. It was the perfect solution. It would destroy all the evidence. It would prevent her reputation from being damned. Who would ever suspect Angela of setting fire to her own townhouse, especially since everyone knew what great pride she took in her home? Her pride was her alibi. House fires happen all the time; it wouldn't seem so strange that it would happen to Angela's house. The more she thought about it, the more confident she became in her perfect solution.

Angela stood up from the bed and opened her dresser drawer. She'd never started a fire before. Not unless you counted that one summer in fourth grade when her mom made her join the Girl Scouts to make friends. They had a campout in the backyard of the unit leader and had to build a fire. Angela didn't do much to help other than gather up small twigs. It seemed like all the other girls had done it a thousand times, but Angela had had to secretly ask the unit leader what "kindling" meant.

Of course, she had to find items around the house that could start a fire. It couldn't look purposeful. If she gathered a bunch of kindling in the yard to start the fire, it could look intentional if any of the twigs survived the blaze. Angela searched drawer after drawer, unsure of what she was seeking but sure she hadn't found it yet. She grew stronger in her belief that fire would save her from this situation. The "accidental" fire would destroy everything, including that thing in the garage. It was the perfect solution.

Angela ran from the bedroom to the kitchen. She began opening cupboards and drawers, throwing bowls and dishtowels on the floor with manic purpose. She couldn't drive out of town to get what she needed. She couldn't walk to the gas station and get kerosene and matches the same day her house accidentally burned down. Angela knew she had to start the fire with something that was already in her house.

Angela had found a solution to that thing in the garage, and she could fake the good life a little bit longer. It was the perfect solution.

47

"I'm going to be a little bit late," Samantha said into her cell phone. Her eyes searched Herbert Street as she rounded the curve in the middle of the block and walked back toward the park and her car.

"How about I come and pick you up?" Doug suggested.

"I'm not that far from my car," Samantha said. Already, Samantha realized she shouldn't have called him.

"Where did you park again?" Doug said.

"On Jefferson Street, in front of Hillside Park," Samantha said.

"I don't know," Doug said. He said this all the time. Samantha knew it was a statement he used to buy himself time to think of an argument. "The park closes at eight o'clock, you know, and it's after eight now. You'd have to walk all the way around."

"Are you serious?" Samantha couldn't help but laugh. "Cops don't enforce that. I'm just walking through to get to my car."

"Yes, they do," Doug said. "I should know. I see them bringing guys in all the time for breaking park curfew."

"True," Samantha said. "If they've been drinking or causing trouble, the police pick them up. But I'm just walking through to get my car."

"I'd feel better if I could come and get you," Doug said.

"You're being unreasonable," Samantha said. "It's not even dark out yet."

"It's getting dark," Doug said. "See, this is exactly what I have been talking about. You shouldn't get so involved."

"I know, Doug," Samantha said nervously. She could hear his voice escalating a little bit, as if on the verge of another high-pitched meltdown. "What can I do to make you happy?"

"Other than coming home right now?" Doug said.

"Yes, other than coming home right now."

"Well, I have been thinking a lot about it today, to be honest," Doug said. "And I decided that if you are going to get so involved with helping these guys out, then maybe I should be involved, too."

"That's not a bad idea," Samantha said. She could feel her shoulders relaxing with relief. It was difficult to imagine Doug at the soup kitchen or overnight shelter, but maybe his involvement would be the perfect solution to their problem. "Listen, I'm almost to the end of Herbert Street. I'll be back at my car in ten minutes."

"Do you want me to come out and help you look for Marty right now?" Doug asked.

"No, I'll just be a few more minutes," Samantha said. "Then I am coming home, and we can talk about your new volunteer schedule."

"OK," Doug said. "Just be careful."

"Of course I will be," Samantha said. "Thanks, Doug."

Samantha said good-bye and ended the call; she couldn't help but exhale a long sigh of relief. For the first time in weeks, it seemed possible that she and Doug would actually be OK. She slowed her pace as she reached the end of Herbert Street. She turned and walked down Bethel Street before crossing toward the park. Samantha studied the ground as she walked, looking up only on occasion to ensure there were no cars coming.

Samantha stopped in the middle of the road. There were tiny spots on the road she and Dogger had not seen before. They were dark stains, two as big as a pencil eraser, but the rest were merely specks that looked like dirt. They almost looked brown. Samantha stooped down low and traced the small dots with her finger. The spots were dry and didn't smear as she ran her finger over them. They trailed in an arc, as if a car was dripping as it slowed to turn from Bethel Street to Herbert Street.

It could have been oil, or maybe even rust-stained water from air-conditioner condensation. It could also have been blood. A car wouldn't just suddenly drip a few spots of oil in the middle of the street. Samantha knelt down and touched the two larger spots with her fingertips. They too were dry and left no mark on her fingertips. They could have been a couple days old or a couple years old.

Momentum, stubbornness, and intuition caused Samantha to turn and walk back toward Herbert Street. She would give Herbert Street one final sweep before leaving. She could still be home in just a matter of minutes, so one more look shouldn't cause any more drama with Doug.

"Come on, Marty," Samantha whispered. "Show me where you are."

48

Marty could hear the sounds of thumping coming through the ceiling in the garage. The thumps were irregular and sounded as if someone were running, then stopping, and then running again. A few thuds indicated that either things were being dropped or someone was falling down. It sounded chaotic and frantic, as if large wild animals were trapped upstairs and running about in a panic. Maybe Sonya had truly lost her sanity. He allowed his mind to think only momentarily about what Sonya must have seen when she walked into the garage. It must have scared her pretty good.

Marty knew that now was the time to make noise, before she came back and while she was still distracted with whatever she was slamming and throwing around. Marty flexed his wrist and began gently knocking on the garage door. The knock was hopefully loud enough to be heard outside, but not so loud as to call Sonya back down there.

The pain was tremendous, but as Marty knocked, a sense of calm overcame him. He knocked rhythmically and focused on the steady and satisfying beat his knuckles made as they tapped the door.

Marty began humming, hoarsely and softly. It was a song he didn't even know he remembered. He listened to the sound of his humming and the soft drumbeat. The words to the song slowly filtered through the pain and drifted into his mind. Marty began singing, although in his hoarse and whispered tone, it sounded more like he was chanting.

Je-sus
What a name to know
Oh Je-sus
Sing it where you go
Oh Je-sus
Savior and my lord
Jesus, what a lov-ing word

He sang that song when he was a little boy. He learned it at vacation Bible school. It wasn't a great song, or a particularly inspiring song. But it was easy to remember, was easy to sing, and had a gentle and easy beat. He used to sing it to himself at night when he was afraid.

The fear he experienced as a child seemed so simple compared with the fear he faced as an adult. He wasn't afraid when he lost his job. He wasn't afraid when weeks quickly became months of unemployment. As an adult, the first time he felt fear that no amount of alcohol could completely shake off was the first night he was alone in the house after Sonya left. She was seven months pregnant with Sonny. He had never felt more inadequate as a man as when Sonya left, and he had never felt more alone.

The terrible fear was that this was, in fact, his life. This wasn't a slump; this wasn't a rough patch. This was it. No amount of drinking could obliterate that fear, even momentarily. What if he truly was meant to be alone? What if the best way he could be a father was to be absent?

Je-sus

What a name to know

After several months of solitude and heavy drinking, Marty made the decision to redefine success in his life. He stopped looking for work because he was "living life to its fullest" by only needing to answer to himself. He stopped paying bills, not only because he did not have the money, but also because he was choosing not to. He chose a life on the streets and decided to be proud of it. The crushing loneliness was lifted only after he met Dogger.

Oh Je-sus

Sing it where you go

Since that time, he had never felt fear. In situations where most people would feel fear, Marty just felt intrigued. Even when his life was in danger, he had no fear of dying because he had no reason to live. He watched his life unfold with only a vague and passive interest.

Now fully sober, in pain, and completely alone, Marty felt fear. This fear could mean only one thing. Marty wanted to live. He wanted to see Dogger and tell him that he was all right. He wanted to maybe even find his son, if for nothing else than to apologize for not being a better man. In fact, he wanted to figure out how to be a better man.

Oh Je-sus

Savior and my lord

Jesus, what a lov-ing word

Marty kept knocking on the garage door and singing softly. He smiled to himself when he realized he felt calm. After all these years, that song still worked.

49

Before he could change his mind, Dogger quickly ascended the metal staircase, which shook and squealed with every step. When he reached the top, he realized the door to the apartment was wide open. The streetlight that shone through the window on the opposite side of the apartment illuminated a small flickering pathway of light from one end of the apartment to the other. He couldn't see anyone inside.

Dogger stepped in the doorway and listened carefully. At first, the apartment seemed to be completely silent. Dogger stood still for a moment, straining to hear any evidence of Steve's presence. Faintly, he could hear low, heavy breathing.

"Hello?" Dogger whispered. The heavy breathing continued steadily. Dogger glanced at the vent on the wall. It was still closed. It had been almost impossible to retrieve the hammer from their stash without having Marty there, but he found that if he stood on tiptoe, he was just barely able to reach the inside. With a lot of jumping and a lot of luck, he had been able to grab the handle of the hammer and pull it out. Dogger ran his fingers over the head of the hammer, carefully feeling the sharp claw before pulling it out of his pocket. The hammer was the only bargaining power he had.

The heavy breathing seemed to be coming from the kitchen area. Dogger walked lightly toward the kitchen, his eyes continuously scanning the entire apartment for any signs of movement. When he reached the long countertop of the island that sat in the middle of the tiled kitchen floor, the breathing was louder. Dogger tightened the grip on his hammer and carefully peered over the counter. On the floor behind the island, he could see the stretched-out body of the traveler.

Dogger soundlessly walked around to Steve's head. His fingertips ran over the cool metal of the claw. It was sharp. Just sharp enough. Dogger crouched down next to Steve and placed one hand on his shoulder and placed the claw of the hammer under Steve's chin. Steve's steady and heavy breathing suddenly stopped with a snort. His eyes popped open and appeared wide and damp in the dim light. Dogger pressed the claw of the hammer deeper into the skin under his chin.

"Don't move," Dogger said. "I'll cut you if you move."

"OK," Steve said. His voice sounded shaken. Dogger tried to suppress a smile. He didn't think using the claw of his hammer would be so convincing.

"Where is Marty?" Dogger said.

"What?" Steve sputtered.

"You're not getting any more money from me," Dogger said. "Here's the new deal. If you tell me where Marty is, I won't cut you."

"I don't know, exactly," Steve said. "Please don't kill me."

"What do you know?" Dogger said. He found himself growing calmer as Steve grew visibly more afraid. "Tell me everything you know. You said you saw him."

"I just got to town," Steve said. His body was stiff, but it seemed as if his entire face was shaking as he spoke. "I was walking through a park when I heard you guys drinking. I saw the cops coming, so I ran out of the park before anyone could see me."

"Did you see Marty run out of the park?" Dogger said.

"No," Steve said. "I got out of there quickly. I was on the street with those rows of fancy-looking houses. I heard a loud crash behind me."

"Did you see the car accident?" Dogger asked. He tried to keep his voice steady and strong, but he felt like crying out. Marty must have been in a car accident. Those bits of headlight he and Samantha saw must have been from Monday night.

"I didn't know it was a car accident," Steve said. "Not at first. I just kept running. Then, suddenly, headlights were on me. I had no idea where I was or where I was going, but I was running like hell because I was sure it was those cops I saw in the park coming after me."

"Did you see Marty?" Dogger said. He felt himself growing impatient and pressed the claw of the hammer firmly into Steve's neck to remind him of the threat.

"I don't know," Steve said, his eyes widening with fear. "I'm not entirely sure of what I saw."

"Why did you tell me that you know where Marty is?" Dogger asked. He could feel his hands shaking with frustration, but he tried to keep his voice even and controlled. "Where is he?"

"The headlights turned away," Steve said. "So I thought the cops had driven down another street behind me. I turned to look, and I saw a car had pulled into a driveway. It was a ways down the block behind me, but I swore I saw someone lying over the hood of the car."

"Was it Marty?" Dogger said. He was afraid he already knew the answer.

"I don't know," Steve said, his voice a nervous vibrato. "I just thought it was some teenage kids playing around. I didn't think much of it until I found out your friend was missing the next morning."

"Which house was it?" Dogger asked. "Which driveway?"

"Jesus, man," Steve said. His eyes had grown wet with tears. "I don't even know what street I was on. I just got to town. It was a street with rows of fancy-looking houses. And the car didn't stop in the driveway; it pulled into the garage."

"I see," Dogger said, taking a shaking breath. "Is that all?"

"That's everything I saw," Steve said. "Everything. I swear it."

"All right," Dogger said. "Listen, you need to leave town. And I mean right now."

"OK, OK," Steve said quickly.

"Richie's down there, and he'll be watching to make sure you go," Dogger said. "In fact, I have guys with knives all over this place who are looking for you to leave town. If you so much as look back, you're a dead man."

"I won't," Steve said.

"I'm going to step back," Dogger said. "You get up and run like hell out of here."

Dogger let go, stood up, and stepped back into the darkness of the apartment. He watched as Steve quickly stood up, grabbed his backpack, and ran out the door. He could hear the stairway creak and rattle as he ran down the steps. Dogger listened carefully, hoping Richie wouldn't say anything to him as Steve ran by. He couldn't hear anything.

Dogger stepped out onto the balcony and looked down. He could faintly see Richie standing underneath the stairs, and there was no sign of Steve.

"Where did he go in such a hurry?" Richie called up to Dogger.

"Out of town," Dogger said, as he quickly descended the staircase.

"Thank God," Richie said.

Dogger began sprinting, with clumsy, manic speed, back to Herbert Street.

***

As the sky grew darker and the streetlights flickered on, Samantha grew more and more desperate and unsure of what she should do. It seemed evident that an accident had taken place at some point, but it wasn't evident if that was related to Marty's disappearance. Doug was expecting her home, but something told her that she was too close to give up just yet.

Samantha wasn't usually too bold, but before she could give it too much thought, she approached the front door of the first home on Herbert Street. If there was an accident that caused the loud sound and left behind a broken headlight, someone surely would have heard or seen it.

The first home was a single-family home—one of only two houses on the street that were not part of the townhouses. Samantha walked up two steps and noticed the cheerful welcome mat outside the door. As if empowered by the mat as a genuine and personal welcome, Samantha rang the doorbell.

A series of chimes, at once ethereal and mechanical, could be heard coming from inside the house. Samantha stood awkwardly, trying to think of what she was going to ask the person that opened the door. No one answered. A little bit relieved to have some time to think about what she was going to say to the residents of Herbert Street, Samantha turned and walked down the steps.

"Hold on," a voice called as a door opened. Samantha turned and saw an elderly woman standing in the doorway, fidgeting with the latch to the screen door.

"Oh, hello," Samantha said. She walked back up the steps. "I didn't think anyone was home."

"I'm here," the woman said. "I'm just slow."

"My name is Samantha," Samantha said. The woman was still fidgeting with the screen door. Samantha pulled the handle and helped her open the door. The old lady looked so alarmed, Samantha realized the she might have been trying to *lock* the door.

"I'm afraid I never buy from door-to-door salespeople," the woman said. "But have a nice night."

"I'm not selling anything," Samantha said. She smiled, and the woman looked at her suspiciously. "Including religion."

"Oh, I see," the woman said. She leaned out of the doorway and looked around outside. Then she looked at Samantha and tilted her head. "I think I recognize you. You work at the big gas station, right?"

"That's right," Samantha said.

"Is everything OK?" the woman asked, once again scanning the street behind Samantha. "Did your car break down or something?"

"No," Samantha said. "I just wanted to ask you a couple of quick questions. It won't take much of your time."

"Are you sure you aren't selling anything?" The woman frowned at Samantha.

"Did you hear or see a car accident two nights ago?" Samantha asked quickly, before the woman could decide to shut the door. "It happened right here at the intersection of Herbert and Bethel."

"No," the woman said, but her eyes lit up. She was suddenly very interested. "There was an accident? Was it one of those hot-dogging kids from Jewel Street? They drive pretty crazy—and at all hours."

"So you didn't hear or see any car accident Monday night?" Samantha said.

"What time?" the woman asked.

"Very late at night," Samantha said. "After midnight."

"Oh no," the woman said. "I would have been in bed. I haven't been sleeping too well lately. I finally took some of those sleeping pills my doctor prescribed. I don't think anything could have woken me up before the sun rose."

"Have you noticed any of your neighbors acting unusual?" Samantha asked.

"They all seem unusual to me," the woman said. "But no one has been acting any more unusual than usual."

"Have you seen any cars with broken headlights or damage?" Samantha questioned.

"No," the woman said. "But I don't really spend all my time inspecting other people's cars."

"Thanks for your time," Samantha said. She let go of the screen door, and it slowly closed behind her. Samantha turned when she reached the bottom of the stairs. The woman was frowning again but waved good-bye.

She walked to the next single-family house. This house also had a small staircase leading to the front door. Samantha rang the doorbell; this time, the standard two-tone *ding-dong* sounded. She waited until it seemed certain that either no one was home, or they were choosing not to answer the door. She rang the doorbell one more time before walking back down the driveway to the sidewalk.

It seemed so fruitless. Samantha stood at the end of the driveway for several moments. The sky was already getting dark, and she didn't have time to knock on every door tonight, especially given that she had almost no reason other than a hunch to think anyone in this neighborhood would know anything about Marty.

"Just one more," Samantha said to herself quietly.

As Samantha walked to the first townhouse in the long row of homes that lined Herbert Street, she studied the pavement. She was looking for any unusual spots or evidence of a car that might have been dropping bits of its headlight on the ground.

Samantha knocked on the door. Very quickly, a short and fit older gentleman opened the door. It was as if he had been waiting by the door. He looked at her with puzzled uncertainly but returned Samantha's smile.

"Good evening," Samantha said, already feeling rehearsed. "I'm sorry to bother you, but I am asking folks in your neighborhood if they either heard or saw a car accident two nights ago."

The man grimaced in a look of strained thought, but he shook his head. "No, I'm sorry."

"Are you sure?" Samantha asked. "You haven't seen or heard anything unusual in the last couple of days?"

"This is a pretty quiet neighborhood," the man said. "It's a good neighborhood with nice people that keep to themselves. Sorry I can't help."

The man began to close the door, but Samantha put her hand on the door and said, "Do you know your neighbors pretty well?"

The man seemed to reluctantly reopen the door.

"I don't know them very well," the man said. "But I know most of my neighbors."

"Have any of them been acting unusual? Or have you seen any cars in the neighborhood with any damage?" Samantha said.

"No one has been acting unusual, and I haven't seen any damaged cars," the man said. "Everyone takes pride in this neighborhood and in their possessions."

"I understand," Samantha said. "It is a lovely neighborhood. So you haven't seen any cars with missing headlights or damage?"

"No, nothing new," the man said slowly. "What is it that you are looking for?"

"A missing person," Samantha said.

"I wouldn't know anything about that," the man said quickly.

Samantha thanked the man, and she could sense him watching her as she walked away. She quickly glanced down the length of Herbert

Street and sighed. Maybe she could talk to the other neighbors tomorrow. She took her cell phone out of her purse and dialed as she walked.

"Sorry, I got delayed a bit longer than expected," Samantha said sweetly into the phone. "But I'm coming home now, Doug."

50

Angela had moved from the bedroom to the kitchen to the linen closet and back to the bedroom in her search. The image of that thing in the garage, broken and splayed on the floor, always threatened to show itself in her mind again. It was the anticipation of seeing that image that made her the most afraid and made her hands tremor violently as she searched.

Angela's fingers picked through T-shirts and panties as she dug her way to the bottom of the dresser drawer. When she reached the pink floral drawer liner, she slammed the door shut and pulled open the next drawer.

She noticed she was breathing heavily now, and a drop of sweat coolly slid down the side of her face. It seemed there was absolutely nothing in her house that would start a fire. Her sister had even given her a set of three matching blue candles of different heights that sat on a plate of glass as a housewarming gift, but Angela had never bought a lighter to use them. Instead, they just sat collecting dust on top of her dresser, their wicks standing up straight with a stark white contrast to the dark blue wax.

Angela slammed the last drawer shut, rattling the candles on their glass plate. She felt the strain of tears pressing on her eyes. She stepped back from the dresser and leaned against the wall next to her closet, allowing herself to slide to the floor in a crumpled pile of sickness, worry, and fear.

Loud sobs filled the air, and she was only able to control them when she realized that Bob Barker, aka Dave, might be able to hear.

"Keep it together, Angela," she whispered. "You'll find something." From the floor, Angela scanned the bedroom. There, under her bed, she spotted what could be her salvation.

Angela crawled toward the bed, reached her arm under, and strained before her fingertips touched the box of Marlboro Lights. She pulled them out. Angela wasn't a smoker, unless she had been drinking. One night at Hysteria, Angela was bumming so many smokes off of Jason that he finally just gave her his pack. That had been months ago, and she had completely forgotten she still had the half-empty pack.

Angela opened the box, and a smile spread across her face. Jason had also given her his lighter. His engagement was almost forgivable. A short yellow Bic lighter sat in the box with seven cigarettes. This was almost too perfect. Just two years ago, someone's house burned down in Mason because they didn't extinguish a cigarette. It was literally burned to the ground, and the family lost everything they owned. It was as if their entire life had been erased. It was exactly what Angela needed.

The scenario quickly developed in Angela's mind. She would make it look as if she fell asleep on the couch, or in bed, with a lit cigarette. She just needed something flammable to ensure the fire spread in the right direction and at least destroyed that thing that needed to be destroyed.

Standing up, Angela whistled mindlessly as she walked back to the kitchen, where she had left the can of Lysol. She turned the can around in her hand, reading the warning label on the back. *Caution: Contents highly flammable.*

Angela walked to the living room, shaking the can of Lysol as she moved. She lifted the thin cotton throw off the back of the couch and began to spray it with the Lysol. This would be the perfect way to ensure the flames devoured the evidence that needed to be devoured.

The blanket began to grow heavy in her hand as it soaked up the spray, but she only paused in her spraying once to quickly give the can a shake. She needed the entire throw to be completely soaked. Her nostrils began to burn from the lemon-scented vapors. She turned her head and continued spraying. Lysol seemed like such a cleansing and appropriate choice for the task. Her plan seemed so perfect. Her only regret was that she could never tell anyone about her perfect solution.

Even Bob Barker was playing along with her plan, although he didn't know it. If the police later found a suspicious amount of Lysol residue, Bob Barker would testify that she told him she was cleaning earlier that day. It would corroborate Angela's story that after a tough day of house cleaning, she relaxed and had a cigarette and dozed off on the couch.

"The cigarette must have dropped from my hand," Angela said. The blanket felt cold and heavy with dampness. Angela sat the blanket down and began to spray the carpet from the couch to the top of the stairs to the garage door. "And the flame followed the path I had most recently been scrubbing: the stairs and into the garage."

After she finished spraying the entryway, she trotted back up the stairs. Returning to the living room, Angela realized the can of Lysol was significantly lighter and colder than when she had begun. The smell of the spray filled her house, filled her lungs, and burned her eyes. She would have to use the remaining amount of Lysol to give a last spray to the couch. This was, after all, the wick.

51

Dogger's limbs were almost out of control as he ran. He had been out of breath for the last three blocks, and his chest and legs burned with exhaustion, but he couldn't stop or even slow down. The image of Marty lying on the hood of a car as it pulled into a garage was playing over and over in Dogger's mind as he ran. It seemed too impossible to be real, but Steve had no reason to lie when he thought his life was being threatened. Plus, he had no way of knowing Dogger and Marty had been chased out of the park by cops on Monday night unless he had actually seen them. Steve must have been telling the truth.

Dogger rounded the corner to Herbert Street. He was on the end of the street furthest from the park. This was probably about where Steve had been when he turned and saw the car with someone lying on the hood being driven into a garage.

Dogger ran past the first two townhouses. Steve had said the car was going into a garage that was well behind him, so surely he wouldn't be in the first two. Dogger ran to the garage of the third townhouse. The house looked dark and empty and seemed almost eerie in its stillness.

"Marty!" Dogger shouted as he knocked on the garage door. He voice was loud and echoed down the neighborhood. He couldn't be too loud, or the neighbors would call the police and report Dogger for creating a disturbance. There was no way that Henry Gates would believe Dogger's story, especially since it was based on the word of a traveler. He pressed his ear to the garage, which felt warm on his cheek from soaking in the sun all afternoon and early evening. Dogger heard nothing.

Dogger ran to the next garage and began knocking. Of course, Marty might not be in the garage any longer. He could be in the house, or maybe in a hospital. Samantha said she checked the hospital, but maybe they had Marty under a false name.

"Marty!" Dogger called through the garage door. He waited for a moment before he began knocking again.

"Hey!" a voice shouted, startling Dogger. He turned away from the garage door to see a tall, thin man with a beard standing on the sidewalk leading to the front door. He was wearing plaid boxer shorts and white T-shirt, and he looked as if he had just gotten out of bed.

"What the hell do you think you're doing?" the man said. His hands were on his hips, and even in the dim light of the early night's sky, Dogger could see the man's face had quickly grown to a ruddy color.

"Looking for my friend," Dogger said, stepping away from the garage door.

"He's not here," the man said. "Leave before I call the police."

Dogger began to inch away from the garage door. How could he know this man was telling the truth? This man could be the one that hit Marty on Monday night.

"Were you in a car accident Monday night?" Dogger said.

"What?" The man squinted at Dogger and shook his head. "No. What's wrong with you? Get out of here."

Dogger turned and walked down the man's driveway. When he reached the sidewalk, he turned and saw the man was still standing and watching Dogger.

"Have a good night," Dogger said. "Sorry to bother you."

Dogger continued walking down the sidewalk as slowly as he could walk without looking like he was stalling. When he heard the door close, he quickly and quietly backtracked on the sidewalk to go up to the next garage in line.

"Marty," Dogger whispered as he gently tapped on the garage door. He pressed his ear to the door. He could hear nothing. He carefully and quietly walked to the next garage, being vigilant for any other watchful neighbors. The next garage also seemed to be silent.

As Dogger rounded the slight curve on Herbert Street, he could see the park up ahead. It looked as if someone were walking across the street and was about to enter the woods. Dogger squinted. It was a woman with long blonde hair. It looked like it could be Samantha.

Dogger ran to the middle of Herbert Street, brought his fingers up to his lips, and blew a loud, screeching whistle. The woman stopped walking and turned. It was definitely Samantha. Dogger waved his arms wildly over his head, and then motioned her to come over. Samantha waved back and trotted over.

Dogger glanced back behind him to ensure the angry man with the beard and plaid boxer shorts hadn't been called back out of the house by the whistle. The street and sidewalks looked empty. Dogger quickly jogged off the street, back onto the sidewalk, and up the driveway to the next garage.

"Marty," Dogger whispered loudly. "Marty, are you in there? It's Dogger." He pressed his ear to the door and listened for several moments before moving on. There weren't too many townhouses left. Although Dogger fought to push the thought away, it was beginning to feel like a real possibility that he might not be able to find Marty at all tonight. He might not be able to ever find Marty.

"What are you doing back here?" Samantha asked breathlessly. Her cheeks were slightly flushed from running. "I thought you were waiting at Berler Bridge."

"A traveler told me he may have seen Marty on Monday night," Dogger said. As he spoke, he walked to the next townhouse and pressed his ear to the garage door. Samantha followed. "He thinks he saw someone lying on the hood of a car that pulled into one of these garages."

"Oh, my God," Samantha said. "Did he call the police?"

"No," Dogger scoffed. He walked quickly to the next garage.

Dogger suddenly became aware of a tapping sound. At first, he thought it was his own heartbeat, and then he thought it could have been the distant rhythm of someone lightly hammering—slowly tapping a small nail into a wall for a picture frame. He pressed his ear to the garage door of the second-to-last townhouse on the block. The tapping was definitely coming from the garage.

"I think someone is knocking on this garage door," Dogger said.

"What?" Samantha's eyes widened, and she ran up to the door and pressed her ear against it, next to Dogger.

"Marty," Dogger whispered. The tapping stopped. "Is that you?"

52

Marty's vision had dimmed to gray, and he wanted nothing more than to stop knocking and simply fall asleep. A few times, his tapping slowed to a stop for what could have been several seconds or several hours. He was blacking out. He tried to keep his faithful, albeit weak, rhythm as long as he was lucid. He no longer had the strength to sing, but he tried to keep humming his childhood hymn.

The words played in his mind as the tapped the garage door. He was sure he could hear his own young voice singing.

Je-sus
What a name to know
Oh Je-sus
Sing it where you go

He allowed his mind to imagine and believe that he was in his small bed in the two-bedroom brick house in Mason. He let himself believe that his mom was in the next room, and he didn't want to wake her to tell her that he was afraid of the dark. He let the words of the song soothe and protect him.

Oh Je-sus
Savior and my lord
Jesus, what a lov-ing word

A knock much stronger than his own knock startled Marty. He opened his eyes wide and stopped knocking. He was in a state of semiconsciousness, close to falling asleep, so it could have been his own hopeful imagination trying to mercifully encourage him. Marty listened. Silence.

Flexing his wrist, Marty tapped on the garage door once. The loud knock replied. Marty tapped twice. The louder knock replied with two identical taps. Marty's dry lips stretched painfully into a grin.

With a bang, the side door burst open. It could only be Sonya. Only Sonya could burst into a room with such fury. Although Marty's back was to the side door, he knew Sonya had an agenda. She had come through that door with a reason, and it wasn't just morbid curiosity, like her last peek. Marty froze and closed his eyes. Playing dead had seemed to work last time.

The sound of her feet shuffling up to him was enough to make Marty want to cry out in horror. But he remained silent. Something was thrown on top of him, touching his face first before slowly falling over the rest of his body and completely enveloping him.

Marty could hear the side door slam and the sound of footsteps running up a staircase before he felt the terrible burn set in. Whatever was on this blanket felt like pure acid on his broken face and body. Marty struggled to lift the blanket off, but he didn't have the strength. The fumes were suffocating. It smelled like ammonia or a cleaning product. Sonya had something crazy planned, and it couldn't be good.

53

Angela quickly felt the damp floor up the staircase. It should be a sufficient trail for the flame to follow.

"I was just cleaning," Angela said as she continued up the stairs to the living room. "And I was tired, so I sat down on the couch and had a cigarette. No, I don't usually smoke. I know it's unhealthy, but I thought it would revive me. The next thing I knew, I woke up, and the house was in flames. I can't believe I lost everything."

Angela sat on the couch. She reached into her pocket, pulled out the pack of Marlboro Lights, and removed the lighter. Placing the stale-tasting cigarette in her mouth, she lit it. She inhaled a long, slow drag of heavy smoke and coughed hoarsely.

"I must have fallen asleep," Angela said. On the armrest of the couch, she could see the irregular circular stain where she had sprayed the couch with Lysol. She touched the glowing end of the cigarette to the spot. Nothing happened. Angela lifted her cigarette and saw a black smudge where it had touched the fabric. There was a burn mark and a small hole, but no fire.

Angela touched the cigarette once again to the couch. The result was the same. She flicked the small lighter, still in her other hand, and held the flame directly to the oddly shaped stain.

The arm quickly ignited, burning in the defined circle of Lysol she had sprayed. Angela jumped up and stepped away from the couch. The small fire on the arm of the couch grew to the back of the couch and down the front leg.

Angela grabbed a *TV Guide* from the top of her TV and fanned the flames in one large, arcing motion. The fire alarm sounded, piercing her ears with a loud sting of high-pitched beeps. She smiled and laughed gleefully when the fire continued to grow and began heading down the stairs. It was following the path she had created.

"Perfect!" Angela couldn't help but shout. The fire was doing exactly what she had hoped. The heat suddenly became intense, and Angela felt mild panic. The plan was working well, but she didn't realize the fire would spread quite so quickly or feel quite so hot. She had to get out faster than she had anticipated.

Angela dropped the *TV Guide* and ran to the top of the stairs. Each step was narrowing as the fire deviated from the path she had created with Lysol and engulfed the surrounding carpet and walls.

Angela turned and ran through the small kitchen to the back porch. She opened the glass door and could feel an intense whoosh of heat behind her. Stepping on to the porch, she realized the second story was much higher than she remembered. As the heat pressed behind her, Angela climbed over the rail.

54

"Ever since we heard that door close, I haven't heard a thing," Samantha said. "I bet whoever was working in the garage has left. They were probably making that knocking sound."

"Listen," Dogger said, looking around. "Do you hear some kind of beeping?"

It sounded as if an alarm were going off. At first Samantha thought it was the sound of a microwave timer, but then as it continued, it sounded more like a loud alarm clock. She stepped back from the garage door and looked up at the townhouse. She couldn't see anyone through the windows, although there was a soft glow of light.

"Maybe it's someone's alarm clock," she said.

"I don't know," Dogger said. "Maybe." He pressed his ear to the garage door and lightly tapped.

"Do you want to check the next garage?" Samantha said.

Dogger seemed to be ignoring her. "Marty," he whispered loudly. He pressed his face against the garage door so firmly that his cheek slid his mouth up into a crooked smile. He lightly tapped three times in quick succession. There was a pause, a pause so long that Samantha was about to step away and walk toward the last townhouse. But then she heard three knocks, an imitation of Dogger's rhythm. Dogger's eyes widened.

"Hello?" Dogger said. "Marty?"

"It could just be a kid playing in the garage," Samantha said, but she could hear the uncertainty in her own voice.

"Marty?" Dogger repeated. There was no response.

"Anybody in there?" Samantha asked, trying to force a cheerful tone. She strained to listen but could not hear any response. As she leaned in, pressing her ear to the garage door, she heard three soft knocks. There was a pause, and then three slower knocks, another pause, and three more soft and quick knocks.

"SOS," Dogger gasped. "It's gotta be Marty."

Samantha pressed her hands on the garage door and pushed up. The garage door didn't move. Dogger noticed what Samantha was doing and pressed his hands to the garage door and grunted with futile effort. It was either locked or too heavy to open manually.

Three quick knocks, three slow knocks, and three quick knocks sounded again.

"We hear you," Samantha said. "We're getting help."

"Hang in there, Marty," Dogger said loudly, pressing his forehead on the garage door and cupping his hands around his mouth. "We'll get you out."

Samantha pulled out her cell phone and dialed 911.

"I believe someone is trapped in a garage," Samantha said into her phone as soon as the operator picked up. "It's on Herbert Street. Eighty-five Herbert Street in Mason."

"We have the police on the way," the operator said. "Do you have reason to believe there are any injuries?"

"I don't know," Samantha said. She stepped back and looked up at the window on the second floor. A small amount of smoke was seeping through one corner. She suddenly realized that the beeping alarm clock she was hearing was actually a smoke detector.

"There's a fire!" Samantha yelled into the phone. Dogger ran toward the front door of the house. "Send a fire truck and ambulance as well!"

"The ambulance has already been dispatched," the operator said. "A fire truck will also be on the way."

Samantha dropped her cell phone to the ground and placed both hands on the garage door. She pushed up, but her hands couldn't find traction and slid up the garage door. The door just couldn't be opened like this.

"Youch!" Dogger screamed. He came running back into view. "The doorknob is burning. The fire must be right on the other side of the front door!"

"Was it locked?" Samantha said.

"I couldn't get it open," Dogger said, shaking his right hand in the air as if to cool it off.

"Marty!" Samantha yelled. She didn't want to believe it, but she knew Marty had to be in this garage. There was no response. She tried to lift the door once more, and Dogger immediately helped. It wasn't moving.

"Are you OK?" the next-door neighbor, the man Samantha had spoken with only minutes ago, stepped out of his front door.

"Help us get this garage door open," Samantha said.

The man ran to Samantha and gave a strange sideways look in Dogger's direction. He looked up toward the smoke that was now billowing out of the second-floor window.

"Is Angela in there?" the man asked when he reached Samantha.

"I don't know, but there is someone in the garage," Dogger said. "Help us lift this."

The garage door shuddered under the persistence of Samantha, Dogger, and the neighbor. Finally, the door shimmied up a fraction of an inch. Noticing the small gap, Samantha forcefully and painfully wedged her foot underneath.

"You guys keep pushing from there," Samantha said to Dogger and the neighbor. "Don't let go."

Samantha quickly walked her hands down the front of the garage door, attempting to place as much force on the door as possible. When she reached the bottom of the door, she stuck her fingertips underneath and gripped.

"Hang in there, Marty," Samantha said. "OK, now lift."

The garage door made a grinding sound as it slowly lifted. Once the door was approximately six inches off the ground, something gave way, and it lifted with ease.

Smoke was seeping through the side door from the house into the garage. Samantha could smell an odd mix of cleaning fluid, smoke, and sickness. At first, she didn't see anyone, and she wondered if the knocking sounds were coming from somewhere other than the garage. In the small garage was a black Chrysler Sebring. She could see from the side that the front end of the car was damaged. The rest of the garage was almost completely empty. The floor was a mess, stained with a dark substance. There was another stain that looked like vomit by the front of the car, and a folded-up lawn chair on the floor. There was a blanket on the ground in front of her.

"Oh, my God," Dogger gasped, stepping back from the garage.

Looking more closely at the blanket, she saw fingertips poking through an opening. It was a body. There was a dark trail from the car to the covered body. She realized that what she had first thought was dirt or oil on the garage floor was blood.

"Marty?" Samantha said.

"What in God's name is this?" the neighbor said.

Samantha knelt next to the blanket and lifted it off. It was damp and smelled of cleaner. Samantha felt a deep chill travel through her body when she saw the face underneath. The parts that weren't covered with dried blood were gray and hollow. He looked dead.

"Marty?" Samantha said. His eyes opened. He looked at Samantha without recognition for a moment.

"Marty!" Dogger knelt down next to Samantha and gingerly touched Marty's forehead. Marty's face lifted, his eyes looking up as if he had just walked through a fog.

"Thank you," Marty whispered hoarsely. "I'm an entirely different bag of bones."

"What?" Dogger stammered. He turned to Samantha before directing his attention back toward Marty. "What does that mean?"

"An ambulance is on its way," Samantha said. She searched Marty's eyes for any sign of lucidity. "Just hang in there."

"Thank you," Marty whispered, and then closed his eyes.

55

Angela's ankle burned with pain. The balcony was so much higher than she'd expected. She stayed crouched low in her backyard, listening to the high-pitched beeping of her fire alarm while testing how much weight she could put on her ankle.

Ideally, she wanted to wait until the townhouse was nearly burned to its foundation before limping to her neighbors' and asking them to call the fire department. She didn't realize how strongly the fire would smell, which could cause Bob Barker to stick his nose out his window at any time. He'd see the smoke and call 911 and expect Angela to thank him for being neighborly.

Angela could see through Bob Barker's sliding-glass window on his second-story balcony and into his kitchen. His house had the exact same layout as Angela's, except he had left all of his walls white. The dome of his kitchen light glowed brightly, illuminating a sparsely decorated and immaculately clean kitchen. There was no sign of him looking out his window.

Putting all of her weight on her left leg, Angela managed to stand up. She hopped a small half-turn to look at her house. The sheer curtains that framed the sliding-glass doors billowed and danced as the orange and yellow colors of the fire glowed in the background. Even in the dark sky, Angela could see the black smoke that rolled off the roof, coming from somewhere in the front. She prayed that somewhere in that smoke were the final remains of incriminating evidence. It seemed that her plan was going to work just perfectly.

Angela could hear her fire alarm beeping, but now she was hearing something else. A long and sustained mechanical cry. At first she couldn't be sure, but soon it became evident that the long wails she was hearing were sirens. Someone had already called the fire department. Angela panicked and turned to run. She momentarily forgot her injured right foot and fell on the grass. The sirens were getting louder. In fact, it sounded as if several emergency vehicles were coming, as the wail of the sirens overlapped and horns honked to create an eerie and urgent symphony.

Angela scrambled on her hands and knees, crawling toward the row of four bushes that separated her backyard from the backyard of her neighbor. She could see the red and blue lights shining over her townhouse and splaying across her backyard. They were there already.

It was too soon. That thing in the garage might not have disappeared yet. There might still be evidence.

Angela pressed her back up against the row of bushes, breathing heavily. She could hear the sound of car doors closing loudly. One … two … three … four doors closing. Then there were two more. It sounded as if more vehicles were arriving every second as the sirens became impossibly loud before shutting off as they likely pulled in front of her house.

Angela had only two choices right now. She could walk through Bob Barker's backyard, tell everyone out there how she narrowly escaped the fire, and just pray that thing in her garage was gone, or she could try to make a run for it right now. She closed her eyes and tried to steady her breathing and gather her thoughts. This was all happening much faster than it was supposed to.

Suddenly, the sound of footsteps brushing quickly through the grass could be heard behind her. She pressed up against a bush, as if she could disappear into its engulfing and scratchy branches.

"You all right, ma'am?"

Angela looked up with a start. It was Officer Jake, the short officer who had stopped by Fashionable Finds earlier that day. Angela felt her face twitching involuntarily as her mind scrambled to determine the right thing to say. An overweight police officer with a pockmarked face came around the bushes and stood in front of her. His name badge said *Henry Gates*.

"Can I help you up?" Officer Henry held out his thick hand to Angela.

"I'm lucky to be alive," Angela said. She found the words spilling quickly out of her mouth, almost out of her control. "I was just cleaning, and I took a nap. I must have left a cigarette lit by accident."

Angela reached to take Officer Henry's hand. When she did, he clasped a cold metal handcuff to her wrist.

56

To Marty, the moment felt like a new awakening. Dogger and Samantha were there, kneeling over his broken body, with looks of profound care on their faces. He had been lifted out of the bizarre and otherworldly realm of the garage and back to reality.

"I knew we'd find you," Dogger said. Marty could see tears in his eyes.

"The ambulance is here," Samantha said. "You're going to be fine."

"Thank you," was all Marty could think to say.

Flashing red lights filled the air, and Marty closed his eyes for a moment to shield his vision from their dizzying spiral around the garage. When he opened his eyes, Dogger and Samantha were standing up, and two young men were kneeling down in their place. His eyes closed heavily again, and he felt his body being moved and lifted. Marty managed to remain silent even through the most painful twists and pokes of the paramedics transporting him onto a gurney. A cool plastic mask was put over Marty's mouth, and he drew in a clean and sweet breath.

"Marty," Samantha said. Marty opened his eyes and saw Samantha standing over him. He realized he had been lifted up onto a gurney and was now laid out several feet off the ground. He struggled to focus on Samantha, who gently touched his shoulder as she spoke. "Marty, would you like for me to call your son?"

"Don't worry about it." Dogger stepped up. "I'll call him for Marty."

"No," Marty said. He noticed his clear plastic mask fogged up as he spoke. "Don't call him. I don't even know him."

"What?" Samantha asked. She looked at Dogger, who just shrugged and looked surprised.

"I'm a liar. I'm sorry, Samantha," Marty said weakly. "I've never met my son. I don't even know what his name is—I just always call him Sonny."

"One, two, three," one of the paramedics barked, and Marty suddenly had the sensation of a bumpy flight backward into the ambulance. His view of the night's sky was replaced with a metallic ceiling that glowed brightly with tract lighting.

"I can find him for you, Marty," Samantha said as she and Dogger stood in the driveway and watched the paramedics securing Marty for the ride to the hospital. The kindness in her voice never faltered. "Wendy, Doug, and I can help you find him. We have resources."

"I'd like that," Marty said as the paramedics waved Samantha and Dogger out of the way to close the back door. "I'm an entirely different bag of bones ... I can be a better man than he expects."

www.ingramcontent.com/pod-product-compliance
Lightning Source LLC
Chambersburg PA
CBHW021036130626
46552CB00005B/1868